W9-CLB-920

WICKED STEPMOTHER

MICHAEL MCDOWELL was born in 1950 in Enterprise, Alabama and attended public schools in southern Alabama until 1968. He graduated with a bachelor's degree and a master's degree in English from Harvard, and in 1978 he was awarded his Ph.D. in English and American Literature from Brandeis.

His seventh novel written and first to be sold, *The Amulet*, was published in 1979 and would be followed by over thirty additional volumes of fiction written under his own name or the pseudonyms Nathan Aldyne, Axel Young, Mike McCray, and Preston MacAdam. His notable works include the Southern Gothic horror novels *Cold Moon Over Babylon* (1980) and *The Elementals* (1981), the serial novel *Blackwater* (1983), which was first published in a series of six paperback volumes, and the trilogy of "Jack & Susan" books.

By 1985 McDowell was writing screenplays for television, including episodes for a number of anthology series such as *Tales from the Darkside*, *Amazing Stories*, *Tales from the Crypt*, and *Alfred Hitchcock Presents*. He went on to write the screenplays for Tim Burton's *Beetlejuice* (1988) and *The Nightmare Before Christmas* (1993), as well as the script for *Thinner* (1996). McDowell died in 1999 from AIDS-related illness. Tabitha King, wife of author Stephen King, completed an unfinished McDowell novel, *Candles Burning*, which was published in 2006.

DENNIS SCHUETZ was born in 1946 in Parkersburg, West Virginia. He graduated from West Virginia University and later moved to Boston, where he attended the Orson Welles Film School and began to write fiction. He collaborated with Michael McDowell on six novels (the two "Axel Young" books and a series of gay-themed mysteries published under the name "Nathan Aldyne.") For the last ten years of his life, Schuetz worked for the Massachusetts Department of Public Works. He died of a brain tumor in 1989.

Also Available by Michael McDowell

The Amulet
Cold Moon Over Babylon
Gilded Needles
The Elementals
Katie
Toplin
Blood Rubies (with Dennis Schuetz)*

* Forthcoming.

Wicked Stepmother

MICHAEL McDOWELL
& DENNIS SCHUETZ

(*writing as* AXEL YOUNG)

VALANCOURT BOOKS

Dedication: For Eric Shifler

Originally published by Avon Books in 1983
First Valancourt Books edition 2016

Copyright © 1983 by Michael McDowell and Dennis Schuetz

Published by Valancourt Books, Richmond, Virginia
http://www.valancourtbooks.com

All rights reserved. In accordance with the U.S. Copyright Act of 1976, the copying, scanning, uploading, and/or electronic sharing of any part of this book without the permission of the publisher constitutes unlawful piracy and theft of the author's intellectual property. If you would like to use material from the book (other than for review purposes), prior written permission must be obtained by contacting the publisher.

ISBN 978-1-943910-34-2 (*trade paperback*)
ISBN 978-1-954321-37-3 (*trade hardcover*)
Also available as an electronic book.

Cover by Henry Petrides
Set in Dante MT

In the winter a blanket of snow was laid over the grave, and when the sun lifted it off in the spring, the man married a second wife.

"Aschenputtel"

PART ONE

The Firstborn

I

On the twenty-second ring of the telephone, Verity Hawke Larner finally leaned over the edge of the bed and swatted the receiver off the cradle. She yawned dramatically, fumbled for the receiver, and answered in a drowsy—even catatonic—voice, "Hmmmmmmm . . ."

"Hello, Verity!" a cheerful female voice exclaimed on the other end.

Verity yawned again, cleared her throat, and accidentally dropped the telephone. Then she picked it up and pressed it to her ear. "What?" she whispered hoarsely.

"It's me, Verity—Louise. I've been ringing and ringing."

"I was here. I was asleep. It's the middle of the night."

"It's one o'clock in the afternoon in Boston." Louise's voice was crisper now. "That means it's noon in Kansas City. This is *not* the middle of the night. Open your blinds."

Verity crawled out of bed and went to the window. With one crooked finger she pulled down a single slat of the Levolors. Searing sunlight flooded the room. "Oh, God," cried Verity into the telephone, "you must be psychic! It *is* day!"

"Why aren't you at work?" Louise demanded.

"No work today. Louise, why have you called?"

"You ought not sleep away your day off. I'll bet there's plenty of interesting things to do in Kansas City on a sunny afternoon."

"How did you know it was sunny here?" Verity said after a pause. "You *are* calling long distance, aren't you? I mean, you're *not* in Kansas City, are you?"

"No, of course not, I'm at the office. Your father asked me to call. . . . I thought *Saturday* was your day off."

"I have every day off."

There was no commiseration in Louise's voice when she asked, "Were you fired again?"—only surprise at the unvarying repetition of an old pattern.

Verity slid down into the pillows.

"No, I quit."

Louise began a little sermon, the highlights of which were inflation, the job market, and the importance of a goal in life.

Louise played a double role in Verity's existence. She was her widowed father's business partner—in a real-estate agency that handled some of the most exclusive properties in Boston—and she was Verity's mother-in-law. Three and a half years before, Verity had married Louise's only son, Eric. Verity had been in Kansas City for two years; Eric was still in Boston.

Without interrupting her mother-in-law, Verity pulled her dark glasses from the drawer of the nightstand and put them on to cut the glare of the sunlight falling in strips through the opened Levolors. She looked at the man in bed beside her and tried to remember his name. "It starts with a B," she murmured.

Louise's lecture droned on.

"Blond hair," Verity whispered, with her hand over the mouthpiece, staring with a creased brow at her sleeping companion. "*Who* do I know with blond hair?" Gently Verity pried open one of the man's eyes: the iris was dark brown; she decided that the blond hair must be bleached. She cautiously lifted the sheet and peered beneath it. "Definitely bleached," she concluded, then said to her mother-in-law:

"Job burnout, that's why I quit. Do you know what job burnout is like?"

"Of course I do. Channel Five had a five-part series on the eleven o'clock news."

"Then will you *please* stop with this inane lecture? If I need a lecture, I'll call Father. If I want to be bored, I'll call Eric."

When her marriage to Louise's son failed after only a year and a half, Verity arranged with the Hawke family lawyer to have separation papers executed. She withdrew what little personal funds she had in her savings accounts, climbed into her car, and drove west. She settled in Kansas City because that was where the car broke down. In two years she had had seven different jobs.

Verity slid out of the bed, grabbed a robe from a pile of clothes on her desk chair, and pulled it on.

"I hope you're eating right, Verity. You shouldn't get too thin —it makes you look haggard."

"I look fine, Louise."

Verity peered out of the window again. Her orange Lotus was angled up over the curb and onto the sidewalk in front of the apartment building. She looked back at the man in the bed, wondering whether he were responsible for that, or whether it had been her own doing.

"Louise," said Verity, "is there a reason for this call, other than to annoy me?"

"Yes," replied Louise, "I'm calling about your sister."

Verity roamed into the kitchen, still with the receiver cradled at her ear.

"If it's about Cassandra, why didn't Father call?"

"Richard is out closing a deal this afternoon," Louise said coolly, "and he asked me to speak to you. Besides, Verity, I'm part of your family too, you know."

Verity opened the refrigerator and took out a carton of orange juice.

"All right, Louise, I'm sorry. I didn't mean to heap insults on your permanent wave. Now what about Cassandra?"

Verity flipped open the spout and took a long swallow straight from the carton.

"She was made managing-editor of *Iphigenia* this week."

"Great," said Verity impassively. "The entire readership of that magazine could sit down to dinner around a card table. Have you ever looked at that thing?"

"Of course I have. We have a complete run of it right here in the office."

"Have you actually sat down and *read* it?"

"I skimmed a few of the issues that Cassandra edited," Louise replied testily. "I don't really understand poetry. The point is, Verity, your father thinks a little celebration is in order for Cassandra and he wants you here for it. He thinks two years is long enough to stay away. Besides, you haven't proved a thing. Your brother wants to see you again too."

"How is Jonathan?"

"Fine. So what's your answer, Verity?"

Verity sat at the kitchen table, tracing a nail over the features of the leering orange face on the waxed juice carton.

"Well," Louise persisted, "will you come home?"

"Sure," said Verity at last. "I'll come. It's a good excuse not to look for another job. Besides," she added after a moment, "I would like to see Father again. And Cassandra. And Jonathan. And—I guess that's all."

"Do you want me to have one of the secretaries make plane reservations? What airlines fly out of Kansas City?"

"Don't bother, I'll be driving. It'll give me a chance to stop in New York to see some old friends."

"Just make sure you're in Boston by the time of the party—it's planned for the second. Oh, and as long as we're on the subject, why don't I ask your father to look around and see if he can find a position for you somewhere, something that—"

"Don't bother!" said Verity sharply. "Why don't you ask Father if he can find Eric a job instead?"

The man—whoever he was—walked in naked from the bedroom. Verity looked over her shoulder. He grinned, stretched, and yawned magnificently—it was more of a roar.

"*What* was that?" asked Louise.

"The dog," said Verity.

"It didn't sound like a dog."

"The dog has a cold."

"I didn't know you liked pets. What kind is it?"

"Mongrel," Verity replied dryly. The man reached for the orange juice; Verity snatched it away from him.

"Are you going to bring him with you?"

"He goes straight back to the kennel," Verity replied. "I have to go, Louise. I'll probably leave tomorrow. I may be in New York for two or three days, and then I'll come straight on up to Boston. When is this party again?"

"A week from Saturday."

"I'll be there for sure. Give Father my love."

Louise hung up without reply.

Verity turned to the man sitting across from her at the table.

"Have we been introduced?" she asked coldly.

On a balmy Sunday afternoon when the Japanese magnolias were in full bloom all over greater Boston, Verity Hawke Larner turned her orange Lotus into the horseshoe drive of her father's home. Where the drive widened before the house, she was distressed to find no space available to park. She pulled slowly around, ticking off the family cars, frowning at Louise Larner's lime-green Toronado, wondering at the unfamiliar yellow Cadillac. Verity reached the other end of the drive. She was about to turn into the street and park beside the cobblestone wall, when she suddenly changed her mind, shifted into reverse, and screeched backward over the gravel. She pulled to a stop right up beside her mother-in-law's Toronado, braked, and turned off the ignition.

Verity pulled a small brush from the glove compartment and ran it quickly through her thick, medium-length sandy hair. Then she withdrew a small, square envelope of leather. Unsnapping this, she took out a vial of white powder and a tiny slender spoon. Leaning down over the passenger seat, she quickly and expertly scooped out two mounds of cocaine, and snorted them up. She replaced the envelope, then looked into the mirror, and dabbed with a wet finger at all the stray grains of the drug. From the glove compartment she took a tube of ruby lipstick and applied it lightly to her mouth. Then she brushed her cheeks with just enough rouge to provide a natural-looking flush. After that, she readjusted her large-framed dark glasses. She grabbed her red leather jacket from the front seat and got out, leaving her bags in the back seat for one of the servants. She passed by the unfamiliar Cadillac, and peered at the address on an envelope that had been left face up on the dashboard: the car belonged to Eugene Strable, the Hawkes' friend and lawyer. Eugene Strable, Verity remembered, bought a new Cadillac every year.

The front doors of the house were unlocked. Verity slipped inside and closed them quickly behind her. Mechanically, she dropped her keys in the basket on the marble half-table in the foyer. She stopped and listened as she checked her outfit before going farther into the house. She wore black wool trousers tapered at the ankles and a red silk mandarin-style blouse beneath her red leather jacket. A gold chain rested about her neck, and more gold shone in the woven belt wrapped about her slender waist. Given the number of cars in the driveway, the house was curiously quiet. After a moment, Verity realized that the slight hum she heard was the sound of muted voices at the back of the house. She opened the door of the living room, walked its length, wondering a little at its consummate neatness, then stood at the closed doors of the formal dining room.

When Verity cocked her ear toward the doors, she could make out her sister Cassandra's voice, then Eugene Strable's—but why was everyone in the dining room at three o'clock in the afternoon? "My God," she murmured, "I'll bet they've waited luncheon on me!"

Verity took a deep breath—drawing a little more of the calming cocaine into her system—engineered an engaging smile, and wrapped her hands about the doorknobs. She turned them and thrust the doors wide. "Well, Father," she said, "I'm home. Have you killed the fatted calf?"

After her speech there was nothing to be heard in the room but the sharp tick of the mantel clock.

Verity looked around. The table was not set for luncheon. Eugene Strable stood at the fireplace. Jonathan knelt at the hearth and was lighting a small fire of kindling and cedar. Cassandra stood at the French windows, fingering the drapery cord. Louise sat fidgeting at the head of the table.

They all continued to gaze at her without speaking.

"Is there a reason," said Verity after a moment, "why you're all dressed in black?"

2

Verity had not been a month old when her parents purchased the house. Margaret Hawke, employing her considerable taste and her greater fortune, found exactly the place to suit them in a moneyed, well-managed, and discreet neighborhood at the southern extremity of Brookline, Massachusetts. Boston was less than fifteen minutes away by automobile, and at night the clouded sky might be red with the city's reflection, yet the setting was one of strictly European formality.

The oldest part of the house had been built in the early 1920s, in the French Provincial style. The façade was narrow, uninviting, private. The house stretched far back, and then turned left into an L. The grounds were a modest three acres, and neighboring homes had at least as much to boast; privacy was as much thought of in the area as fine views and the right gardener. In the front of the house vast chestnuts stood resolutely in a graveled parterre. In the summer these ancient trees masked the house entirely from the private road on which the property was set, and in the winter their stark, tan, leafless forms lent the place an air of well-bred bleakness. In the back of the house, however, were thick stands of spruce, maple, dogwood, and mimosa. In her first season there, Margaret Hawke planted five Japanese magnolias between the garage and the kitchen garden, to remind her of Marlborough Street, where she had grown up and where the magnolias bloomed in profusion every March.

A nine-foot cobblestone wall—constructed before zoning laws constrained fencing to a meager six feet—surrounded the property. An arced gravel driveway went right up to the double-door entrance of the house.

The formal rooms of the house were long, rather low-ceilinged, and elegant. The hallway floors were marble, and the walls were painted a soft gray. The living room was in blue and orchid, and Margaret Hawke had furnished it with pieces taken from her grandmother's house in Back Bay. The room was stately but comfortable. There were a maple-paneled office and two walk-in cloakrooms—one for men and one for women—at the very front, and at the back, a large dining room with a carved marble fireplace and three sets of French windows opening onto the back lawn; its walls were painted with the scenery of the upper Charles River. This entire floor, with suitable decorations, was prominently featured in the Christmas issue of *Architectural Digest* for 1965.

Two guest rooms and the master bedroom suite were located above this formal part of the house.

The stem of the L contained the kitchen, the breakfast room, and the servants' rooms—it was thought innovative in 1922 to have the servants sleep on the ground floor. Upstairs were the four bedrooms, playroom, nursery, and three baths in which the three Hawke children were brought up.

Jonathan now lived in Back Bay, in a condominium in one of the Prudential Center residential towers. His father had gotten it for him at a ridiculously low price. Cassandra still occupied the bedroom she had had since infancy, and Verity's, at her father's order, was kept always in readiness—with weekly airings and changing of linens—against her unexpected but always hoped-for return.

Two of the family's boats were kept in the garage, and the third space was taken up by Richard's Mercedes. Jonathan's yellow Porsche, Cassandra's black Audi, the Buick station wagon that was kept for the use of the servants, and Louise's lime-green Toronado were often arranged in a curved line along the gravel drive. The keys to all these vehicles were kept in a basket on the table in the front hall, so that the cars could be used or moved about at will.

The entire household worked that smoothly. There were dates, inexorable as Christmas, when the winter drapes were taken down and the summer drapes put up, when the gardener was sent down to Truro to open up the summer house, when the iron garden furniture was repainted for the coming season, when furs were taken out of storage for the winter. All this was now Cassandra's province. Richard rarely concerned himself with the workings of the house, but turned his energies to the running of his prestigious Newbury Street realty office. In colder months he often worked well into the night and on weekends. Late spring through early autumn, his spare time was devoted to navigating his sailboat along the upper reaches of the Charles River. To his children, Richard Hawke was a polite handsome stranger who knew a lot about winds and tides and each year at Christmas took them to the Boston Ballet's production of the *Nutcracker*.

The relationship of the Hawke children to their late mother

had been no less distant. Verity, Jonathan, and Cassandra had
spent their first years under the loving care of a nurse and gover-
ness. Their mother they remembered best appearing in the bedroom door, kneeling to kiss them, smiling—and saying good-
bye. The only time that Margaret Hawke spent six consecutive
months in the house was the last year of her life, when she was
confined to her bedroom with the cancer that killed her. When
she died, Verity was eleven, Jonathan ten, and Cassandra eight. At
her funeral none of the children displayed any emotion over their
loss. Not long after, Verity and Jonathan were sent off to private
schools in Vermont and New Hampshire. Cassandra followed
them within a year. Verity, who eventually went to Bennington,
was a fine student, and would have been a brilliant one if she
had only applied herself. Jonathan was best in the sciences, and
eventually graduated cum laude from Harvard, with a degree in
anthropology. Cassandra went to Radcliffe and worked for a spe-
cialized major of comparative literature. She managed to gradu-
ate summa cum laude and Phi Beta Kappa. After college Verity
and Jonathan had returned, at least for a time, to the mansion in
Brookline. But with their father they maintained relationships of
only the politest forms of affection. Verity moved out at the time
of her marriage and did not return when the marriage broke up.
Jonathan left following a terrible argument with his father, begun
around a disagreement on what shoes to wear to church. For the
past year Cassandra had lived alone with her father, but without
any increased intimacy.

Verity pushed the doors of the dining room shut behind her.
She slid her hands into the pockets of her slacks and waited for
someone to speak.

"All right," she said. "I know. I missed the party. I'm sorry."

Verity pushed at the bridge of her dark glasses and looked her
sister over. Cassandra was dressed in a white silk high-necked
blouse with ribs of lace down the front. Her black skirt uncharacteristically touched just above the calf. She wore conservative
gray-toned hose and square-toed, heavy-heeled shoes of black
leather. Her thick auburn waves were brushed back from her
pale, sharp-featured face.

"We've just come back from Mount Auburn," said Eugene Strable.

"The cemetery?" asked Verity in a small voice. She was suddenly aware that the family lawyer seemed much older than when she'd last seen him. The lines about his mouth and forehead were more pronounced and his short dark hair had grayed at the temple.

Cassandra moved across the room toward her sister, but Verity became suddenly very stiff. "Am I going to have to play Twenty Questions?" she asked, then demanded, "Where's Father?"

"Father died on Wednesday night," said Cassandra. "In Atlantic City."

"Atlantic City!" repeated Verity in surprise.

"Father and Louise went down for a three-day convention of real-estate brokers," Cassandra explained.

Verity turned to Louise Larner, who had remained seated at the head of the table.

"Brokers of *luxury* properties," added Louise, her expression betraying no emotion.

Louise was tall and slender with a ruddy, smooth complexion. Her figure was shapely, and she did not show all of her forty-five years. Her hair was jet black, glossy, and fell in thick waves that just brushed her shoulders. Louise spent at least two lunch hours a week in a fashionable beauty salon three doors down from the Hawke Associates Realty Company.

"How did Father die, Louise?" Verity asked levelly.

"It was his heart," Louise returned quickly, "but you see ..." Louise looked at the three Hawkes, and went suddenly silent. She slipped forward a little in her chair, as if waiting anxiously to be prodded to speak more.

"His *heart?*" Verity cried. "He never—"

"It was completely unexpected," Eugene Strable said gently. His eye, however, was on Louise. "It took us all by surprise. When I heard ..."

Verity moved distractedly away from her sister, shunning her touch. At the French doors, she stopped and turned back to the lawyer. Then she looked at Louise. "Tell me how it happened."

Louise began to speak, but Jonathan stood up from the hearth, where the fire had begun to blaze. "Now isn't the time, Verity," he said.

Louise sat back in the chair. She tugged at one of her wide shirt cuffs.

Verity looked up at him. "Now *is* the time. I want to know exactly what happened." Verity closed her eyes a moment, then sat down at the end of the table, directly opposite Louise Larner. Cassandra came forward and placed her hand on her elder sister's shoulder, but Verity writhed out from under it.

"I think," the lawyer said to no one in particular, "she probably *should* hear about Richard, even though . . ."

"Even though *what?*" demanded Verity. "Why isn't anyone speaking?" Verity looked straight at each person in the room.

"Your father and I flew down to Atlantic City last Monday," Louise began, before anyone else spoke. "Richard and I have been involved for some time in a big new development project. So much of our time has been spent in lining up investors—wooing them, Richard called it. And as it turned out, two of our biggest prospects are real dyed-in-the-wool gamblers, so Richard thought it would be a good idea if we met them down at Atlantic City, so—"

"For God's sake, Louise!" snapped Verity. "Nobody cares about that!"

Louise took a noisy little breath expressive of having taken offense, but she went on more to the point: "Anyway, Richard and I were in Atlantic City, on business. And you know how your father was when he traveled—no matter how tired he was, it was almost impossible for him to get to sleep. Wednesday night we had dinner and your father wanted to get up early the next morning so he went to bed and took sleeping pills. Sleeping pills don't always work, you know, and this time they didn't work at all. I guess he took some more of them, without thinking, of course, and they still didn't work, so he got up and dressed and went down to the lobby to have a few drinks and do a little gambling."

Louise paused in a show of consternation.

"Go on," said Verity.

"He had a heart attack," said Louise slowly. She touched a hand to her neck, fingering the large onyx broach there. "At the blackjack table," she added with a grimace.

"My God," whispered Verity faintly and sadly. "Where were you? Why didn't you stop him from drinking after he took those pills; he—"

"Verity, I didn't know he had done it! I was so exhausted by all the meetings that day. I didn't find out about it until they came upstairs to get me. I don't need to tell you that I was devastated! I still am." Her voice rose in pitch and strength: *"Especially* since—" Louise left off abruptly, and glanced questioningly at the lawyer. "I think *now* is the time to tell them, don't you?" she said in a low voice. "Now that Verity's here?"

"Tell us what?" demanded Verity. "There's more? What more could there be? Father's dead."

"Now," sighed the lawyer.

Cassandra and Jonathan exchanged puzzled looks. Eugene Strable stepped up to the table and rested his hands on the back of a chair. Louise sat up straight and stiff. Her stockings whined as she uncrossed her legs.

"Louise and your father were married last Saturday," said Eugene Strable. "It was a civil ceremony in the Brookline town hall. Jeannette and I were witnesses." There was a long moment of stunned silence.

"It was very solemn and lovely," said Louise quietly. She folded one hand over the other in her lap.

Jonathan sat slowly in one of the wingbacks by the hearth. Cassandra drew her breath loudly. Verity mumbled, "Oh, Jesus! Last week?"

Louise nodded. "The trip to Atlantic City was business, of course, but it was a sort of honeymoon too. We were going to announce the marriage at Cassandra's party. Then of course Richard died. We couldn't find you, Verity, because you were on the road, but you promised to be here in time for the party. That's why we scheduled the funeral today," she added with a touch of reproach, "because you had *promised* you'd be back." She looked from one to the other of Richard's children. "I know this won't mean much to you right now, but I want you all to know that Richard was very, very happy this past week. We only had four days together—but they were perfect days."

The fire popped and crackled, and quickly the room became

too warm. Louise sat very still and expectant, most evidently waiting for someone to speak words of welcome to the family, or words of consolation on the loss of her husband. Jonathan, Verity, and Cassandra all maintained their silence, until it became oppressive. Louise rose and hurried through the swinging door into the kitchen. Verity sat at one end of the Sheraton dining table, well away from the fire. Cassandra took the chair next to her. Jonathan described the well-attended public funeral and the private graveside service at Mount Auburn.

When he was done, Eugene Strable turned so that he faced the three of them. There was genuine concern in his pale gray eyes. "I want you to do me and yourselves a favor. The three of you have lost your father, and I've lost my best friend—but Louise has lost her husband. She's trying hard to maintain her composure, but I know for a fact that she is deeply grieved. I know that there's been a little friction between you and Louise, but I'm going to ask you to put that aside for now." He looked from one to the other.

"I can't deal with this," said Verity, turning away.

A moment later, Louise came back into the dining room, bearing a large silver tray laden with cups, a steaming silver pot, half a dozen tiny spoons, and a silver sugar and creamer. The tray was obviously heavy. Eugene Strable made a quick movement to assist her, but she motioned him out of the way. She placed the tray on one corner of the table.

"I thought we all could use a little bolstering," she announced with cold dignity. "The cemetery was very damp, after all."

Cassandra made a distracted, almost imperceptible nod of her head.

Louise poured and Eugene passed out cups. When everyone had been served, Verity took a single sip from her cup and grimaced. "God," she said, "this tastes like creosote."

"It's Lapsang Souchong," said Louise defensively. "It's all I could find. I'm not as familiar with the house as I should be . . ."

A few minutes later, Eugene Strable got up to go. Verity politely stood and shook his hand. Grasping her hand in both of his, he again offered his sympathy and his regret that it had all come as such a shock to her. He left, refusing Louise's offer to see him to the door.

Richard Hawke's three children and his widow remained in a rigid and lengthening silence in the dining room.

"You haven't asked about Eric," Louise said to Verity at last.

"I didn't intend to."

"He was at the funeral, of course. I'll be seeing him again this evening. I'll tell him to be sure and call you tonight."

"Please don't, Louise. I've had enough to contend with today."

"All right, dear." Louise was silent a moment, then said, "But I'll leave his number on the hall table, in case you change your mind. He lives in Cambridge now."

When she still got no reaction, Louise went on, in a slightly offended voice. "I think you owe it to Eric. Owe it to him for what happened at the funeral today. He was horribly embarrassed."

Jonathan and Cassandra looked up sharply and questioningly at this.

"What on earth happened?" asked Verity curiously. "I've never seen Eric embarrassed."

"*That man* you had an affair with showed up at the cemetery, looking for you."

"Which one?" Verity pursued dryly.

"Ben James," said Cassandra. "Louise, Ben James was a friend of Father's. *That's* why he was at the funeral."

Ben James had been at Harvard with Richard Hawke, and his daughter had been Verity's Bennington roommate. His affair with Verity had ended shortly before her marriage.

"I told him you were out of town," said Louise. Then she sighed. "It was a terrible moment for Eric."

"I told Ben to call tomorrow," said Jonathan.

"Good," said Verity, smiling at her brother.

"I'm going to run out to the greengrocer's now," said Louise, standing. "I volunteered to fix dinner for the four of us this evening."

"Where's Ida?" asked Verity. "And Serena? And Cara?"

"The servants are off, of course," replied Louise. "I suggested Cassandra let them have the day off to mourn in their own fashion."

"I see," said Verity.

"Is there anything you want me to pick up?"

Cassandra and Jonathan replied in the negative, and Louise started out. She had just opened the double doors and was stepping through, when Verity's voice halted her. "Oh, Louise!"

"Yes?"

"I think my car's blocking yours. The keys are in the hall basket. Don't bother about the bags in the backseat, I'll have someone bring them in later."

Cassandra stepped closer to the fire, staring into the flames for a long moment before shifting her glance to her sister. The fire was reflected in the large dark lenses of Verity's glasses.

Verity smiled ruefully. "I feel as if I've just been trampled by all ten thousand runners in the Boston Marathon."

"I need a drink," said Jonathan. He knelt before a Chippendale commode and opened the doors. Second of the three children, he was twenty-seven, tall, thin, and clean-shaven, with sandy hair a shade lighter than Verity's. When he smiled he was almost handsome, for a smile showed off his perfectly aligned teeth and gave definition to his jaw. He had the same sharp nose and highly defined cheek lines of his sisters—these they had all inherited from their mother. "Who else wants one?"

"I do," said Verity. "A vodka gimlet."

"I don't know how to mix that."

"Then Canadian Club and Seven. Light on the Seven and skip the ice."

"Verity," Jonathan said, rummaging for the whiskey, "I get the distinct idea that you saw the inside of a lot of bars in Kansas City."

"I did. Bar crawling is the favored sport of the elite in Kansas City."

"Are you going back?" Cassandra asked.

"I would rather walk naked through the fires of hell on a Saturday night than go back to Missouri." She took a long swallow of the drink.

"So you'll stay on for a while?" Jonathan asked.

"At least until the reading of the will, I guess."

Cassandra seated herself on the floor beside her sister's chair, her legs folded beneath her. The firelight played about her face and made glossy highlights in her hair. Verity absently reached down and grazed her sister's cheek with the back of her hand.

"I could get you a good position in the company," Jonathan offered. His company was the Commonwealth & Providential Life Assurance Corporation, headquartered in Boston. For the last three years he had had a job as an assistant director of personnel; he had already found cushy jobs for half-a-dozen Exeter and Harvard classmates.

"Thank you, Jonathan. Really," said Verity after a disapproving moment. "But I've suffered terrible job burnout recently, and it may take me a while to get over it."

"Cassandra, do you want a drink?" asked Jonathan.

"Sherry," she replied.

Verity shook her head. "So, what are we going to do about dinner?"

"Louise is fixing dinner," said Cassandra.

"Not for me, she's not. She going to show up with Eric and an armful of broccoli. I'm going out; who's going with me?"

"I will," said Jonathan.

They both turned to Cassandra. "It wouldn't be right," she said. "Not *this* evening."

Verity shrugged. "If you think I'm going to spend this evening watching Louise smile bravely in her tacky widow's weeds, you're out of your head. I certainly do not want to hear her version of the last four days of Father's life."

Cassandra tossed her hair and looked up at her sister and brother, Jonathan standing with his back to the fire, his shadow falling across Verity's face. "All right, we'll go out. After all, it's not Father's death that's upset me so much, it's the prospect of having Louise underfoot from now on." She took a breath, and said, "Poor Father." But there was no regret or remorse in her voice. "I haven't been able to mourn him at all yet. I guess I keep expecting him to come back from Atlantic City. I don't know who I thought it was they were burying in that casket today! The funeral home put rouge on his cheeks, and they parted his hair on the wrong side."

"Do you know what I'm going to miss most?" said Jonathan.

"I'm going to miss the calls to tell me there's a sale on at Louis or at Brooks Brothers."

Cassandra's laugh was short and bitter. "And his giving me advice on how to hire and fire."

"He didn't actually know us very well," mused Verity. "Nor we him."

"I wonder what's in the will?" said Jonathan.

"Knowing Louise," said Verity, "don't you imagine that she got Father to change it in her favor?"

"They were only married for four days," exclaimed Cassandra. "There wouldn't have been time."

"Well," said Jonathan reassuringly, "even if Father left everything he had to Louise, none of us is going to be left out in the cold exactly. Father's death doesn't affect the trust fund." He paused a moment, and then glanced at his sisters. "At least I don't think it does. We should be all right, even if worst comes to worst and Father didn't leave us anything at all."

"Don't say that," said Verity. "Father did leave us something —something very important."

"What?" asked both Jonathan and Cassandra.

"Well," said Verity bitterly, "Father's left us Louise Larner Hawke—our very own wicked stepmother."

3

"I can't help feeling guilty," Cassandra admitted.

"Guilty?" asked Verity. "About what?"

They were seated in the curve of a red-leather booth in a small Middle Eastern restaurant nestled beneath the elevated subway tracks in Boston's South End. Business was slow this evening, and now that some secretary's farewell party had staggered out after consuming a quarter of an hour trying to divide the check, there was only one other table occupied, and that was on the other side of the room. The lighting was so soft that Verity had removed her dark glasses. Her eyes were large, pale blue, and a little unfocused. Jonathan had left the table in order to make a telephone call.

"About going out on the night that Father was buried. And for not telling Louise we wouldn't be there for dinner after she went to so much trouble."

Verity shrugged nonchalantly, and remarked, "You know what I was thinking? I'll bet that when Louise gets laid she's like a lifer's wife on a conjugal visit."

Cassandra took a sip of wine and remarked, "When Jonathan gets back to the table, we'll give you a hand and lift you out of the gutter."

"I'll bet Father and Louise did it on the floor. That's more comfortable anyway, if she's on top. And I imagine that she *was* on top."

"Verity, you're being disgusting. You're talking about our *father!*"

"Honestly, Cassandra, you sound as if you thought the man didn't have any sexual urges. The only unnatural thing about Father was that he found Louise Larner desirable. And that he married her. God! My mother-in-law is now my stepmother! I feel as if I were living in darkest Appalachia." She took a sip of wine, glanced around to see if Jonathan was off the telephone yet, and then looked back to Cassandra. She said thoughtfully, "Louise was bad enough when she was only father's business partner. She was considerably worse in the part of my mother-in-law. Now in the third act she comes on stage triumphant in the simultaneous roles of widow and stepmother. She's a woman who wants her name all over the program of a very cheap melodrama."

Cassandra was silent a moment. She averted her eyes, and then asked in a low voice, "Don't you think Father's death rather . . . strange?"

"Do you?" Verity returned flatly.

Cassandra nodded her head slowly. "Yes. It was just so odd, the whole Atlantic City business."

"Too odd," Verity agreed. "I don't buy Louise's story either. It's too pat, too—I don't know—too *something.*"

"What do you mean?" said Jonathan, slipping back into the booth.

"Would anybody who knew Father," said Cassandra, "ever imagine that he would die in Atlantic City, of all places, slumped across a blackjack table?"

"Absolutely not," said Verity, "but Louise said they were there on business—that investment nonsense she was babbling on about. Do you think she was lying?"

"Things just don't seem to add up," said Cassandra hesitantly. "Father *did* occasionally take sleeping pills, and of course he liked his brandy and soda after dinner—but he wasn't the type to get things mixed up, and forget what he had taken and what he hadn't. Father could recite the name of every client he had for the past ten years, and then tell what they paid for their property. He could have listed what every one of us got for Christmas in nineteen sixty-two. Father was hardly the type to forget he had just swallowed a handful of sleeping pills."

"That's true," said Verity after a moment. "What do you think really happened?"

"Do you think . . . ," Jonathan began, then trailed off.

"Think what?" prompted Verity.

"That he committed suicide?" said Jonathan. "It had certainly occurred to me."

"No," Cassandra exclaimed. "Father thought suicide was cowardly and selfish and not respectable."

"After a few days of marriage to Louise," Verity offered, "he may very well have changed his mind."

"If he was going to commit suicide he wouldn't have married Louise first," said Cassandra. "And he certainly wouldn't have killed himself in New Jersey."

"There wasn't an autopsy, was there?" asked Verity.

"Of course not!" exclaimed Cassandra. "Why should there have been?"

"To find out exactly how he died," said Cassandra.

"He died of a heart attack," said Jonathan. "That much was obvious, I guess."

"Right," said Verity glumly.

"Are you actually thinking that Louise . . . ?" Cassandra began, but she didn't finish.

"No, not really," sighed Verity. "I'm no fan of Louise's, but I don't think she's stupid enough to murder Father only four days after she married him. I'm not sure I believe her story, but I can't figure out why she'd lie about it either."

"Louise is willing to fight for what she wants, but I don't think she's willing to risk murder for it."

"*It*," repeated Jonathan. "That's the question. Just what is it that Louise does want?"

"I'm not worried about that," said Cassandra. "But this whole business with Father bothers me. I wish there were some way we could find out what really did happen in Atlantic City."

"Just wait," said Verity. "If Louise is lying about something, she'll trip up. Just pay attention to what she says and does. If there was something funny going on, we'll figure it out sooner or later. Louise isn't *that* smart."

They finished their wine in silence.

"Did you get hold of Apple?" Cassandra asked Jonathan suddenly.

He nodded, and drained his glass.

"Apple?" Verity inquired.

"Jonathan's new girl friend," explained Cassandra.

"*Miriam* Apple," said Jonathan. "But she thinks Miriam sounds too biblical. Everybody calls her Apple."

"She used to have a band," added Cassandra with a smile. "They were called Apple and the Corps."

"Very cute," said Verity impassively. "Jonathan, do you mean to tell me that you are actually dating a woman who sang in a rock group?"

"Sings," said Jonathan, with a small smile of pride.

"She's still in a band," added Cassandra.

"Good God," said Verity. "I'm going to have to revise my entire opinion of you, Jonathan."

"Apple and I get along just fine."

"Are you living together?"

"Sort of," he replied, wagging his head. "We still keep separate apartments, though."

"I see," said Verity. "You know, this really is very interesting, Jonathan. And after all those boring 'Cliffies' you used to drag through the house. What kind of group does she have?"

"Punk!" said Cassandra.

"Dear God!" cried Verity, sitting back suddenly and laughing. "Can I take this? You're actually going out with a singer in a punk rock band? After six years of Exeter, four years of Harvard, and three salary reviews at Commonwealth & Providential you now decide to consort with an eighteen-year-old woman with a green and purple Mohawk? I'll bet she dresses head to toe in leather—or dyed buckskin, probably—and wears lucite platform shoes with goldfish in the heels. Probably got a tattoo of a skull in flames across her shoulders. And her great ambition in life is to shove Nancy Reagan's face into a paper shredder. Have I described her perfectly?"

"No," said Jonathan coldly. "I'll have you know that she's pleasant and intelligent. She holds down a very good job, at a publishing house. Her last promotion was announced in *Publishers Weekly*. And she is *not* eighteen."

The waiter laid the check on the table.

Cassandra picked it up, and both Jonathan and Verity allowed her to do so without protest.

"This is on me," said Cassandra, unnecessarily.

"Where does she live," Verity asked, "this punk singer?"

"Commonwealth Avenue, near Exeter," replied Jonathan. "She shares the place with her drummer."

"Male?"

"Yes."

Verity shook her head. "I don't know about you, Jonathan."

"What do you mean?"

"You always used to be such a preppie. Now you've got a girl friend who has a male roommate, and it doesn't seem to bother you at all. A real preppie wouldn't allow his fiancée to share an apartment with another man. Is he gay?"

"Hardly," said Jonathan. "He and Apple used to be lovers when they were students at Emerson, then they broke up, and now they're just friends."

Cassandra had paid the check and received her change. She figured out a tip, placed it on the tray, and sighed. "Well, I suppose it's time to go home and sit around the living room and talk about how wonderful Father really was."

"I don't want to go back to the house," said Verity firmly. "At least not until I'm sure that Louise has gone home. The one thing to be grateful for in all this is that Father didn't have time to move Louise into the house before he died."

"I don't want to go back there either," Jonathan admitted.

"What we need," Verity suggested, "is a bar that's dark and loud."

"And all stagger home drunk at two in the morning?" Cassandra asked.

"We don't have to stay for last call," Verity pointed out.

"And we don't have to get drunk either," said Jonathan.

"*I* do!" said Verity, lifting Cassandra's wineglass and drinking off the little that remained. Cassandra still hesitated to give her sanction to the plan.

"I guess we could go to Betsy's Pit," said Jonathan, "just for a little while, I mean."

"All right," said Cassandra at last.

"Betsy's *what?*" asked Verity with a long sigh.

Dinner that evening for Louise was a dismal affair. Wearing a simple full-length dress of scarlet silk with dolman sleeves and a wide sash tied loosely at the waist, she sat alone at the head of the table in the empty house, and picked at the food she'd so carefully prepared. It grew cold on her plate, until the only smell in the room was the burning paraffin of the chafing-dish candles. She was humiliated and angry that Cassandra, Jonathan, and Verity had left for the evening when she had specifically announced her intention to fix dinner for them. No amount of distress, no unwillingness to remain in the house could excuse such crass impoliteness. As their father's widow, Louise thought, smoldering, she deserved a lot more consideration than she was getting.

Louise put down her fork and dropped her folded napkin beside her plate. If her stepchildren chose to snub her, then she would simply revel in the luxury of being alone in the house that would be hers when the will was read. She sat back and glanced about the dining room. Then she turned slightly and stared down the long marble-floored hallway. She got up and went to the French doors. Pulling aside the draperies, she gazed out into the moonlit gardens. The shrubs and bed of daffodils and tulips were all black and pale gray. She turned back and, placing both her hands on the table, looked about the room again with satisfaction. Leaving her food untasted on her plate, she wandered about the first floor of the house, wondering at the space and the luxurious emptiness of it. Twenty principal rooms, three acres of ground, stone walls nine feet high to protect her privacy—Louise could scarcely believe her good fortune.

All her life Louise had been thrust into apartments. Each had seemed tinier than the last. Her father had been custodian of a large apartment building in Philadelphia, and as part of his salary got a two-bedroom basement flat rent-free. In one of those bedrooms, with a single horizontal window looking out onto a concrete walk where the residents walked their dogs, Louise had lived seventeen years with sisters one and two years older than herself. Both her father and mother had been at home all day. The place was never empty. Louise might not have gotten along with her sisters under any circumstances, but their cramped quarters ensured years-long battles between them.

To escape that bedroom and that basement flat, Louise married a construction worker named Fred Larner. He was twenty-two, she was eighteen, and the day before their wedding he made a down payment on a house in a subdivision he was helping to build in the town of King of Prussia, near Philadelphia. Louise would not only leave her apartment, her parents, and her sisters —she would leave the claustrophobic city as well. Until the house was finished, however, she lived with her husband in a single room over a corner grocery two blocks from her old home. Here at least there were times during the day when she had the place to herself, and when she looked out of the window she saw sky. She had often dreamed of going to college, but with her family's straitened finances there had been no possibility of that.

Three weeks before she and Fred were scheduled to move into the house in King of Prussia, she was brought word that he had been killed on the job. A crane cable, lifting a prefabricated roof into position, had snapped. Fred was crushed by a corner of the falling roof.

Louise wept bitterly, less for her husband than for the house she was now convinced she would never have. She remained another week in the room above the grocery before moving back in with her parents.

Fred had carried a fifty-thousand dollar life insurance policy on himself, but he had failed to sign this over to his wife. His mother and father were beneficiary, and refused to help their daughter-in-law even when Louise informed them that she was pregnant.

Fearing the medical consequences of an illegal abortion, and hoping that a grandchild would charm some of Fred's insurance money out of his parents, Louise went through with the pregnancy. Eight months after Fred's death, Louise gave birth to a boy, whom she named Eric. By the time Eric was christened, his Larner grandparents had moved to Florida on Fred's insurance money, and did not even send a silver spoon.

On the day after that christening ceremony, Louise packed a small suitcase and took the train to Boston, leaving her infant son in the care of her mother and father. She secured a rented room in the West End of the city, and took a job as a secretary in a small South End realty firm. Monthly she sent forty dollars home to reimburse her parents for their care of her child, but she called only on Christmas and her own birthday, and even then never asked after the boy.

Eleven years after her arrival in Boston, she applied for and received her realtor's license. The office where she was employed went out of business when the owner was jailed in a kickback scheme involving plumbers and electricians. Louise got a job with the Hawke agency in Back Bay, and was able to take a lot of the burden off the shoulders of the recently widowed Richard Hawke. After delivering some papers to her employer's home in Brookline, and seeing in what style the widower lived, Louise vowed to herself that she would marry the man come hell or high water.

Although Richard Hawke had allowed himself to be consoled by a succession of handsome women, he looked on Louise as a valuable company employee and not a bedmate. Louise bided her time. She moved from the West End to Back Bay. Her new apartment was very small, but it had an unimpeachable address. She had looked into the possibility of purchasing a house for herself, but Boston prices were prohibitively high, and, as a single woman, Louise was considered a bad credit risk.

One day, when she had been working at the Hawke agency for

a little more than five years, she came home and found a strange teenager loitering about the entrance to her building. She said to him, "Don't you have anything better to do?"

He said to her, "Ma?"

Her parents had died together in the wreck of a chartered bus carrying nuns and local parishioners on a tour of springtime Washington, D.C. Eric hadn't discovered his mother's address until after the funeral.

Louise took her son in because she didn't know what else to do with him. He turned out to be ill-tempered, spoiled, and generally difficult to manage. She soon discovered that his bouts of ill-temper coincided with his monetary needs. She learned that she could stave off almost any amount of bad behavior with a five-dollar bill. When he was eighteen she found him a rent-controlled apartment, and installed him in it. "You keep up the payments," she said. "Because if you don't, you won't come back to live with me."

Eric, in three stormy years of living with his mother, had acquired a certain superficial polish. He was very good-looking, and his manners, when he wanted something, could be charming. He found jobs with no difficulty, but his innate laziness usually prevented his holding on to them for long. Despite her threats, Louise often helped him out with his rent.

Neither Louise nor Richard understood why her son and his daughter should get married, but they did so, when they were both twenty-five. Eric later confessed that Verity had been pregnant, but had miscarried on the honeymoon. Louise never told her employer of this, despite the intimacy that had crept up on them after fourteen years together in the office.

At a realtors' convention in New York City, Louise finally managed to seduce a very drunk Richard Hawke. She never allowed him to forget that one moment of intimacy. After a time there were others, and Louise began to talk about marriage. In lieu of that, Richard offered her a partnership in the firm. Louise took it, and didn't mention marriage for fully two years. Then she resumed her assault with increased vigor. Richard eventually relented and agreed to wed her the following autumn. Louise didn't want to wait that long, and finally persuaded Richard to marry her a week before the celebration of Cassandra's promotion.

Four days later Richard Hawke collapsed across a blackjack table in Atlantic City and died.

When it became apparent to Louise that the trio would not return even in time for dessert, she propped open the kitchen door and carried all the food back in. Rather than preserving it, she very carefully scraped it into the disposal and methodically destroyed all trace of the meal she'd prepared. If they apologized later, she'd say that she hadn't done a thing. She washed the dishes and placed them in their proper cabinets. Through all this her expression was grim. When she had finished in the kitchen, she went to the small telephone niche beneath the stairs, snapped on the green-shaded table lamp, and shut herself in. As she dialed she yanked a clip-on earring from her lobe, and shoved her hair back over her ear.

The line connected after two rings, and without waiting for a greeting, Louise said—in her coolest business tone—"Eric, it's Mother."

"Hold on a minute, Mrs. Larner, and I'll get him," said a hesitant female voice.

"Barbara?" Louise asked, with unrepressed irritation.

"How are you, Mrs. Larner? Eric told me about Mr. Hawke. I was sorry to hear about it. He said you had only been married a few days, I'm so—"

"Barbara, I thought you had gone off to Nepal for a year." There was no masking the accusatory style of the inquiry.

"It was Senegal. And it was awful. So now I'm back."

"Oh," said Louise. "I knew you gave up your apartment when you went away—have you found another place to live yet?"

"Here's Eric now, Mrs. Larner," said Barbara quickly. "It was nice to talk to you."

Louise pursed her lips and waited for her son to come on. She listened intently, hearing muffled voices for a moment, then nothing, as the receiver was covered up. The silence lengthened. Louise tapped the heel of her shoe on the polished oaken floor.

"Yeah, Ma?" said Eric unenthusiastically.

"The word is *yes* and I am your *mother*," said Louise.

"*Yes, Mother*," replied Eric distinctly and sarcastically. "What's up? Why'd you call?"

"Verity's back."

"She wasn't at the funeral."

"She didn't even know Richard was dead until she walked in the house this afternoon. You should have been at the house too."

"I was at the funeral," he returned mildly. "Besides, Richard hated my guts. You told Verity I was broke, didn't you? You told her I had lost my job and didn't have any money?"

"I told her that you went right from the funeral to an important interview. How did it go?"

"How did what go?"

"Your interview! Though I don't know who gives job interviews on Sundays."

"I didn't have an interview today."

"Eric, you *told* me you had to 'see a man about a deal' you were working on. I assumed you meant something about a new job."

After a moment, Eric replied, "Oh, that's right. I met with him. Maybe something'll come through."

"I certainly hope so."

"Ma, is there some particular reason you called? Barbara and I were just on our way out—"

"I called to talk about your marriage, that's why I called."

"Why? Has that bitch finally decided that she wants a divorce?"

"You better hope she doesn't!"

"Why not? I don't want to be tied to her for the rest of my life."

"You listen to me, Eric." Her voice was brittle. "You've got a rich wife. Her mother left her a fortune in that trust fund, and next year sometime Verity comes into the whole thing. I know she walked out on you, but now she's back and I think she's going to be here for a while. Take advantage of the fact. After the will's read, this house will be mine."

"Are you sure about that?" asked Eric.

"Of course I'm sure! I was Richard's wife. This was Richard's house, so the house comes to me. And when the time comes—and the time will come pretty soon, I can tell you—I shall very politely ask Cassandra and Verity to pack up their old kit bags and get out. That's the perfect opportunity for you to step forward and offer Verity the hospitality of your apartment."

"Verity hates my guts."

"She fell in love with you once, she can fall in love with you again. Put on a little charm for once."

"I don't think my charm works on Verity, Ma—*Mother.*"

"Think of something that will."

"I'll try."

"You'll do it!"

"All right, all right. Did you tell them yet? About your having married Richard?"

"Yes."

Eric laughed sharply. "I'll bet three jaws hit the floor."

"It was a surprise," Louise admitted. "Don't try to change the subject. We were talking about you and Verity."

After a pause Eric said, "Why are you so interested in Verity and me all of a sudden, Ma? I'd have thought you would still be playing the bereaved widow."

"I *am* bereaved," snapped Louise. "But Richard is dead and there's nothing I can do about it. There *is* something that can be done about you and Verity. And one more thing."

"What?"

"Get rid of Barbara. Tonight."

"She doesn't have anywhere to go! She just got back from Senegal."

"Get rid of her, Eric. She's very pretty. She'll find a place to sleep. Drop her off in front of a bar."

"I can't just toss her out tonight. . . ." He whispered this last; evidently Barbara was not in the same room, but nearby.

"Tomorrow then."

"Tomorrow," Eric sighed.

"Right after you do that, call Verity. Ask her out to dinner at a nice restaurant. I'll pay. Do you understand?"

"I guess."

"You do or you don't!"

"I understand."

"Good-bye, darling," she said, and hung up the telephone.

For the next half hour Louise wandered through the darkened house, peering into rooms she already considered to be her own.

4

Betsy's Pit was located on the edge of a desolate field of stiff grass and broken bottles in East Cambridge, in the basement of a vast and mostly empty warehouse. For several decades—the decor was original thirties mahogany and cast iron—it had been the hangout for blue-collar workers and truck drivers in Cambridge's small bleak industrial sector. They drank beer, ate sandwiches prepared by the waitresses in a tiny back room, and played on the cheapest pinball games in Cambridge—still three games for a quarter. In more recent times, the management of Betsy's Pit, realizing that no matter how good their weekday business was, their evening and weekend business stank, decided to establish an additional clientele. They built a small stage, and began to bring in bands—the rawest sort of local band, that would play for nothing but the exposure. But even the rawest bands have their followings—there being a fair segment of the sophisticated Boston pop-music crowd who will go to hear *anyone* in order to be able to say, "Oh, yes, I heard them when they were nothing, and playing —God, can you believe it?—Betsy's Pit." Soon the Pits, as it was affectionately called, became *the* place to try out a first band; the management turned no one away, and some sort of crowd gathered there every night. There was even a legend that a scout from EMI Records, visiting Betsy's Pit incognito, had signed a band on the evening of its first and only public performance. On the weekends, the better bands played. Even for those groups that had attained a certain position in the Boston hierarchy of new music, the exposure was still good, the audience knowledgeable and enthusiastic; more often than not, Betsy's Pit deserved their sincerest gratitude.

The Pits had a vast floor covered in linoleum tile. The paneled walls were painted black once a year; the ceiling was of patterned tin. Along one wall was a long mahogany bar with mirrors, and a tiny stage was jammed in the opposite corner between the doors of the bathrooms. Two waitresses patrolled the entire floor: bleached blondes in their early forties, they wore shiny black uniforms stretched over their corpulent figures. Their hospital shoes had been painted black with shoe polish, and year in and year out they wore corsages of plastic Christmas poinsettias. Darlene was a very good waitress; Susan couldn't get an order straight for two pitchers of draft beer.

Verity loved the place immediately. When Jonathan stated his preference for a table well back and in a shadowed corner, she protested, and led him and Cassandra to a tiny table disconcertingly near the stage. One band had just finished its set; the players were putting away their instruments.

"That was Boys Say Go," said Jonathan.

Verity looked at her brother in surprise. "You've been here before," she said. He nodded. Darlene came to the table and took orders.

When she went away, Jonathan said, "I've got a surprise. Apple's band is playing here tonight."

"Oh," cried Verity, "then I get to meet her! I suppose she'll be kicking her spiked-heel boots right in my face." She reached out and touched the stage; she didn't even have to lean forward. "I can hardly wait—Apple and the Corps, huh?"

"No," said Cassandra, "that was the old group. They broke up."

"I can't begin to guess what they're called now," said Verity, and speculated: "The Slaves of Fashion? The Self-Inflicted Wounds?"

"People Buying Things," said Jonathan.

"Not bad," Verity considered. Darlene appeared and distributed their drinks. Cassandra handed the woman a ten-dollar bill.

Jonathan checked his watch. "They'll be on in about twenty minutes . . ."

"Good," said Verity, rising with her drink. "That gives me time to look this crowd over."

She went straight to the bar, and planted herself next to a tall, slender, black-bearded man who had just walked in the door and was ordering his first drink. Verity adjusted her dark glasses, smiled, and said, "Hi, I've never been here before. . . ."

"Did you know," said Cassandra slowly, as she turned in her

chair to watch her sister at the bar, "that Verity lost her virginity on the day that Fluellen was run over?"

Fluellen had been the Hawkes' Welsh terrier; he died when Verity was fourteen.

"So?"

"They say that sex and death are intertwined," said Cassandra, rather mysteriously.

Jonathan considered this a moment. "I think you're having to read too much poetry at *Iphigenia*."

Boys Say Go had gotten its instruments off the stage, and, after a few minutes' pause in which nothing at all transpired, two tall, slender, clean-shaven men came out and stood together whispering, seemingly oblivious to the fact that they were standing on a spotlit stage in front of a hundred and fifty people. Desultorily, and with many pauses between their many whispered and quite relaxed exchanges, they set up the band's equipment. Finally, one of them slid the strap of his electric guitar over his shoulder and dropped his fingers across the strings. His friend idly experimented with volume and vibrato on the electric keyboard.

A third man came onto the stage. He was short and well built, with a swarthy complexion. His curly chestnut hair fell softly about a face displaying distinctly Italian features—large, thickly lashed eyes a shade darker than his hair, and a full mustache above a sensual full mouth. He wore a light blue tank top and white painter's pants. Out of a back pocket jutted a set of drumsticks. He crossed the stage, pausing first to speak to the keyboard man and then to the guitarist. He looked over the crowd, then nodded and smiled at Jonathan.

Then Cassandra felt the man's eyes upon her. His broad smile narrowed and faded for a moment.

Cassandra flinched from his stare.

He winked solemnly, then returned his attention to the other musicians.

Cassandra laughed nervously. "That's the new drummer?"

Jonathan nodded.

"What's his name?"

"Rocco. Rocco DiRico."

"Sounds like a gangster," said Verity, suddenly appearing at tableside and sitting down again. "Is that his real name?"

"What happened to your new friend?" asked Jonathan.

"He wasn't as good-looking as the gentleman in question." She lifted her glasses, leaned slightly forward toward the stage, and stared unabashedly at the man who had winked at Cassandra. "He's beautiful," she pronounced. "However," she went on, "now that I see him up close, I find he's a bit too hairy for my taste. Cassandra, what's your opinion?"

"I think he's very good-looking."

"He's just your type," said Verity flatly. "Or don't you still fantasize about being ravaged into oblivion by a dusky, handsome Mediterranean man?"

"You've had too much to drink."

"Actually, I've had very little to drink. My shamelessness is entirely a result of some cocaine I snorted with my new friend over there. I just came over for a few minutes so that he could engineer a little purchase for me from that bartender."

"I take it," said Cassandra, "that you don't intend to end up in Brookline tonight?"

"I told him I wanted to hear this next set, and then I'd go back with him to Porter Square."

"You should have asked him to join us," said Jonathan politely.

"Not on your life. He's sweet, but not the type you introduce to your family. Besides, I don't want him to find out that Father was buried today—it might inhibit him. By the way, Cassandra, what's cab fare from Porter Square to our house?"

"At least fifteen, probably twenty."

"Lend me forty, will you? I'm full of plastic, but I gave my last cash for the coke."

Cassandra opened her wallet and took out two bills, folding them up and handing them to her sister beneath the table. Verity passed the back of her hand beneath her nose, inhaling sharply. "Oh that's better," she murmured. "I never get it quite right the first time. So," she went on, "the band is called People Buying Things. The lead singer's name is Apple, and the drummer is Rocco DiRico. Who's the red-and-yellow afro on guitar? And the platinum whiffle on keyboard?"

"Bert and Ian," said Jonathan. "I'm not sure which is which.

I don't think they have separate personalities. Apple just always says, 'Bert and Ian this' and 'Bert and Ian that.' They're lovers, and very jealous. Besides each other, all they care about is music and speed."

"So where's this fruitful fiancée of yours? Are we supposed to bang on the table and demand Apples?"

"No," said Jonathan. "Here she is." He pointed to the door of the ladies' room, from which Miriam Apple was just emerging. She was tall, with a pretty and intelligent face framed in a mass of hennaed ringlets. She wore bright ruby lipstick, pale pearl-gray eye shadow, and four tiny hoops piercing her left ear. Her blouse was of fitted gold lamé, gathered at the wrists and tucked into a pair of wine-colored harem pants. Her gold lamé slippers curled upward from the toes.

Apple carried a cordless microphone in her left hand. She stood at the edge of the stage and extended her right arm expectantly. The guitarist reached down and pulled her up onto the platform in one sure motion. The lights lowered by quick degrees. A drum roll sounded. With a flourish, the keyboardist punched a violently dissonant chord just as Apple, feet spread, back arched, and head thrown dramatically back, screamed directly into the microphone.

Verity, unprepared for the violence of the noise, choked on her Scotch. Jonathan smiled with pride. Cassandra stared at the drummer.

The guitar brought up and replaced Apple's scream. The drums came in full force, and Apple jumped high into the air. When she came down again, she belted:

> I don't want your bread,
> I don't want your pity.
> I just wanna string myself
> From the roofs of Psycho City.
>
> Gonna slash my fucking mom.
> Get your knife and hold it steady.
> Wanna spill my daddy's blood
> From the walls of Psycho City.

We're gonna waste the halt and blind,
So guess you better be ready
To see a million corpses piled
On the streets of Psycho City.

At the song's finish, beneath the wild applause, Jonathan leaned over and shouted in Verity's ear: "Apple wrote the lyrics —isn't she great!"

During the day Miriam Apple was an assistant editor for a prestigious publishing house in Boston, where she made herself invaluable in three principal ways. She was an exhaustive line editor who could knock into shape a piece of narrative trash that made the senior editors of the firm shudder. She handled difficult authors no one else in the firm would even shake hands with. And she could make *any* book sound good on its back cover or jacket flaps. Moreover, and of equal if not greater importance to her superiors, Miriam Apple had no particular regard for credit being given where credit was due. She was perfectly willing for some- one else to be congratulated for a job she had done superbly; this was not because Miriam Apple was timid, or naturally self-effac- ing, but only because she had, when it came down to it, no inter- est at all in the publishing industry. She cared about her music, and the job at the publishing house was no more than that—a job. As far as she was concerned, it was simply easier to perform her duties very well than it was to shirk them. She had started out woefully underpaid, as was the case with every female employed by a Boston publishing house, but now she commanded quite a respectable salary. She was given a raise every time she received an offer from another firm—for her publishing house lived in intermittent terror that Miriam Apple would be snatched away, and that her onerous duties would have to be divided among the remainder of the staff.

Her co-workers were aware that Apple had some interest in music but were wholly ignorant of the fact that she was lead singer with her own band, a band that—marginally—made money, a band whose name was advertised—about every other week—in the Arts section of the *Phoenix*. Apple's energy was apparently inexhaustible; but, of late, she had turned over to Rocco DiRico a number of the duties she had formerly assumed herself. It was now Rocco who dealt with Lenny Able, the manager of People Buying Things and of a number of other bands just starting up in the Boston area. Rocco argued less with Lenny than Apple did, but this was probably because Rocco hadn't know Lenny as long as she had.

It wasn't entirely clear to those who knew them what Apple and Jonathan saw in one another. They didn't seem at all alike. It had at first been conjectured that Apple was after Jonathan's money; but Jonathan, though of a rich family, had no idea of personal finances and was always borrowing ten- and twenty-dollar bills from Apple, and never remembering to pay them back. Apple had great affection for Jonathan and he for her.

Between her music and her work at the publishing house, Apple had very little time to spare. What time she and Jonathan did have together was spent at carefully selected films or plays, gallery exhibits, and their favorite restaurants, making love, and casually planning their future together. The congruence of taste and desire, they had decided nearly six months before, warranted an engagement.

5

Next morning, Louise walked into the dining room just as Cassandra was finishing her breakfast. She took Cassandra to task for having gone off on the very night of her father's funeral. "I was going to fix dinner for the three of you. I went to a great deal of trouble, because I thought it was important that the family should be together at a time like this."

"The family *was* together," Cassandra pointed out. "I'm sorry you were left all alone here, Louise, but we had already made other plans."

"You might have told me about them!" Louise protested.

"You didn't ask us," Cassandra returned placidly. "You simply announced what your plans were without asking what *we* intended to do."

Louise closed her mouth very tightly. "Where's Verity?" she demanded.

"Right here," said Verity, from the doorway. Her dark glasses rested on the top of her head, but after one glance at Louise, she pulled them down onto the bridge of her nose.

Louise looked Verity up and down. "Those are the same clothes you had on yesterday. You spent the night out, didn't you?"

"Oh, Louise," sighed Verity. "Really." She crossed to the buffet and poured a cup of coffee for herself, generously spooning in cream and sugar.

"You did, didn't you?" persisted Louise angrily.

Verity sat down at the table. "I'm a physical wreck," she remarked to Cassandra. "But I feel great."

"Where were you?" cried Louise.

Verity turned slowly. "Do you really want me to answer that?"

"Yes, of course I do."

"All right. I went home to Porter Square with a complete stranger. I think his name was Jack. He was very nice. I had taxi fare, but he drove me home anyway."

Louise drew in her breath sharply. "Are you actually admitting to me that you were unfaithful to Eric?"

"You asked. I'm too hung over to lie."

"And on the night your father was buried?!"

"Christ, Louise, give me the confession and I'll sign it. Just lower your voice. You're rattling my contacts."

"I can't believe this," cried Louise. "I can't believe the way you two girls are acting."

"I'm twenty-five," said Cassandra. "Verity's twenty-eight. We're not girls anymore." Her glance at her stepmother was hard. "Louise, what are you doing over here at this hour, anyway?"

"I *came* to see if I could do anything for you. This is a house of mourning. I *came* to see if I couldn't be of some help. After the death of a husband and father, a family has to draw together."

In one parallel motion, the two women looked at Louise sharply, glanced at one another, and then turned away.

"We're fine," said Cassandra grimly.

"We're fine," echoed Verity. She rose to pour out another

cup of coffee. "Louise, aren't you going to be late opening the office?"

Louise marched out of the room without another word. Verity returned to the table.

"How long has she been here?" Verity asked.

"She's been skulking around the house all morning. In and out of rooms. Up and down the stairs. She's been driving Cara and Serena crazy."

"Giving them orders?"

"Trying to," said Cassandra. "I put a stop to that. I told them to ignore everything Louise said."

"Louise covets this house," mused Verity. "You can see it in the way she walks through the rooms."

"I have no intention of turning it over to her," said Cassandra flatly. "Nor of asking her to move in, either. Although I think that's what she's after."

"No, of course you mustn't," said Verity absently. "Last night, I was thinking. . . ."

"Thinking what?"

"That one of us ought to go down to Atlantic City," said Verity, almost shyly.

Cassandra nodded her understanding. "To see what really happened?"

"Yes," said Verity. "Talk to people."

"Jonathan and I spoke about this last night after you had gone off," said Cassandra.

"And?"

"And it wouldn't do any good. A resort hotel hushes these things up. They don't stay in business by advertising how many customers fall dead in their casinos, or how many people get shot up in their dining rooms."

"We could talk to the police," said Verity. "Or hire a detective."

"Sam Spade or Philip Marlowe?" Cassandra's laugh was melancholy. "I'm not making fun or anything. Jonathan and I thought about the same thing. It's just that all that's so melodramatic. Finding out exactly *which* blackjack table Father died at, hiring a private eye. This isn't a melodramatic family. We've never done things like that. We'd never do it right if we tried."

"Maybe," said Verity. "So what do we do?"

"Nothing, for the time being. I mean, we don't really believe that Louise *killed* Father, do we?"

Verity didn't reply. She merely got up and closed the dining room doors. Then she went to the swinging door and peered into the kitchen. Only Ida, the cook, was there.

"What are you doing?" Cassandra asked.

"Louise may be lacking in tact, but she's not deaf," shrugged Verity. "I just wanted to make sure she wasn't hanging around."

"And," Cassandra went on, "if Louise did do something stupid in Atlantic City, she'll probably do something stupid again. We'll just have to watch her closely, that's all."

Verity considered this as she poured out a third cup of coffee. At last she nodded her acquiescence.

After another few moments, Cassandra asked, "Did you at least have a good time last night?"

"I think so," said Verity after a moment of hesitation.

"You don't know?"

"Well, we did a lot of coke, and then we drank something that—Cassandra, honest to God it was bright green, and I *know* it wasn't crème de menthe." With two fingers she rubbed the skin just beneath her nostrils. "And I've got nose-burn from the amyl nitrate."

Cassandra raised her eyebrows and shook her head.

"Are you shocked?" asked Verity, peering at her sister over the top of her dark glasses.

"No," sighed Cassandra. "Just surprised that in the midst of all that, you still had time to think about Father, and Louise, and Atlantic City."

Verity shook her head slowly. "I couldn't think about anything else." She took the last coffee roll from the plate on the table and spread it with butter. There was a lull as the two sisters gazed out the open French doors at the morning-lit garden. Right outside was a plot of King Alfreds. The flowers were thick now, and on a slight breeze their bright fragrance was blown into the dining room. For a moment it even covered the smell of the freshly brewed coffee.

"Should we apologize to Louise?" Cassandra asked.

"I think it might be a good idea," said Verity. "For appearances. I have no scruples about that sort of thing, do you?"

"I suppose we ought to apologize. She's going to be enough trouble around here without our starting fights about nothing."

"Why," Verity wondered aloud, "would Father actually *marry* her? He was obviously sleeping with her—probably he had been sleeping with her since Mother died. Why didn't he just leave it at that?"

"I don't know. She talked him into it, I guess. At the funeral I kept thinking, well, at least Louise won't be underfoot anymore. Ironic, isn't it?"

Verity wrinkled her nose. "This room reeks of that awful perfume she wears. Where does she buy it—J. C. Penney's? I can't believe she was here at breakfast. It's just what I need to start the day—my mother-in-law accusing me of infidelity to her rotten son."

"Your *stepmother*," Cassandra corrected.

The offices of the Menelaus Press occupied the second floor of an eighteenth-century building on Brattle Street in Cambridge, just on the edge of Harvard Square. Cassandra's office, as managing editor of the quarterly journal of the arts and letters, *Iphigenia*, had two large unshaded multipaned windows that overlooked Brattle Street. Three walls of the room were covered floor to ceiling with bookshelves. A long oaken table behind Cassandra's desk was laden with magazines, bound galleys, loose galleys, manuscript boxes, and stacks of manila envelopes containing unsolicited submissions.

Cassandra returned to work a few days after her father's death and found her already cluttered desk piled high with mail, all of it, doubtless, requiring replies. She worked all morning on correspondence, lunched with the artist who had brought preliminary sketches for the artwork of the September issue, and spent the afternoon at her desk, feet up and coffee in hand, grimly perusing an ample and badly typed manuscript. Every minute or two she'd look up—at the clock, at the budding trees that appeared through one window, at the wooden shingle reading MENELAUS PRESS EST. 1942 that appeared through the other. Whenever she finished one page of typed poetry, she'd place it carefully atop a pile on the far side of her desk, and riffle through what remained to be read.

A crisp spring breeze creaked the shingle, and automobile traffic and students' voices around Harvard Square were a pleasant murmur. As had been the tradition for many years, in celebrating the end of the long Boston winter, large numbers of students had stuck their stereo speakers in the dorm windows and were playing the Beatles' "Here Comes the Sun" at full blast. When she finished the last page, she sighed, sat wearily back, and called out, "Sarah!" She waited, but did not bother to call again.

After a minute or so, a short, squat woman of about twenty-seven appeared in the doorway of Cassandra's office. She had waist-length dull brown hair, and wore wire-rimmed glasses, an ill-fitting cowl-neck sweater, and a pleated plaid skirt.

Cassandra waved a hand toward the manuscript.

"You wrote the report on this?"

"That's Mary Scott-Trout?" asked Sarah, and when Cassandra nodded grimly, Sarah said, "Yes, I did."

"Did you actually read it?"

"Of course! I thought it was a darkly fragmented statement of the condition of the artist as societal mentor, fragmented yet—"

"I read your report," interrupted Cassandra. "I also read the poetry. They're both total nonsense."

"Oh," said Sarah weakly, "do you really think so?"

"I do."

Sarah clucked her tongue. "You know, that could be a real problem. Her new book just got that wonderful review in the *New York Review* and there was this big article on her home life in the *Globe Magazine* last Sunday."

"Why is that a problem?"

"Because in the *Globe* article, she told the interviewer that *Iphigenia* was going to publish her entire new cycle of poems as a special issue."

Cassandra smiled. "She actually said that?"

"Yes." Sarah shifted uncomfortably, and leaned against the doorjamb.

"Where on earth would she have gotten an idea like that?"

"I don't know. I didn't say anything to her about it. Really, I didn't."

"I believe you," said Cassandra. Sarah looked very relieved. "Ms. Scott-Trout and her fans at the *Globe* are just going to have to be disappointed."

"Should I write her or call her?" Sarah's tone of voice betrayed with what little pleasure she anticipated the task.

"I'll take care of it," said Cassandra, and reached into the drawer of her desk for a sheet of the journal's notepaper, embossed in the upper-left-hand corner with the figure of a young woman standing despondently on the seashore.

"You don't mind?" asked Sarah incredulously. "I *hate* writing rejection letters."

"So do I," said Cassandra. "I hate doing things like this. And I'm terrible at it, but if someone is going to waste our time by presenting a patently unpublishable manuscript, I don't mind telling her I feel that my time has been wasted."

"You won't say that!"

"No, I'll be very polite, and I certainly won't mention what she said in the *Globe* interview."

"She's going to be very very upset," warned Sarah, edging out of the room. "You know how obnoxious she can be."

Cassandra had already begun to type.

"It's not our problem," said Cassandra. "*Iphigenia* wasn't founded so that we could devote entire issues to the fourth-rate poetry of minor celebrities of the local literary scene."

Sarah paused at the door. "I just wonder where she got the idea that we were going to publish her."

Cassandra paused in her typing. "It's not important, Sarah. Forget it. Some people just have a talent for making trouble."

At five-thirty, Cassandra dropped the letter to Ms. Scott-Trout into a mailbox, then walked over to the Harvard Faculty Club and took part in a small dinner symposium on the state of Boston literary arts.

It was nearly 10:00 p.m. when Cassandra parted from a noisy group at the door of the Faculty Club. She got wearily into her car and was about to cross the river on her way home to Brookline when she quite suddenly changed her mind and turned left onto Storrow Drive. Ten minutes later, she pulled into a free spot in front of Betsy's Pit.

Inside, Boys Say Go was in the midst of the same set it had played the last time she'd been to the place. Cassandra slipped off her quilted leather jacket and draped it over the back of an empty chair at the bar. She slid up onto the stool and ordered a glass of white wine. For a long while she sat, lost in thought, neglecting not only the band behind her but the glass of wine in front of her.

She didn't even turn around until twenty minutes later, when the drummer smashed his cymbals with such force that his drumsticks snapped apart. She politely joined the audience in applause. She watched as the band packed up their instruments and drifted off the stage, and looked expectantly for Rocco DiRico and People Buying Things to come drifting on.

Instead, six women appeared, wearing puce body stockings and knee-high lace-up high-heeled boots. All of them had teased green hair, white pancake makeup, black eyeshadow, and crimson lipstick.

Puzzled, Cassandra called the bartender over.

He was young, burly, and sandy-haired. When Cassandra smiled at him, he returned her smile with suggestive warmth.

"What's the name of that group setting up now?" she asked.

"Vera and the Swamp Pussies. That's Vera with the green hair."

"They all have green hair."

"Vera's the tall one. Ever seen 'em before?"

"No, I haven't. I thought People Buying Things would be playing here tonight. That's why I came. Will they be on later?"

"No, but why don't you hang around anyway—I get off at two."

"Do you know if they're playing anywhere tonight?"

"Who?"

"People Buying Things."

"The Rat."

"The what?"

"The Rat. The Rathskeller," he explained. "Kenmore Square."

"Oh," said Cassandra uncertainly. "Yes . . ."

"You come to a place like this, and you don't know the Rat?" He shrugged and was called away to fill an order. When he returned he asked, "Are you going to wait for me tonight?"

Cassandra shook her head with a smile. "I can't," she said in a soft voice. "Sorry."

The bartender shrugged. "You know Rocco?" he asked.

"Yes," replied Cassandra. "But not well," she added after a moment.

The bartender swept his eyes from Cassandra's face down to her breasts and then back up again. "Rocco and I have the same taste." He paused, evidently waiting for a response. But when none came he took up his towel, which had lain on the bar beneath his fist, and said, "Go over to the Rat. If you can believe it, the place is even scruffier than here. Don't go in the front; you'll never get a table, you won't get near the stage, and Rocco won't even know you're there. Go around the back, tell 'em Andy sent you. That'll get you in. He may be in the dressing room, but if he's not, wait for him there."

Cassandra smiled sincerely. "Thank you," she said.

"You don't look like a groupie."

"I am *not* a groupie," said Cassandra pointedly.

Andy shrugged. "If it doesn't pan out, come on back over here. I get off at two."

Cassandra pulled the coat over her shoulders, smiled a farewell, and left the bar without answering him.

"Andy? Who's Andy?"

The broad woman dressed in the none-too-clean waitress's uniform blocked Cassandra's way in the rear entrance to the Rat. She had already gotten by two sixteen-year-old girls sharing a joint with a young man relieving himself loudly against the lid of a garbage can.

"Andy works at Betsy's Pit," Cassandra explained. "He told me to give his name as a password."

The waitress regarded Cassandra skeptically. She was in her mid-twenties, with a greasy yellow beehive and vivid blue Cleopatra eye shadow. A wad of gum ballooned her right cheek. Her hands were on her hips and her feet spread wide, one heel tapping rhythmically to the muffled beat of the band playing behind the wall of concrete just to their right.

"Andy," the waitress repeated.

"You know him?" Cassandra asked uneasily. She wasn't in the habit of going to bars at all, much less sneaking in the back way.

"Used to work here," the woman said sourly, shifting the wad of gum to her other cheek. "Punched me out one night."

"Oh," said Cassandra quietly, "that's terrible."

"I dislocated his jaw. I broke his toes," the woman said. She waited for Cassandra to speak again.

"Look, I'm not trying to avoid paying the cover, I'm just trying to find Rocco. That's who I came to see. And Andy is *not* a friend of mine—he just told me to use his name—if that makes any difference."

"It does." The waitress stepped aside. "Dressing room's down front. That door to the right of the front stairs."

As Cassandra slipped past her, the waitress grabbed her arm, pulled her up short, and hissed in her face, "You tell Andy for me: he comes around here I'll break his face into little pieces and stuff 'em in his shoes!"

Cassandra gently pried her arm free. She found the dressing room, which the performers shared with the furnace for the entire building, but hearing several male voices raised in heated discussion behind its closed door, she went out to the bar. She took a stool next to a mirrored wall, and ordered a white wine.

"They're fabulous!" shouted the man sitting next to her, referring to the group then playing on the stage at the opposite end of the room.

"Who are they?" Cassandra shouted back.

"The Instant Spellers!"

The Instant Spellers were in fact terrible, but Cassandra nursed her wine through the remainder of their set, and waited impatiently for the appearance of People Buying Things. During the break, Cassandra ordered her second glass of wine, and began sipping that.

"Did you catch the first show?" asked a female voice behind her.

Cassandra turned. Miriam Apple stood there, looking softer than she had appeared on the stage of Betsy's Pit.

"I just got here," said Cassandra. "I . . . I had a hard day. A long day. I wanted to hear some music and relax."

Apple smiled wryly, and slid onto the recently vacated stool next to Cassandra. "This place isn't for relaxation," she pointed out. "And you shouldn't have come."

"Why not?" asked Cassandra, surprised.

"Because," said Apple, "Rocco missed two cues the other night."

"I beg your pardon?"

"Staring at you staring at him."

Cassandra blushed and smiled. "I didn't think performers ever really saw who was in the audience."

"Cassandra," said Apple, "I won't go so far as to say that your tongue was draped over the edge of the stage, but . . ."

"Maybe I'm becoming a fan."

"Not exactly. You may admire our work, but you're not a fan."

"I don't understand."

"A fan shows up *every time* we play." Apple nodded thanks to the bartender who had brought her a glass of Scotch and ice. She took a swallow and sighed. "I just wish fans paid a little more than the rent. I'd love to quit my job." She waved a hand toward the stage, and then extended the motion to take in the bar as well. "My job downtown, I mean. *This* is my work. This is my life. The publishing job—that's support, and that's all it is."

Cassandra looked toward the stage where the guitarist and keyboard man were setting up the instruments. "What kind of jobs do Bert and Ian have?" she asked.

"They both work in a record store, the one down on Boylston Street across from the library, and Rocco's in the men's department at Filene's, third floor. You think he looks good in a leather vest and no shirt—you should see him in a gray wool suit. One night we're going to come here straight from work. I'll wear my little tailored pinstripe, and Rocco will be in gray wool with everything buttoned down, and we'll do twenty-one verses of 'Fuck Until You Faint.' That'll get 'em!"

Cassandra was taken aback. "Is that one of your songs?"

"No, that's a song by Eva and the Perons. Heard of them?"

"No."

"Don't bother. They're low-class druggies and they're not serious about music. They just want to be musicians because they heard that musicians get a lot of free drugs. Once our agent booked us on a double bill with them. I was livid, and Rocco wanted to walk out, but unfortunately we needed the money. Five minutes before they came on, they decided to change their name. You know what they changed their name to? Surgical Penis Clinic. Then they came out and the lead guitarist got into a fistfight with a man sitting at the front table. She hit him with a mike base. He had to have three stitches. And we had to come on *after* all that."

"You lead an interesting life," Cassandra remarked. "Jonathan never told me those kinds of things."

Apple shrugged. "Our lives are all work. We work at our nine-to-fives and then we play music all night. If we're not in a club, we're practicing. If we're not in a club *or* practicing, then Rocco and I work on new material. I don't know why Jonathan puts up with it. But he does. Our real problem is Lenny."

"Lenny?"

"Our agent," Apple explained with a frown. "He's an idiot. He gets us play dates, but always on the same round: here, the Pits, Jack's in Cambridge, and then some godawful place out in Saugus where nobody in the audience weighs less than three hundred pounds. Lenny has never understood the concept of upgrading. We take turns fighting with him. Tonight it was Ian and Bert's turn."

"I think I heard them earlier," said Cassandra, "when I went by the dressing room. Why don't you change agents?"

"Easier said than done. I've told you how busy we are—there's not much time to go out looking. And do you have any idea how many bands there are in this town? Outside of New York, Boston probably has the best new music scene in the country. But there aren't that many agents. And the ones there are, aren't that good. The good ones all go to New York."

"I don't understand why you don't manage yourselves. What is Lenny doing that you and Rocco couldn't do better?"

Apple shook her head. "I could do it if I quit work, and Rocco could do it if he quit work—but it would take time to get established, to get things going. And who'd support us in the meantime? Lenny's terrible, but at least he keeps us employed. The fact is, we're in a bind." She raised her finger for another drink, and while it was being poured, looked around the bar.

"I don't mean to pry or to give advice when it's not wanted, but . . ."

"Give it," said Apple.

"Why don't you listen to what you're saying?" said Cassandra earnestly. "You're in a bind, but you also know what will get you out of that bind. If Lenny isn't doing his job, then you ought to get rid of him. If you want another agent badly enough, you'll find him and you'll get him. And if you don't, then you'll manage it yourself. Right now you're stagnating. You're playing three dates a week—"

"Sometimes four."

"—four dates a week, but it's going in a circle. You said it yourself—no upgrading. You make your own luck, you know."

"I had no idea that working at a classy little magazine like *Iphigenia* could teach you so much about the real world."

Cassandra laughed. "You should hear me on the subject of unsolicited manuscripts!"

"You're right, though," said Apple, nodding ruefully, "about all of this."

"I know I am," said Cassandra. "Lately I've been thinking about becoming an agent myself—a literary agent, I mean. I'm not a good writer—I have the craft, but not the talent. I am a very good editor, but I don't find editing all that exciting—you're too hemmed in by authors. What I really love is contracts, terms, fighting for percentages and publication dates and all that sort of thing."

"You do all that at *Iphigenia?*"

"I do a little of it. Enough to whet my appetite for more."

"'Knowledge and Logic and a Heart of Ice,'" quoted Apple.

"What's that?"

"A good agent," replied Apple. "You know, we really *should* get rid of Lenny. Rocco and I get up in the morning, and we harp on

Lenny. We meet for lunch and all we talk about is Lenny."

"That's a lot of wasted energy," said Cassandra.

Apple finished her second drink, and put her glass down. "Time for me to go." She looked around the bar. "I don't know *where* Rocco is. He wanted to meet you the other night, but I told him there had been a death in the family, and that you were distracted and another night would be better."

"I wasn't distracted."

"I know," said Apple thoughtfully. "Neither was Jonathan. I don't understand your family."

"What do you mean?"

"I understand Jonathan, of course, but by himself, not in combination with the rest of you. Oh, of course, I like all of you, but . . ."

"But what?" asked Cassandra curiously.

"I don't know—I guess I was just brought up differently. We didn't have money."

Cassandra laughed. "What difference does that make?"

"All the difference in the world." The voice came from behind them. Cassandra and Apple turned on their stools. Rocco stood between them. He wore a pale blue tuxedo shirt beneath a pair of tailored white farmer's overalls, his hands pushed deep into the back pockets.

"You're late," said Apple, sliding off the stool. "You've made this nice young woman wait. She had to talk to me for twenty minutes, and she hated every minute of it." Apple introduced them quickly. She said, as she started to walk away, "We're on in ten." Then she stopped, looking at the stage. "Where are Bert and Ian?"

"Screaming at Lenny," replied Rocco.

Above the noise of conversation, above the jukebox, above the rattle of glasses behind the bar, came the sound of a harsh male voice shouting: "Fuck you both!" A short wiry man with close-cropped hair, wearing denim pants and a stiff new denim jacket with an open-collared patterned shirt and some small quantity of gold around his neck, flew out of the dressing room. He shoved his way through the crowd and out the back door exit, briefly setting off a fire alarm.

"That was Lenny," said Apple with a smile, and left. Bert and Ian had come out of the dressing room, evidently quite unperturbed, and were beginning to tune up. Rocco took his drumsticks from his back pocket and held them parallel to the floor between the palms of his hands.

"We meet at last," he said.

"At last?"

"I hear Jonathan talk about you. Apple too. You're the literary wiz, right?"

Cassandra smiled. "So I tell myself."

They were silent a moment. Rocco turned his hands so that the drumsticks were perpendicular to the floor. "Listen," he said, "Apple's spending the night at your brother's place. I've got a fireplace and a bed that sleeps two."

Cassandra blushed and laughed. "You work fast." She didn't reply to his proposition, but she didn't look away from his eyes either.

"We'll be done in a little over an hour," he said. "We can cab from here, unless you don't mind walking down to Exeter Street."

Cassandra continued to look at him for a moment, then she said, "I'm parked out back."

6

Cassandra rolled over in the bed, moaning in half-sleep. As she stretched across the rumpled sheet, the spread and patchwork quilt fell away from her breasts. Wondering why Cara had not yet called her—she instinctively felt it to be past her usual time for rising—she yawned, took a deep breath, and opened her eyes.

Someone had changed her curtains.

The last vestiges of sleep were suddenly purged from her mind, as she realized she was not in her own bedroom. For one thing, her own curtains were large-patterned, and these were solid ocher. For another, her own blanket was deeply quilted, and satin, not cotton.

She grabbed the spread and held it against her breasts as she sat up in the bed. She looked across the room and saw her clothing draped neatly over the ladderback of a rush chair to one side of an oak bureau with black knobs. On an identical chair on the other side of the bureau was a set of men's clothes, even more neatly folded. She examined them: white overalls and a blue formal shirt.

She had spent the night with Rocco DiRico.

It seemed so obvious, once she had figured it out—she wondered how she could have forgotten.

She looked at the door, watched it for a moment to see whether it would open. It did not. She got up quickly, strode across the room, and took from a white porcelain hook on the back of the door a red velour dressing gown. The polished oak floor was cool beneath her feet. She stood before a beveled mirror over the bureau, took a brush and ran it through her thick hair until she felt presentable.

She opened the door of the bedroom, and stepped out into the hallway.

The apartment was quiet. Passing down the hallway, she peered first into the bathroom and then into Apple's bedroom, which looked as if it hadn't been slept in the night before. She went into the living room. Three high, curtainless windows fronted Exeter Street on this side of the building, and the sun shone brightly through a dozen very healthy spider plants, whose tendrils cast delicate shadows across a white shag rug. She heard music, not hard rock, but something familiar and rather cheap.

She turned to the kitchen door. Behind it a radio played a muzaked version of " 'Drink to Me Only With Thine Eyes'," and Rocco DiRico hummed along. Cassandra nudged open the door, and was overwhelmed with the odor of freshly brewed coffee.

Rocco, seeing her, suddenly broke into the words:

> Drink to me only with thine eyes
> And I will pledge with mine,
> Or leave a kiss within the cup,
> And I'll not look for wine.

Rocco stood at the counter, blindingly bright where the sunlight struck the white formica, and began filling small yellow glasses with orange juice from a yellow pitcher. He was bare-footed and bare-chested, wearing only a pair of jeans riding low upon his hips.

"Good morning," whispered Cassandra, who hadn't found her voice yet. She made a small cry as her feet touched the cold linoleum. Rocco put down the pitcher, turned, and took her unexpectedly in his arms. She pressed her hands against his chest in an automatic gesture of defense, but then relaxed as her fingers were ground against the thick chestnut hair there. Rocco studied her face, smiling and still humming along with the song.

"That was our lullaby," said Cassandra.

"Really?" asked Rocco, pausing in his humming only long enough to put the question to her. "Strange lullaby."

"It was the only song my father knew how to sing. I think I was in college before I realized it was a love song."

He leaned forward and kissed her hard, one hand gently caressing her neck. She laughed deeply in her throat, a laugh that was strangled beneath his kiss. Rocco's other hand slid up from her hip and unfastened the loosely tied sash of the robe. As the garment fell open, he pressed her closer, massaging her breasts against his own chest; she could feel the growing hardness beneath his jeans chafing against her thigh. She put her arms about his neck, twining her fingers into the thickness of his curly hair. "Now I remember last night," said she, drawing her head back a moment.

Rocco moved his hand from her breast, down across the flatness of her stomach and abdomen, and into the auburn hair between her legs. Cassandra lifted one leg and wrapped it around his calf. She pulled her mouth away from his and let her head loll back, eyes half-lidded, as he bit and kissed lightly at her neck and ear.

"Are we filming *God's Little Acre* with hidden cameras, or is this what all city people do before breakfast?" asked Apple, from the open doorway.

Cassandra and Rocco separated without any apparent embarrassment. Cassandra carefully retied the sash of her robe.

"We didn't hear you come in," explained Rocco.

Apple had replaced her large hooped earrings with tiny pearl studs. Her hennaed hair wasn't as fully combed-out as the night before at the Rat. She now wore an open-collared white blouse with tiny pearl buttons, a chocolate skirt, and matching jacket. Jonathan appeared in the doorway behind her, and smiled uncomfortably at his sister.

For a moment, Cassandra stared silently at him. Then she said, in a completely matter-of-fact voice, "Good morning, Jonathan."

"Good morning," he mumbled in return.

They all sat down at the table near the window that looked out over Commonwealth Avenue.

"Why did you come back here?" Cassandra asked Apple. "You're already dressed for work."

"I always feel like a hooker if I go to the office from someplace other than home. Besides, I needed to make plans with Rocco for the evening."

While she and Rocco quickly and expeditiously talked over what they must accomplish during that day on behalf of the band, Jonathan turned to his sister and said, "This has all the earmarks of an embarrassing situation."

Cassandra shook her head. "I certainly don't intend for it to be."

"Okay," said Jonathan, after a moment, "I guess it's not. It's just strange, Cassandra."

"I heard!" cried Apple.

"Heard what?" asked Cassandra.

"Heard you were publishing Scott-Trout's poems in a special issue of *Iphigenia*."

"A vicious rumor," Cassandra sighed, but eagerly took up the abrupt change of subject. "If the postal service is working, she'll have her rejection with her morning coffee."

Rocco had brought heated cinnamon rolls to the table. Apple grabbed one off the plate, took a bite, and pointed the remainder of it at Rocco. "Did he show you how hot he looks in a gray three-piece?"

"Last night?" said Rocco. "Apple, my idea of kinky sex is not walking around the bedroom in a three-piece suit."

"Well, then, what is your idea of kinky sex these days?" demanded Apple.

"Apple!" said Jonathan reprovingly. His face had turned very red.

"Sorry."

There was a moment of silence before Apple spoke again. "Well, Jonathan—you and I are very much in the way here. And I'm late anyway. Can you drop me off at Arlington Street?"

"Sure," he said, rising hastily. He appeared relieved to have found an excuse to leave.

"Get a move on," said Apple to Rocco, as she rose and stuffed the remainder of the cinnamon roll in her mouth. "Or you'll be late too. Cassandra, you and I will have to get together soon and trade literary gossip."

"Get out of here," said Rocco. "Jonathan, see you later."

"See you later, Rocco," said Jonathan, and hustled Apple out of the kitchen. "Bye, Cassandra."

"Bye, Jonathan," his sister said.

Cassandra and Rocco sipped coffee. They heard Apple's low heels clattering across the polished oak floors, then the slam of the apartment door.

"Jonathan was upset to find you here," said Rocco.

"He had no reason to be," said Cassandra stiffly.

Rocco smiled. "You're his little sister. He's worried about you. He's afraid someone's going to come along and break your heart. When do I get to see you again?"

"When do you want to see me again?"

"Lunch?"

"All right."

"Dinner?"

"All right."

"After our show?"

"All right. But won't you be tired?"

He leaned forward out of the chair, and scooped her up in his arms. Her head fell delicately against his shoulder. "I've only seen men do this in the movies," she remarked.

"Well, then," said Rocco, "you're in luck, Miss Hawke. I'm showing coming attractions in the bedroom. . . ."

Verity's sleep the night before had been restless, disturbed by dreams of her dead father. After a long hot shower that did little to ease the tension in her shoulders and neck, she breakfasted on toast, coffee, and a screwdriver. Rattling the ice in her half-consumed drink, she wandered into the study and looked over the shelves of two book-lined walls, hoping to find something to interest her for the remainder of the day. Most of the volumes, however, dealt with real estate, New England architecture, or sailing; the novels she had read during her youth and adolescence. The most recent fiction was an early work by Joyce Carol Oates. A calendar bookmark inserted in its pages reminded her that, eight years before, she had given up on page thirty-two.

Verity sighed and resigned herself to the morning paper. She stood for a few moments by the French doors into the garden, and finished off the gin and orange juice in one swallow. She carried the glass to the kitchen, where she'd left Ida in the obituaries. When she emerged with the paper and another drink, Serena came down the hallway toward her.

"Someone to see you," the young woman said softly. "In the living room."

Verity looked at her questioningly. "I didn't hear the bell."

"He came up while I was bringing in the mail."

"Do you know who it is?"

Serena shook her head.

"Good." Handing Serena the drink and the paper, Verity turned toward the living room. "As long as it isn't Eric." She paused a moment before a hall mirror to straighten her blouse and flick back a wave of hair from her forehead.

Ben James was waiting by the unlighted fireplace when Verity stepped into the room. She smiled immediately, as did he. She went to him with her hands extended. He took both, and they exchanged friendly kisses of welcome on either cheek. Ben James was a man who very much resembled Verity's dead father, not so much in specific features, but in dress, carriage, voice, and line-age. Both had been educated at Exeter and at Harvard, and such traces as those schools leave are not eradicated. Ben had gone to Harvard Business School after graduating from the college, specializing in advanced accounting techniques. Now, twenty-five years later, he had his own Manhattan-based firm specializing in managing the personal fortunes of the extraordinarily wealthy and financially naïve—sports stars, widows of foreign dictators, underage heirs, and the like.

"I had to come back up to Boston this week, and just wanted to tell you how sorry I was about Richard. He was a good friend, Verity, a very good friend."

"Thank you," said Verity. "It meant a lot to me to hear that you came to the funeral last week. How did you find out?"

"Find out?" he asked, with a puzzled expression.

"Yes," said Verity, "how did you find out that he was dead?"

She showed him to the couch, and then seated herself in the opposite corner. He settled in, a little uncomfortably, and then said, "Didn't anyone tell you?"

"Tell me what?"

"I was with your father when he died."

"In Atlantic City? I thought Louise . . ."

"Well, Louise was in town, in the hotel. But I was in the casino. At the table with him."

"I didn't realize—" Verity faltered.

"Didn't Louise tell you?"

Verity shook her head.

Ben James smiled and shrugged. "I don't know why she didn't. I was down there consulting with a set of clients—they had a stint at one of the gambling hotels there. It was a big chance for them. And I ran into your father on the boardwalk. So we had lunch, and that night we did a little gambling together. If I had known . . ."

"Known what?"

"Known that he shouldn't have been drinking."

"Father didn't have a bad heart," Verity said. "Or at least not that we knew of."

"It went all at once then, I guess. It does, when you get to be our age."

Verity grimaced. "You're not *that* old, Ben."

"Thanks. I was fishing for that one."

"Did Father seem sick to you that night?"

"Pale, absentminded. He lost pretty bad. He wasn't playing his cards right. And then all at once he had an attack. The casino had a doctor there in about thirty seconds, but your father was already dead. Just like that." James snapped his fingers. "And then they got him out of there. Fast. I went with them, of course. They took us into a back room."

"And then you called Louise?"

"No," said James. "I called here, but there wasn't anybody at home."

"Why didn't you call Louise? She was his wife."

"I didn't know that," said James.

"Father didn't tell you!"

"He didn't say a word about it."

"So you didn't even know that Louise was in town with him, then."

"Well," said James, shifting one leg over the other, "in fact I did. Because I ran into her earlier that day, in a hobby shop, of all places. I was buying a stuffed animal for Beth's little girl—Beth's about to have her third, by the way, and she sends her best—and right in front of me there was a woman I thought I recognized, but I couldn't place her, so when she was signing the credit-card slip I looked over at her name, and it was Louise."

"What on earth was Louise buying in a hobby shop?"

"I don't know," said James. "It was already wrapped up."

"Did you speak to her?"

James shook his head. "I've never cared for Louise. Louise is the type of person who never really listens to you because she's always thinking so hard. Or not thinking, *calculating.*"

"Why do you think Father never mentioned to you that he was in Atlantic City on his honeymoon?"

"Maybe he was embarrassed. I hate to say this about your step-mother, but *I* would have been embarrassed."

Verity stood up abruptly. "I need a drink," she said. "Would you like something?"

"Whatever you're having," he said.

Verity went into the kitchen, and a few minutes later came out with more screwdrivers.

"He talked about you," said Ben James without preamble, when Verity had sat down again.

"About me?"

"About the three of you, his children. He was hoping that you'd all be a family again someday."

Verity's expression over the rim of the glass turned sour. "It's just the sort of thing real-estate men say to old friends in gambling casinos."

Ben seemed embarrassed and said quickly, "I'm sure he meant it."

"I think he probably did," shrugged Verity. "But it wasn't going to happen. Especially not after he had gone off and married Louise." Verity looked up sharply. "Did Father know that you and I had an affair?"

"I don't know," said James. "He never mentioned it if he did. I certainly never mentioned it."

"Louise knew. She threw it in my face after the funeral. I wonder how she found out."

"Maybe Eric told her," said James. "He definitely knew about it. Did you know that he tried to blackmail me?"

Verity sighed loudly. "I'm not one bit surprised. I hope you didn't give him any money."

"I told him that I'd have somebody tear his balls off if he ever called me again. He never called back. I warned you not to marry him."

Verity looked up and took a long swallow of her drink. "How long are you in town?"

"Till tomorrow. I'm staying at the Ritz."

"They still have those cozy little fires at the Ritz?"

Ben James smiled. "Should I call up room service from here, and have them set one up? It'll be bright and warm by the time we get over there."

"Sure," said Verity, "just let me go get a jacket. I know it's spring, but I haven't felt warm since I got to Boston."

7

A week later, by which time spring was firmly entrenched in Boston, Verity sat in a large leather-upholstered wing-backed chair in the living room. Her legs were crossed beneath a full-length teak-and-azure wool skirt. With one hand she tugged at a button of her wide-collared Shaker sweater, while the other rested listlessly in her lap.

The chairs in the room had been drawn out of their positions, and placed to form a crescent with the sofa in the center. Cassandra and Jonathan sat on either side of Verity, and Louise sat directly across from them in a similar wing-back.

Three vases in the room were filled with thick bunches of jonquils and King Alfreds, Cassandra's favorite spring blooms.

Attorney Eugene Strable stood with the open French doors at his back. The sheer curtains had been drawn across the dusky blue twilight and they billowed as a temperate spring breeze wafted inside. He took a sip of the weak Scotch-and-water that rested on the refectory table at his side, and then continued with the reading of the last will and testament of Richard Alexander Hawke.

"I give, devise, and bequeath my entire estate, real, personal, or mixed, of every kind and nature wheresoever located, of which I may die seized or possessed, or over which I may have power of appointment at the time of my death; or to which I may be entitled at the time of my death to LOUISE LARNER HAWKE, provided, however, that she survives me. In the event that she does not survive me then I give, devise, and bequeath my entire estate to be divided equally among my three children, VERITY JANE, JONATHAN ALEXANDER, and CASSANDRA BENT."

Then followed a detailed listing of all Richard's holdings and property. He had a few hundred acres in New York State; the real-estate business, which included the building on Newbury Street that housed it; four apartment buildings in Brookline and Newton; and a small portfolio of municipal bonds handled by Peabody, Kidder and Peabody.

Strable paused. Louise shifted in her chair, her silk dress whining against the chintz. She glanced at Cassandra, sitting near her on the couch.

"What about the house?" Louise asked, when the silence continued. "You didn't say anything about the house."

"What house?" said Eugene.

Louise cleared her throat. "This one, of course. What other house is there?"

The lawyer glanced at Richard Hawke's daughters, but it was Jonathan who spoke. "Louise," he said, "this house didn't belong to Father."

"What?" she cried.

The lawyer shook his head slowly, and his brow bore a puzzled, uneasy expression.

"Who *did* it belong to, I'd like to know, if it wasn't Richard's?" said Louise peremptorily.

"It was Mother's," said Verity, with a sweet smile. "And it was part of the trust that Mother left the three of us. Father of course was allowed to live here, but he couldn't have sold it, and he certainly couldn't have left it to . . . anyone else in his will."

"This house has always belonged to the three of us," said Cassandra. "The place at Truro is ours too. I'm surprised you didn't know that."

"Of course I didn't know that! I just naturally assumed, that as Richard's widow, the house—"

Louise left off abruptly. Her movements had become jerks. All three of the Hawkes were watching her, and she forced a semblance of calm over her features. "Of course it's yours," she said, in a slightly choking voice. "I remember now. Richard told me all about it, some time before we were married. But it didn't make much of an impression. And of course I'm glad it works out this way—I don't know what *I'd* do with a house this size. The upkeep alone . . ." She trailed off, under Verity's knowing smile.

When Louise fell silent, Verity said, "Well, Louise, it's a pity that the house didn't come to you, I suppose. However, I am *so* glad that Father had the forethought to change his will in the first four days of his marriage."

Louise glared at Verity.

Jonathan turned his attention back to the lawyer. "Father was executor of Mother's will," he said. "Who becomes executor now?"

"I do," said the lawyer. "There won't be any changes to speak of, I can assure you, because, for all practical purposes, I was the executor anyway. Richard didn't have the time to look over all the details. I've always overseen that trust."

Cassandra said to the lawyer, "You know, I really don't know anything about this trust. It came as a bit of a shock to me this year when I turned twenty-five and starting getting a check for three thousand dollars a month."

Louise suddenly leaned forward, and adjusted the skirt over her knees, clearing her throat at the same time.

"I don't even have any idea how much money is *in* the trust," Cassandra went on. "I know when Mother died it was about three million dollars. Do you have any idea what it might be now?"

"Yes, in fact I do. The estate held in trust for the three of you has grown steadily. Recently, in fact, we've been averaging about eleven percent a year."

Jonathan whistled. "That's pretty good."

"I would say so," said the lawyer modestly. "And the money's always been completely safe. We didn't once take a loss on any of our investments."

"How much is it worth now?" asked Jonathan.

"Approximately eight-point-seven million."

Louise evinced less surprise at the amount than did Verity, Jonathan, and Cassandra. She smiled knowingly, as if to imply that she and Richard had talked over the matter of the trust in some detail.

"Eight million," remarked Verity, eyeing Louise suspiciously. "It does mount up."

"Taking out thirty-five, seventy, a hundred and five thousand dollars a year as allowances for the three of you didn't even *begin* to make a dent," Eugene continued. "As you know, when each of you reaches twenty-nine, you are to receive your third of the inheritance. Verity, at twenty-eight, you're the eldest. Next February, you'll be able to withdraw your portion of the trust as capital. You can do with it whatever you like. I imagine that by then it will be something just over three million dollars. Jonathan and Cassandra will get proportionately more, because the money will have been set aside for just that much longer."

"I had no idea," said Verity.

"Nobody did," murmured Louise.

"That's why Richard felt no compunction in leaving everything he had to Louise: there was no reason to leave anything to the three of you when you were already so well provided for. Now, with your father gone, I have the responsibility of seeing that the provisions of your mother's will are carried out as specified."

"I still have a couple of questions," said Verity.

"About your father's will?" asked the lawyer.

"No, about the trust," Verity pursued. "Father never really told us anything about it. He seemed to think the whole business was in bad taste." Verity glanced at Louise with a broad smile.

Strable passed over this. "What would you like to know?"

"Why twenty-nine?" asked Jonathan suddenly. "Why do we come into the money at that age particularly? It's such an odd age. Why not thirty?"

"Your mother was twenty-nine when she came into *her* inheritance," explained Strable. "She thought it was a good age to deal with a large amount of money, apparently."

"What would happen if one of us died?" asked Verity. "Who would get the money?"

"Well, that depends entirely on *when* you died."

"How do you mean?" asked Cassandra. She and Jonathan were not uninterested.

"Verity," said the lawyer, "if you died after your twenty-ninth birthday—that is to say, after you had come into your portion of the inheritance outright—then the money would be left according to any will you had made out. If by any chance you *hadn't* made a will, then everything would go to Eric."

Verity winced, and said in a low voice, "I'm drawing up a will tomorrow."

"If, however, you died *before* your twenty-ninth birthday," the lawyer went on, "then the entire fund would simply be divided in two, between Jonathan and Cassandra. Any will, so far as the bulk of the money went, would be invalid. And of course the same holds for you, Jonathan, and you, Cassandra."

"And if two of us died before our twenty-ninth birthdays," prompted Cassandra.

"Then the entire trust fund would revert to the survivor."

"And if all three of us died?" asked Jonathan.

The lawyer demurred. "That's hardly likely."

"Last week," said Jonathan, "a drunk driver ran down and killed four children in the same family. It could happen."

"The money *would* have gone to your father in that case. Now that your father is dead—" The lawyer glanced, almost involuntarily, at Louise.

Louise looked up, and smiled vaguely, as if she understood little of the conversation, and cared even less.

"—the money would go to your father's estate," the lawyer concluded.

"To Louise," said Verity.

"Yes," said the lawyer. "Now," he said quickly and with a reassuring smile, "I'll see that you continue getting your monthly allowances, and I'll be overseeing the administration of the fund. It will be my responsibility to pass judgment on any 'extraordinary expenses' that can't be taken care of by your monthly allowances. But I want the three of you to come to me just as you went to your father. In this, I'm taking his place, and I'd like to think that I have your confidence just as your father did." He made a short nod.

Still thinking about the size of their inheritance, which, unknown to them, had been increasing with such rapidity, Verity, Jonathan, and Cassandra murmured acquiescence to this speech.

Louise Larner Hawke sat glowering in the wing-backed chair, which, contrary to her cherished expectation, did not belong to her after all.

8

"Eric," said Verity with weary patience, "please don't refer to that part of my body again. You haven't seen it in two and a half years. You couldn't possibly remember what it looks like."

Verity was sitting up in bed, resting back into a stack of down pillows, with the bedcovers secured under each arm. She wore nothing but a large black velvet sleep mask. The telephone was cradled between her ear and her shoulder.

"Yes," she said, "I do want to see you again. For about sixty seconds."

She listened to her husband without changing expression. "You're joking," she said after a moment. "Darling, you don't expect *me* to give *you* money, do you?"

There was a tap at the bedroom door.

"Come in!" Verity called, then sarcastically to Eric: "What happened? Were you fired from the massage parlor? Or did Louise cut you off?"

Cassandra stepped quietly into the room.

"Whatever," said Verity into the telephone. "Eric, I have no interest whatsoever in the way you live your life." She pressed the mouthpiece against her neck. "Cara?" she questioned. "Serena?"

Cassandra did not answer.

Verity poked a finger under her sleep mask and raised it a notch. "Oh, Cassandra, good morning."

"It's four o'clock in the afternoon," remarked Cassandra as she went to the windows that overlooked the back gardens. She drew open the draperies, raised the blinds, and then lifted the sash to let in fresh air.

"Yes," said Verity testily into the telephone, "I believe your mother *is* here. I heard her prowling about the hallway a little while ago, making clucking noises because I wasn't out of bed yet." She put her hand over the telephone and said to her sister, "Is Louise's car downstairs?"

"Yes," replied Cassandra.

"Yes, Eric, she's here. No, I will not tell her anything for you. I am not an answering machine or a message service. And I'd rather you didn't come over here.... Eric, I can't believe that you're asking me, your wife, to accompany you to the bar where you pick up all your one-night stands. Make it the Averof at ten.... All right, good-bye."

"Are you thinking of making up with Eric?" asked Cassandra sourly.

"I'm thinking of murdering him in front of a large crowd of strangers. I have to do it myself," Verity explained, "because hit men don't take plastic."

"Honestly, though," said Cassandra, "are you thinking of a reconciliation?"

Verity shook her head vehemently.

"Verity, I wish you'd take that mask off," sighed Cassandra.

Verity slowly raised the mask. The full light of the afternoon shone directly in on her face.

"Oh, God," she moaned, "doesn't this day have a rheostat?" She rolled sideways in the bed and buried her face in the topmost pillow.

"Verity, you really should make an effort to get up a little earlier in the day. It's not as if you were working a job on the graveyard shift, you know. Father always said it might be nice someday to see you for breakfast, and I agree."

"I hate breakfast," Verity moaned. She rolled onto her back. "Besides, I would have been up earlier if a certain stepmother and mother-in-law rolled into one hadn't made a concerted effort to disturb me." She sat up straight, punched the pillows, and then sank back into them again. "Louise has been skulking about since dawn. Has she closed down the agency? Every time I'd doze off, she'd open the door to see if I had gotten up yet. She opened the door of *your* room twenty times."

"I didn't come in last night."

"Oh, yes? Did you catch his name?"

"Rocco DiRico."

"That hunky drummer? Oh, Cassandra, I'm so jealous!" She sank down farther, pulling the mask back over her eyes. "Now I'm distraught. Now I don't think I can get up at all."

"Verity..."

Verity laughed, and pulled off the mask. "Good for you! It's what I've always said: pick out what you like best and then take it down off the shelf."

Cassandra sat on the edge of Verity's bed, looking out the window at the late afternoon sunlight that shone on the tops of the evergreens. "I know why you're going to see Eric," she said unexpectedly.

"Why?"

"To buy coke from him."

"Do you need some?"

"Coke's bad for you," said Cassandra. "It eats away your nose."

Verity slipped farther under the covers. "Oh, God, lecture time. Coke is better than heroin," she pointed out.

Cassandra was silent for a moment. Then she said, "It really *is* about time you got up."

"I know," Verity sighed as she pulled back the covers and edged out of the bed.

"I wonder," said Cassandra at last, "if Louise knows that Eric deals drugs?"

"No," said Verity definitely.

"How can you be so sure?"

"Because," said Verity, walking toward the bathroom, "if she did know, she'd have demanded a cut of his profits."

When she returned from the bathroom a few minutes later, wearing a robe and carrying a brush, she sat on the edge of the bed beside Cassandra. Cassandra took the brush, and ran it again and again through Verity's thick blond hair.

"Just like I used to," she said, with a small smile.

"Guess what I did yesterday," said Verity.

"I wouldn't even *begin* . . ."

"I went to a hobby shop. I went to two hobby shops, in fact. One at the Chestnut Hill mall, and one downtown."

"Why on earth?" asked Cassandra.

"To see what the merchandise was like. To try to figure out what it was that Louise was buying at the hobby shop in Atlantic City."

"Good God!" exclaimed Cassandra. "It could have been *anything.*"

"No, it couldn't have. I called Ben James last night, and asked him how big the package was. He said it was very small. Like a bag for candy or something. So that cut out a lot. I just had to look for small things."

"And what did you find out?" asked Cassandra curiously.

"That Louise was either planning to get high on airplane glue, or else she made a purchase of certain chemicals."

"In a hobby shop? What kind of chemicals?"

"Little tiny bottles. For teenage chemistry sets. I wasn't able to figure out what kind she got."

Cassandra put down the brush. "You think Louise doctored Father's sleeping pills?"

"I think that's more likely than that Louise is sniffing airplane glue."

"Verity, I don't like this."

"Of course not. Murder isn't—"

"That's not what I'm talking about. What I don't like is your going on about this. You can't accuse Louise of *murder*. I mean, that's completely outrageous. I certainly don't like her. I'm certainly not glad that Father married her. But I'm absolutely sure that she didn't *kill* him."

"How can you be so sure?"

"Because there was no *reason* to kill him."

"His money," Verity pointed out.

"Father didn't have any money. Or not much. He had already made Louise a partner in the business. Why should she kill him?"

"Louise thought she was getting this house. Didn't you see her face when Eugene Strable told her that the house belonged to us? That's what she wanted. I'm sure she knew about Mother's trust fund for us. That was common knowledge down at the realty office. But she may have thought Father had a lot more than he did have. He may have married her, but I bet he didn't open the account books on their honeymoon."

Cassandra shook her head. "I think if you had a job, you wouldn't let your imagination get carried away like this. You're brooding!"

"I'm not brooding!" protested Verity. "I think it's sort of fun. I'd love to pin a murder rap on the world's most vulgar woman. She deserves the death penalty for those clothes she wears, anyway."

"See?" said Cassandra. "That's what I mean. You're just stirring up trouble because you're bored."

"You think we ought to have Father exhumed?"

"No!" cried Cassandra. "I do not! What a horrible idea!"

"You'd rather that Louise get away with it, then?"

"She's not getting away with anything!" cried Cassandra. "I don't know why I'm talking to you. You've gone off the deep end. It's all that coke, probably."

Verity took the brush away from her sister. "*You're* the one who's upset," she said with a smile. "You think there's something wrong too. You just won't admit it."

To this Cassandra made no reply.

At ten o'clock that evening, Verity stood beneath the tiny canopy before the door of the Averof Restaurant near Porter Square in Cambridge. She was uncharacteristically on time. Eric, characteristically, was not. In habitual lateness, at least, they had been a well-matched couple. It was raining heavily. Verity tried to protect herself from the downpour, as well as from the water that spilled off the roof, by squeezing between a pyramidal evergreen in a redwood bucket and a cold stuccoed wall next to the wooden door of the restaurant. The cool rain spattered in her face and across her calves beneath her leather trench coat. She took off her dark glasses, squinting against the glare of headlights passing along busy Massachusetts Avenue, and wiped away the water from the lenses with a tissue. She leaned forward and peered up and down the sidewalk. She cursed Eric—not under her breath at all. She was jostled by a party of already drunken patrons scurrying in off the sidewalk, and trying to crowd through the narrow doorway at once. In defense Verity plunged the point of her umbrella into the thigh of the most obnoxious member of the party. He snapped about and glared at her, but she was gazing innocently in another direction.

When the offending party had all squeezed inside the restaurant, Verity turned back—and there stood Eric.

"Why the hell didn't you wait inside?" he asked. "You're fucking soaked."

Beneath his raincoat Eric wore a green Izod pullover and tan dress slacks. The protective awning cast a shadow across the upper portion of his face, hiding his dark-blue eyes and accentuating the sharpness of his handsome features. His dark mustache was full and neatly trimmed.

"I waited out here," Verity continued, "because the smell of Greek food makes me want to throw up. Besides, there's a belly dancer inside. How people can digest their dinner while some woman sidles up to the table and shakes her stomach in their faces is something I can't even *begin* to understand."

"Then why the hell did you suggest the Averof?"

"I was confused."

Eric took a deep breath, evidently trying to stifle some shred of annoyance, or some angry remark. "Why don't we go over to Uno's?"

"Uno's? It sounds like a singles bar for people who want to remain that way. It's not a bar, is it? If you're going to ask me out to dinner on a rainy night, I'm not going to let you off with a pitcher of beer and a bowl of pretzels."

"It's a restaurant. You like Italian, don't you? There's a bar downstairs, but it's quiet. No disco, no belly dancers."

He took her umbrella, snapped it open, and stepped out into the rain. He motioned her to get under with him. "Where's your car?" he asked.

"Across the street," she replied. "Where's yours?"

"Repossessed."

They crossed the rainy street together, and climbed into the Lotus.

"We might as well do our business now," said Verity.

"No," said Eric.

"Why not?"

"Because as soon as you got your coke, you'd say, 'Eric, I don't have any appetite, where do you want me to drop you off?'"

"You know me too well."

"I wanted to see you tonight, Verity. It means a lot to me."

She turned on the ignition. "I hope you'll take a check," she said.

Eric pursed his lips, and exhaled sharply through his nose. He spoke a moment later: "For you, anything . . ."

"Credit?" she asked, pulling out of the parking space.

"Well, no," he conceded. "Not credit."

The rain beat against the roof of the car. Verity stopped suddenly before a changing light.

Eric turned to her. "Can you really see, on a night like this, through those glasses?"

"Like a cat."

Uno's was actually Pizzeria Uno, right in Harvard Square. Verity groaned at the door, but inside, the place was dark-walled, and dimly lighted, and filled with the substantial odor of good

Italian food. After hanging up their coats and leaving the name Larner with the head-waiter, Verity and Eric went downstairs to the bar and picked out a table in a dark corner next to an unplugged Pac-Man machine. She ordered bourbon on the rocks, and he a Heineken. While waiting for their drinks, Verity stood and checked her reflection in one of the mirrors that lined the walls above the wainscoting. She pushed back a strand of wayward blond hair from her forehead and picked at the puffed sleeves of her forties-style white dress, patterned with lines of vivid cherries. When she turned back it was to find Eric's eyes lingering on her breasts. She sat down again, and pointedly adjusted the low-cut bodice upward.

Eric raised his eyes and met hers. He smiled languidly.

Verity twitched the corner of her mouth. She said, in a voice that parodied Eric's, "'Oh, Verity, even after all this time, even after all that's happened, you still turn me on.'"

"You do!" Eric exclaimed sincerely. "You really do still turn me on! God, you're beautiful, Verity. I don't know how I could have let you go out of my life."

Verity groaned softly. "Who writes your dialogue?"

"Why can't you ever accept a compliment about yourself?"

"I can, when it comes from a stranger."

"I want this to be a pleasant evening for us. But you get so fucking defensive, just like when we used to have fights. You always had to pretend you were right, even when you knew you were wrong. I just want you to know you don't have to be defensive with me."

Their drinks were brought, and, as the waitress put them down, Verity said, with some softness in her voice, "You're right, I *was* being defensive, and I apologize."

They talked about what they had been doing during the past two years. Verity told of Kansas City and terminal boredom. Eric had lost his job as a CETA office manager when the program was dismantled. Unable to find anything similar—a good salary and very little work—he had made do with temporary positions obtained through an agency. He had, for instance, been a cutting operator at a postcard factory, and had wrapped packages at Jordan Marsh during the Christmas season.

"But mostly," said Verity, after Eric's recitation, "you deal."

"Some," he admitted.

"Enough that you're not really looking for anything else. Just don't get busted," added Verity earnestly.

"Wha, Miz Verity, ah'm touched deeply," he said, tilting his head, and touching the brim of an imaginary cap.

Verity took a deep breath. "Don't be," she said. "I don't want a husband in jail, even if he's an estranged husband. Besides, it's too much trouble finding a good dealer. I was always getting burned in Kansas City. Jesus, some of those bastards mixed in everything from cornstarch to Dutch Cleanser. If you'd had enough of it, you could have made biscuits. As far as dope goes, you were always faithful to me. Speaking of which, how is Barbara?"

Eric blinked innocently. "Didn't Mother tell you? We broke up some time ago."

"That's a surprise. For a while there I thought you'd developed a Siamese twin."

"I haven't seen Barbara for months," said Eric. He paused thoughtfully. "I think she joined the Peace Corps."

"So you're living alone?"

"After you . . . ," he said gallantly.

Verity rolled her eyes.

"I have some deals going," he added, seriously. "You don't have to worry about me. There are irons in the fire."

"Well," said Verity, "I'll say this in all sincerity, Eric: I hope one of those irons gets hot this time."

They were called upstairs, seated at a table in the corner and given menus. After they had ordered, Eric said, "I really was sorry about your father, you know."

"Thank you," said Verity, as she scanned the menu. "Now let's allow that subject to rest for the evening."

The waiter brought a carafe of red wine. In the conversation that followed, Verity saw flashes—as she might have seen flashes of lightning on a summer night, out of the corner of her eye—of the Eric she had fallen in love with, and the Eric she had married. He was very good-looking, and—she had to admit—still very sexy. He had hardly changed in three years. His hair was cut shorter, he was thinner, and his face had more character. She was almost certain that he could not have fabricated that gaze, which revealed in him a melancholy mixture of regret and longing. At the same time, though, she saw other flashes—and these were brighter—of his cheap sarcasms, his laziness that outdistanced even her own, his inability and unwillingness to give any sort of direction to his life. Eric's basic fault was that he always took the easy way, without regard to even obvious consequences.

When the check was brought, and laid face-down upon the table, Eric said, "Verity, I need to ask you something—"

Interrupting him forcibly, Verity cried, "No! Don't even mention a reconciliation! There have been times, I admit, when I've thought it might be possible, but it wouldn't work out any better a second time around. I'm not going to push for a divorce, not for a while anyway. The separation is fine, and besides, we're going to be seeing one another—after all, you're my dealer again."

"And we both have the same mother now, too."

"That is a revolting thing to say when I have food in my mouth."

"You're my stepsister," said Eric. "As well as my wife."

"I am not amused."

"I still need to ask you something," said Eric.

"What?"

"Can you take care of the check?"

PART TWO

The Only Son

9

"Just what the hell do you know about real art?"

Cassandra swiveled her chair around. Mary Scott-Trout stood framed in the office doorway, trembling with rage. Her feet were implanted against the doorframe.

"You look like Samson," remarked Cassandra, "about to destroy the temple."

Mary Scott-Trout was in her late forties, solidly built, with her gray-streaked hair cut into a no-nonsense page boy. She wore no makeup, and nobody could be sure whether—considering the harsh features of her face—this was a good thing or a bad. Her wardrobe invariably consisted of a white blouse, a gray skirt, dark hose, and low-heeled pumps.

Mary Scott-Trout pulled a crumpled envelope from her purse and flung it across the room at Cassandra. Cassandra didn't even flinch, and the letter fell far short.

"You didn't even have the decency to return my poems. *Not the decency*," she repeated with savage emphasis.

"You didn't include return postage," Cassandra explained.

"I didn't think I'd *need* return postage when I had already been assured that you'd take the poems." She stalked into the room, and threw herself into a chair opposite Cassandra's desk. "I feel betrayed. You know what it's like to feel betrayed? You feel like shit!"

Cassandra said nothing for a moment, then she asked, "Why are you here?"

"To find out what *this* means." She picked up the crumpled

envelope from the floor and smoothed it out on Cassandra's desk.

"It's a rejection letter. The one I sent to you on your most recent cycle of poems. It says that we won't publish them. I'm sorry, I thought the letter was quite straightforward."

Mary Scott-Trout sneered. "Wait'll I tell PEN what you did to me. There'll be an investigation, a real investigation into why a twenty-five-year-old girl without any previous publishing experience is allowed to edit a poetry magazine. We'll see what PEN has to say. I'd advise you not to be at the next meeting, that's what I'd advise."

"I never attend PEN meetings," said Cassandra. "I'm usually too busy reading manuscripts. Mary, I'm still not quite sure I understand. Just what is it I've done to you? How have I 'betrayed' you? Writers get rejection letters all the time. They don't usually storm the editor's office and threaten legal action."

"You *promised!* I told the *Globe*—"

"I didn't promise," said Cassandra calmly. "I didn't even know you had written the poems till I found them on my desk."

"You *did* promise," snarled Mary Scott-Trout. "Louise told me—"

"*Louise?*"

Mary Scott-Trout nodded with satisfaction. "Louise told me you said you'd be proud to publish anything I submitted, and the longer the better."

"When did Louise say this to you, Mary?"

"When I bought my condo from her last month."

"I see," said Cassandra quietly. "Well, Mary, I have to tell you something. Louise Larner—Hawke, excuse me—is not the editor of *Iphigenia. I* am the editor. In your case, I exercised my right to reject manuscripts."

"What about the *Globe?* I told the *Globe* you were going to publish the poems. You'll look stupid, really stupid when you don't."

"*I'm* not the one who's going to look stupid," said Cassandra. "If anyone asks me about the poems, I'll just tell them that the poems were not worth printing, and that you spoke out of line. That's all."

"And I'll tell them about your stepmother, I'll tell them that—"

"My stepmother is hardly a spokeswoman for Menelaus Press," interrupted Cassandra. "You were very foolish to listen to anything she had to say on the subject. And if you tell the story, that's what *other* people are going to think, too. Now, I'm very busy, and you came in without an appointment, Mary. If you'll speak to Sarah there in the outer office, I think she'll be able to give you your poems back. Good-bye, Mary."

"Well," said Eugene Strable, "I think this was a very pleasant idea."

He and Louise were sitting in a cozy, remote corner of the Café Lananas, well away from the other guests and the well-trodden paths of the waiters in the intimate basement restaurant on Newbury Street.

"Oh," said Louise gaily, "I'm so busy these days, running the office all alone, that I hardly ever have time for more than a sandwich. This is quite a treat for me. And I haven't seen you since the reading of the will." A somber expression, as if in remembrance of her dead husband, flitted across Louise's features. She wore a slate-gray dress with a high collar and pleated front. Her black hair was swept back from her face, and she had on tiny black pearl earrings.

Eugene Strable smiled a doleful smile of consolation. The waiter brought menus and took their orders for drinks. Louise looked around the restaurant and then back to Eugene. Her expression had become troubled.

"Is something wrong?" the lawyer asked.

"I've had something on my mind I wanted to discuss with you, but I don't want to spoil the afternoon by talking about it now. . . ."

"Please go on. If there's anything I can help you with . . ."

"It's Verity. I'm worried about her."

"How so?"

"Well," said Louise, "I've been dropping by the house in the afternoons—just to make sure everything's going along all right. I feel *such* responsibility toward Verity and Jonathan and Cassandra, and—"

"Isn't Cassandra taking care of the running of the house?"

interrupted Eugene. "She did that even while Richard was alive. He didn't bother with any of that, I don't think."

"Cassandra's preoccupied these days," said Louise carefully. "With that Italian." She clucked her tongue. "She's let the servants get slack in their work. I drop by now and again to let them know they can't get away with *everything*."

"Oh? But what about Verity?"

Louise murmured thanks to the waiter who brought her martini. When he went away, Louise said, "Verity gets up at three or four in the afternoon. She doesn't even bother to get dressed then. She wanders downstairs, makes herself a drink, and sits out in the garden, or in the living room, until Cassandra comes in and tells her to get dressed for dinner. Then she stays out half the night. Still married to Eric and she stays out half the night drinking with strange men." Louise took a deep breath. "She could very easily become an alcoholic."

Eugene nodded slowly. "Verity was probably very upset by Richard's death. It takes some people longer to deal with grief than others. I'm sure that's all it is," he added reassuringly.

"I don't think so," said Louise, shaking her head. "I think it's more. I *know* it's more than that by the way she treats me."

"What do you mean?"

"If Verity's problem were just the grief she felt for Richard's death, then she'd be treating me a whole lot better than she does. All three of them, in fact, would be treating me better. I don't think they loved Richard at all."

"Louise—"

"They resent me. They resent me horribly. And they don't hesitate to let me know it, either. I'm embarrassed for them, for their behavior."

"Your marriage came as such a surprise," Eugene pointed out. "Maybe if they had found out about it *before* Richard died."

Louise, clearly preferring not to hear this explanation, offered her own: "I think Verity's real problem is something else altogether. I think her drinking problem has been brought on by her failed marriage. In fact, I'm almost sure of it."

Eugene Strable wasn't able to disguise a glint of skepticism in his eye.

Louise saw it and said, "No, you don't know her the way I do, Eugene. She's proud and vain and she'd never admit that it's her fault her marriage went on the rocks. I think what Verity really needs is to get back together with Eric."

"Louise," the lawyer began hesitantly, then paused altogether when the waiter brought their appetizers.

"What?" said Louise when the waiter had gone away.

"There's something I think you should know about your son. I hadn't wanted to have to tell you. . . ."

"Tell me," said Louise, her mouth set.

"Last week," said Strable, "a friend of mine came to me and said he had discovered that his daughter was using cocaine. He had also found out where she got it. He wanted my advice on the best way of turning the dealer in."

Louise picked at her shrimp with a fork. "Yes?" she said. "What has this got to do with Eric?"

"Eric was the dealer he wanted to turn in to the police."

Louise looked up quickly. "What did you tell him to do?"

"I talked him out of it. I didn't tell him that I knew Eric either. I don't need *that* kind of reputation among my clients. Louise, did you know that your son was selling drugs?"

Louise hesitated. "This girl must have been a friend of Eric's, and he got it for her as a favor. I'm sure that's all it was. Eric is not a professional at this. I'm sure it was just Eric doing this girl a favor."

"Are you sure he's not working on a slightly larger scale than that?"

Louise grimaced. "Yes. If he were doing it on any scale at all, he'd be making a fortune. As it is, he comes to me for money."

Eugene spoke with a cynicism to match Louise's: "You ought to have a talk with him. Either get him to stop doing 'favors' for friends, or have him go into this business all the way. If he's caught, he'll do ten to twenty years—so he might as well get rich."

Louise looked up astonished. "Are you joking?"

The lawyer paused and smiled before answering. "Of course," he said. "I would never advise anyone to break the law."

"Of course not. But you see what my problem is. He's a grown man now. I can't stand him in the corner because he's selling hard drugs. That's why I'm so anxious for him and Verity to get their marriage together again."

"An alcoholic and a drug dealer?"

With affronted dignity, Louise replied, "That's cruel. They're just young people with problems. I think they could help each other out. I don't know why you're so down on Eric. I know he thinks very highly of you, Eugene."

"I'm sorry, Louise. I do realize the value of their trying to resuscitate the marriage."

"Then you'll speak to Verity?"

The lawyer laughed. "I thought you said you knew Verity. There's no talking to her about something like that. She has to see it for herself. If I were you, I'd leave the whole business alone, and let it evolve. Verity hasn't left town. So far as I'm concerned, that's a very good sign. And Eric's gone to see her, hasn't he?"

"Yes."

"Then I'd leave it at that. I wouldn't say anything to Verity, Louise. You might just set her off. Don't antagonize her. Just try to make yourself as pleasant as possible. Richard wasn't an interfering father. Those kids are used to doing pretty much what they want to."

After a moment, Louise said, "Maybe you're right. I won't push it—for now."

"But if I were you, Louise—"

"Yes?"

"I *would* speak to Eric. I'd tell him to be more careful in choosing his clientele."

When Cassandra came home from work that afternoon, she stopped in the kitchen to speak to Ida. She found the cook standing near the kitchen ovens, with her heavy arms crossed and a perplexed expression on her face. Louise sat perched over the vast butcher-block worktable that was at the center of the room. She was trying to cut small red radishes into the semblance of roses with a shiny new implement meant precisely for that purpose. Beside her was a large orange casserole dish, already filled with some blend of foods that was pale yellow with flecks of orange. Opened cans and discarded packages suggested that the casserole dish might contain a combination of pineapple, carrots, and grapefruit juice. Cassandra's mouth tightened and her eyes hardened, but she said nothing at first.

Louise looked up. "I can't get the hang of this." She held up her latest experiment. It didn't look at all like a rose—in fact, it didn't even look like a radish anymore. Louise went over to the sink and dropped it into the disposal.

She turned back to Cassandra. "I guess we'll have to have the casserole without the garnish." She nodded in the direction of the pot on the table. "I'm just waiting for the oven to get to the right temperature. Ida, what's the thermometer say?"

Ida turned, opened the door of one of the three ovens in the wall, and mumbled, "Three seventy-five." Clearly agitated, she let the door slam shut. She fussed with a strand of white hair that had come loose from the tight bun at the back of her head.

"A few minutes more," said Louise. "The casserole should cook at four hundred."

"It's carrots and pineapple?" asked Cassandra after a moment, and glancing at Ida.

"I found the recipe in this month's *Bon Appétit*."

"Louise," said Cassandra, with a perplexed brow, "why are you making a casserole?"

"Helping Ida, of course," said Louise with a smile. "We've been getting along fine all afternoon—haven't we, Ida?"

Ida made a vague noise of agreement.

"No," said Cassandra. "What I mean is, *why* are you here in the kitchen at all?"

Ida sighed loudly.

"For dinner, of course! I thought it was time we all sat down together and talked things out." She picked up another whole radish and looked at it speculatively. "Maybe I should try once more. . . ."

Cassandra blinked rapidly. "Louise," she said calmly, "you have no business being in here."

Louise's mouth twitched. "I'm trying to *help out*, Cassandra."

"Ida is here," said Cassandra. "Serena is polishing the woodwork in the study. Cara is upstairs doing the bathrooms. If we had anybody else 'helping out,' we'd have to build a new wing."

"A household gets out of kilter . . . ," said Louise.

"Out of kilter?"

"After a death," Louise continued tonelessly. "Especially when you're not here half the time."

"What do you mean by that?"

"Your bed wasn't slept in at all last night."

Cassandra didn't reply to this charge directly. "Why aren't you at the office?" she asked.

"I took the afternoon off."

"Well," said Cassandra after a moment, "if the realty office can run without your assistance, Louise, so can this house. Verity and I are quite capable of taking care of things." She went to the refrigerator, opened it, and looked inside. "I know exactly what to do. Besides, you're wasting your time with this dinner."

Louise put the radish cutter down with a bang. "What do you mean?"

"Verity has a dinner date."

"With who?" Louise demanded angrily.

"With Eric," replied Cassandra with a sly smile.

"And it's not their first, either," said Louise, mollified. "I guess it'll be just you and me."

Cassandra turned with a carton of milk in her hand. "No," she said coolly, "I'll be out too."

Ida, flushed, hurried through the swinging door into the dining room.

Cassandra watched her go, sighed, and poured milk into a glass she took from the cabinet. She had her back to Louise.

"This past week," Louise said matter-of-factly, "you and Jonathan and Verity have gone out of your way to be rude to me."

Cassandra turned and looked at Louise over the rim of her glass. She did not answer.

"I'm thinking of what your father would have said about the way you three have been treating me," said Louise, letting her voice drop.

"I'm thinking of what Father would have said if he had known you were interfering in my work at the press."

"What does that mean?"

"It means that you told Mary Scott-Trout that I would be happy to publish her poems."

Louise was silent a moment, then she said, "I didn't tell her that."

"You obviously did, Louise. Otherwise, she certainly wouldn't have mentioned it to the *Globe*. You sold her a condominium last month, didn't you?"

"Yes. It had only been on the market for three—"

"And you told her that I'd publish her poems—as an inducement to buy, right?"

"Of course not! I just told her—"

"Told her what?" prompted Cassandra.

"That you had mentioned her in conversation," said Louise carefully, "and that you liked her work, and would like to publish her sometime. As soon as you could." Then, more sure of her ground, Louise went on quickly: "She misunderstood me. She did it on purpose. It wasn't my fault, Cassandra. She deliberately took what I said and twisted it, and now she's made a real fool out of you, but it's not my fault."

Cassandra smiled. "She hasn't made a fool out of me. But I'd be very surprised if you don't hear from her in the next few days, Louise. So you better get your story straight for *her*."

Cassandra drained the glass and placed it in the sink. She went to a drawer on the other side of the room, and fished about among the utensils there. She didn't find what she wanted, and opened another drawer next to it.

Louise in the meantime went over to the sink, turned on the hot water, dribbled a little soap into the glass, washed it, rinsed it out with cold water, and then dried it with a towel. She placed it upside down in the rack. "You know, Cassandra, I'd do anything for this family."

"Louise, you can think about what Father might have done, and what Father might have said, all you like. You can comfort and console yourself until you choke on it. But *you cannot interfere in my life.* You cannot barge in here any day of the week, start fixing dinner, and then get upset because we won't rearrange our schedules for you. And also, it's no concern of yours whether I sleep in my bed, someone else's bed, or in a doorway on lower Washington Street." Out of the second drawer, Cassandra withdrew a utensil, darkened with age and use, which was the counterpart of the one Louise had been deploying with such difficulty and so little success.

"You're treating me as if I were a stranger! I'm not a stranger! I'm part of this family now!"

"That's unfortunately true."

Louise's eyes fell hard upon Cassandra. "You're being deliberately unpleasant. You're going out of your way to upset me. Your father loved you very much, but if he could hear the way you're talking to me, he'd be horrified. Except, if he were here, you wouldn't dare to say these things to me, or to anybody else. I try to help you out and you accuse me of interfering. I know you say ugly things about me when the doors are closed. Well, let me tell you, young lady, I am your father's widow and that entitles me to a say in what goes on around here!"

"A very limited say," said Cassandra. "We've decided to let you choose the monument to go over his grave." She had moved around the butcher-block table, and picked up one of the radishes. While Louise talked on, Cassandra carved a perfect rose with the older implement. She set the radish down neatly, and with a small flourish, next to the casserole, then picked up another. "This is a very unpleasant conversation," she said.

"I'm not the one who made it unpleasant!" cried Louise. Her voice was strident, brittle.

"I have no interest in fighting," remarked Cassandra. "I'm not used to it, and I don't like it." Cassandra spoke slowly. She finished a second perfect radish, and placed it beside the other. She picked up a third, and began on that. "As far as running the house goes, one thing Father would never do is interfere with Ida here in the kitchen. And Father never said anything tasteless such as 'You were out all night last night. Where were you?' Father said, 'Verity, there are circles under your eyes. Are you sure you're getting enough sleep?' Father didn't care what we did so long as we were polite and did it in the right places. Actually, I don't think he cared about anything but selling houses at the top of the market, and sailing when the weather was good. If he hadn't insisted we all learn to handle a boat, we wouldn't have seen him at all while we were growing up."

"He loved you, Cassandra. All of you!"

"In his way, I suppose he did," replied Cassandra mildly. She picked up a fourth radish. "And we loved him, in our own way. But Verity and Jonathan and I have no intention of allowing him to run our lives from the grave through you."

Louise's expression hardened.

Cassandra finished off the last radish quickly, and put it down with the others. She closed her eyes and rubbed her temples with the thumb and middle fingers of her right hand. "I hope you don't need any more rosettes than that, Louise, because I have a terrible headache. I really do hate having to say these things aloud."

Louise shook her head. "I don't like being talked down to like this."

"I just want you to understand that this is the way things are," returned Cassandra. "I had to make it plain, for Verity, and Jonathan, and myself. Now, if you'll excuse me, I think I had better go and apologize to Ida. She's not used to being made to listen to family arguments."

Cassandra walked out of the kitchen and into the dining room.

Louise flung the four carved radishes into the garbage disposal.

10

For some time, Jonathan had been putting pressure on Apple to move in with him. He no longer saw anything but inconvenience in their maintaining separate residences. Apple was willing to move into Jonathan's apartment in the Prudential Towers only after she was certain that she would not be leaving Rocco in the lurch. She knew that his salary at Filene's was insufficient to pay the rent on their two-bedroom place on Commonwealth, but when she raised the matter with him, Rocco only said mysteriously, "I'll be able to manage."

"Do you have a source of income I don't know anything about? Are you running numbers? Have you won the lottery?"

"No," said Rocco. "But I'll manage."

On the first Saturday in May, Cassandra and Jonathan went

over to the Commonwealth apartment directly after breakfast. Apple had been up much earlier packing boxes and suitcases.

She stood in the center of her bedroom, looking around her carefully. It was bare of all the personal belongings that had adorned the bureau, nightstand, and windowsill. The closet door was open and held only black hangers. The bed had been stripped of its coverings. Three small embroidered Middle Eastern rugs were rolled up and tied together near the door to the hallway. The walls were bare and even the picture hooks had been removed. A spider plant in a forlorn cracked pot was tilted into a dusty corner. "I'm leaving that," said Apple. "I always hated that plant."

"Let's get going," said Jonathan.

Rocco came up behind Cassandra and put his hands around her waist and hugged her. He wore an army surplus khaki shirt and a green cloth marine cap. "Let's get a move on," he said. "I've waited three years to get rid of this woman. Thank God she's finally moving out."

"Are you getting another roommate?" asked Jonathan, picking up a box.

Cassandra shook her head. "We like the privacy."

"Oh, ho!" said Apple, following Jonathan out with the rugs under her arm. "That explains . . ."

She and Jonathan were out the door before she finished the sentence.

"Explains what?" Cassandra asked Rocco.

"She was asking how I'd be able to afford this place by myself."

"Did you tell her I was going to help you out?"

Rocco shook his head. "She just figured it out." Cassandra had just picked up two shopping bags filled with toiletries and clothing. Rocco took them from her, and put them down again. He threw his arms loosely over her shoulders and kissed her.

"Do you mind?" Cassandra asked.

"Mind what?"

"That I'll be helping you with the rent?"

"Why should I mind?"

"Some people would."

"Does it bother you?" Rocco asked.

"Of course not. I *do* like the privacy when I come here. And

I'm willing to pay for it. And if I'm smart, I'll figure out some way to take it off on my taxes—my office in the city, or something."

"Christ," breathed Rocco with a laugh, "you rich people!"

They were still locked in an embrace when Apple and Jonathan returned for a second load.

"Wait till I'm out before you do it on the bare floor, would you, please?" sighed Apple.

"The sooner we're out," said Jonathan meaningfully, "the sooner you two will have the place to yourselves."

"All right," said Cassandra, taking the hint. She and Rocco filled their arms, and trudged downstairs behind Apple and Jonathan. When the car was packed, and the apartment was checked to make certain she was leaving nothing behind, Apple turned to Rocco and Cassandra standing together on the sidewalk.

"Come over to dinner tonight."

"You sure you want us?" said Rocco to Jonathan, who was revving the car.

"Yes," Jonathan replied. "I'm going out to Brookline this afternoon, and I'll ask Verity if she wants to come too. Our housewarming."

A few minutes later, upstairs, Rocco removed his hat and tossed it into a chair in the hallway, on top of several other of his garments.

"How about some coffee?" asked Cassandra.

"Not now." He moved into the living room, looking around. "This place is all ours now." He threw himself sideways into a chair and motioned Cassandra over. She stood beside him, and he pulled her down beside him. They kissed for a long moment, holding hands, until she nestled her face against his shoulder. She felt him tense up as a drum solo, off the radio, filled the room.

"What's wrong?" she said, looking up.

"That's Danny Longo."

"You know him?"

"He used to be with the Normal Mailers until they broke up. Then he formed his own group—the Monotones."

"Can you actually tell it's him playing?"

"Can you actually tell it's Liza Minelli when she sings *New*

York, New York? Of course I can. Just listen to that," Rocco sighed. "Longo plays like his sticks are lead pipes. And the Monotones are getting *air play?*"

Cassandra sat up. "Why haven't People Buying Things cut a single?"

Rocco raised his eyebrows. "It's not quite like publishing a book, you know."

"No, I didn't know."

"When you get a manuscript and you can see some potential in it, you work with the writer for a while, suggesting rewrites and so forth, and he looks at it again, and maybe another editor sees it, and a copy editor, and so forth—it goes through a hundred stages before it gets to the public, right?"

"Close enough."

"Well, when we play an audition, the man booking us doesn't give us the chance to make rewrites. He listens to what we've got and it's thumbs up or thumbs down. No editing, no consensus of opinion. Same with a record. A real chancy proposition. Say we took it to one of the really progressive rock stations, ERS or ZBC, and the producer says, okay, we'll give it air play—they spin it once at two a.m., and if forty-seven people don't call up immediately and say, 'Oh, God, that song has changed my life,' then it never gets played again. God forbid somebody should call up and say he hates the disc—then you won't even be able to get in the door of the station again. And a bad disc on the radio will keep people away from a gig in droves."

"What are you saying? That it's not worth the risk?"

"Of course it's worth the risk. It just has to be done *right*."

"What does doing it right entail?"

He smiled at her, and undid two buttons of her blouse. He slipped his hand inside to cup one of her breasts. "Don't you want to take advantage of this empty apartment?"

"Later," said Cassandra, removing his hand and closing the buttons. "This is very interesting. Come in the kitchen with me while I make hot chocolate. Keep talking."

He followed her into the kitchen, saying, "You need quality engineers all the way down the line. Boston must have seven or eight recording studios that are capable of putting out a flexi-disc, but there's probably only one that's exactly right for us. And of course it's bound to be the most expensive. You need a good cover for it, and that means the right illustrator, or the right photographer. Advertising—a poster that will make people remember us and forget everybody else. Twenty-seven college freshmen to tack up the fliers on every pole in town, and even somebody to take 'em down to New York. And above everything else, an agent or manager who can get us decent gigs."

"It's *just* like publishing a book—a commercial book, at any rate."

"Except we're supposed to do all this ourselves. It costs money, that kind of push—and there are other things we need."

"Like new equipment."

"Yes."

"And a rehearsal studio."

"Yes."

The kettle whistled and Cassandra poured the boiling water into cups set up with cocoa, sugar, and cream. As she stirred the mixture together, her expression was thoughtful and distant.

"What's wrong?" asked Rocco.

"Nothing," she replied hastily. "I'm just thinking."

"About what?"

"People Buying Things."

Rocco nodded. "We're in a rut. We were coming along quickly there for a while, but then we got in a rut. I don't know what happened. It seems like all the bands that were coming up with us are going right on ahead. Like the Monotones—that burns me up. I'm not sure what we can do about it."

"I'll tell you one thing you can do—"

The telephone rang, interrupting her. She answered it and, after a moment, handed the receiver to Rocco. "It's the root of your problem," she said with distaste.

"Hello, Lenny," said Rocco. "What's up?"

As Rocco listened, Cassandra stood by, watching him intently.

"Providence is all right. Let me speak to Apple, though, she . . . What do you mean, no guaranteed base? Christ, Lenny, this is *not* a major opportunity—*Providence?*"

"Tell him no," said Cassandra quietly.

Rocco continued to listen to the manager, and finally he said, "No. No way. Not without guaranteed base. Just *something* for our dignity, for God's sake. . . . Apple's not here. She's moved out. . . . She's living with her boyfriend now. . . . No, I won't give you her number, you can get it from her tonight. Besides, my decision goes in this case."

Cassandra nodded approval.

After more argument, to no purpose, Rocco said good-bye abruptly and hung up.

"Lenny's the reason you're not going anywhere," said Cassandra.

Rocco nodded ruefully. "But what do we do? We've got to have an agent, and you're going to find this hard to believe, but Lenny's not the worst agent in town. Hey, let's go in the bedroom, and see what the ceiling looks like from the point of view of a couple of pillows."

"I'm too distracted," she said, shaking her head.

"About what?"

"The group."

Rocco laughed. "Are you going to get us on the fast track to success?"

"Maybe," said Cassandra seriously. She put down her cup unfinished. "Listen, I'm sorry, but I'm going to go now. I want to look into something."

"Man," said Rocco, "when you get something in your head, romance goes right out the window, doesn't it?"

"Getting things right takes time. And nobody's got time to waste. If you want something, then you've got to go after it."

"What are you going to do?" he asked.

She smiled and said, "Shoot Lenny."

That afternoon, when Jonathan arrived at the house in Brookline, he was startled to find a moving truck in the drive. Uniformed workmen were loading a tall piece of furniture, wrapped in pads and loosely covered with a sheet. Jonathan looked closely, and ruminated, and then realized that the piece was the highboy from his parents' bedroom. Amazed, Jonathan followed the men inside the house and up the stairs to the second floor. As the moving men went into the master bedroom, he heard Louise's voice. "All right, the vanity next."

Jonathan saw the door of Verity's room opened. He stepped inside, and found Verity sitting on her window seat, drink in hand, wrapped in a shawl, looking out at the moving van. "I always loved moving days," remarked Verity. "Even when I was little I loved to watch things carried in and out of the house. Maybe I should have been an interior decorator."

"What the hell is she doing?" asked Jonathan.

"Louise is redecorating her bedroom over on Marlborough," said Verity, with an ironic smile.

"Why?" demanded Jonathan in open-mouthed astonishment.

"Because she likes our furniture better, I suppose."

"By what right, I mean!"

Verity shrugged. "Louise thinks she has the right to do anything she wants around here. She just gets up out of the chair and does it."

"Have you spoken to her?"

"As little as possible."

"Does Cassandra know about this?"

"Yes," said Verity, "I believe she does."

"Is she here?"

"Maybe," replied Verity vaguely. "I don't know."

"Well, if nobody else cares what happens to this house, I do. *I'll* speak to Louise," said Jonathan.

"She's in there, directing the action. You know, if I were stronger," said Verity thoughtfully, still looking out the window, "I think I'd be a moving man. I think it would be great to go in strange people's houses, and lift their most treasured belongings." She looked around, but Jonathan was gone.

The moving men, carrying Margaret Hawke's vanity, nodded to Jonathan on their way down the steps. Jonathan went into the master bedroom, and found his stepmother standing in the center of the room, her hands on her hips, looking proudly around at the nearly empty space. Nothing remained but the family photographs on the near wall, and the carpet on the floor. The fragments of a Chinese vase littered a corner by the window.

"Oh, hello, Jonathan!" Louise cried. "I didn't know you were coming here today. It's so nice to see you!"

"Louise," said Jonathan, looking around the room and shaking his head, "what do you think you're doing?"

"What?"

"You think you can simply walk in here with moving men, and take away all of my mother's furniture?"

Louise winced at the word *mother*, and fielded his question by saying flatly, "It was your *father's* furniture. And because of that, it was very dear to me. I want it as something to remember him by."

"Louise," said Jonathan slowly, "you have no right to do this. This furniture is part of the house. And the house, as you know, does not belong to you. It belongs to Verity, to Cassandra, and to me."

"I got permission," said Louise distastefully, as if she thought Jonathan had no right to question her so.

"From whom?"

"From Verity. She said I could do whatever I wanted in here."

"Verity owns one-third of this house. Cassandra owns one-third. I own one-third. You certainly didn't get *my* permission to move Mother's furniture out."

"It was your *father's* furniture," Louise snapped. "And as his widow, I have claim on it. Besides, I don't know why you care anyway, Jonathan. You don't live here. You haven't been in this house in a month, I don't think. What difference could it make to you what furniture is in here? Those rooms above the garage out there are *filled* with furniture. If you're so upset, then all you have to do is move some of that stuff in here. It's as simple as that."

"You have one hell of a nerve to pull something like this!"

"Like *what?!*" cried Louise. "You keep saying I did something bad, and I didn't. I just came to get a few of the things that are particularly dear to me because of your father."

"Dear is certainly the right word. You just carted away some of the most valuable pieces of furniture in the house."

Louise hesitated. "I didn't know that. I don't care about that. I just want them because they were your father's." She went to the window and looked out. She took a breath and then said with some satisfaction, "Anyway, it's too late to do anything now, Jonathan. The moving van's already driven off."

Jonathan, still standing in the doorway, was silent for a moment. He appeared to be gathering his thoughts as he looked over the empty room, and then back to Louise, who was lifting a corner of the carpet with the toe of her shoe. "Why didn't you take the carpet too?" he asked sarcastically.

"I don't have a room big enough for it," replied Louise absently.

Jonathan shook his head. He looked at his stepmother and said quietly, "You have been using Father's death as if it were a springboard. His name, *our* name, has given you social respectability, I guess—but it will never make you respectable. You got a little money, a little property, and you got the real-estate office—but you wanted more than that. You wanted *our* fortune, but it was tied up in trust. You wanted *our* house, but it belongs to the three of us. So now you're going to loot it room by room, and then I guess you'll try to take it away, stone by stone, brick by brick, and board by board."

Louise looked at Jonathan coolly. "You have a very nasty streak in you. You didn't used to be this way. I'm going to ignore it. I know you're still upset about your father's death. We all are."

"Are we?"

"What?"

"Are we *all* upset?" asked Jonathan.

"What's that supposed to mean?"

Jonathan shrugged. "Yes, of course," he said, "we're all upset. It was horrible what happened to Father in Atlantic City. The way he died."

He smiled at Louise. Louise said nothing.

"So suddenly," Jonathan went on. "So strangely. So mysteriously."

"Heart attacks are terrible," said Louise nervously. "How do you think I felt? Down there, away from home, on our *honeymoon*, for God's sake!"

"I wondered that myself," said Jonathan.

"Wondered what?"

"Wondered how you felt when you found out Father was dead. Down there, away from home, on your *honeymoon*."

The mimicry hung in the air between them. Louise turned away and examined the family photographs on the wall.

"Well," said Jonathan, breaking the silence with a show of amiability, "I'm sorry that you went to this much trouble."

"Oh, it was no trouble—"

"Well, it's going to be. I want all those things returned. You have four months' grace time—until the first of September, to be precise."

"Thank you very much," Louise snorted, then asked warily. "Why September first? Why so exact?"

"Because that's when Apple and I are getting married." He smiled broadly. "And moving into this house. And this room. With my mother's furniture put back in it."

"You're getting married?" Louise asked, her tone of anger instantly giving way to shock.

"Yes."

Louise's face froze. "I never heard about these plans."

"The date's been set for a long time."

"You might have told me."

"We hardly need your permission. And I'm telling you now."

"Why don't you keep your old apartment?"

"It's too small. Apple and I want to live here, in this house. And we're going to, on September first."

"Then why," Louise said distractedly, "why don't you both live in your old room?"

"Because," said Jonathan carefully, "I'm coming back here with a wife. My old room doesn't have a bath attached to it. And this room has a dressing room, a bath, and two walk-in closets. It's perfect for Apple and me."

Louise stood very still at the corner of the Oriental rug. She toed a shard of the broken porcelain vase. "You want to bring a —a punk-rock singer to live in your father's house?"

"What do you mean by that?"

"I'm just wondering if you've really thought things through."

Jonathan looked at Louise closely. "You think I'd be injuring the reputation of the family if I married a woman who's a rock singer?"

"Apple's smart, she's a smart young woman, but she's not. . ."

"Not what?"

Louise took a breath and then said pointedly, "Not up to the standards of this family."

Jonathan stared at Louise. Then he laughed, and there was amusement in his voice. "*You're* saying Apple is not good enough to marry into this family. *You!*"

"What's that supposed to mean, Jonathan?"

"What do you think it's supposed to mean?"

"You don't think I'm good enough to carry your last name, is that it?"

"No, as a matter of fact, I don't, but I was referring to Eric, not to you."

"Eric?"

"It's not nearly as bad for me to be married to a rock musician as it is for Verity to be married to a drug dealer."

"What?" cried Louise, stepping forward, and crushing one of the shards of the broken porcelain vase beneath her foot. "What do you mean by that?"

"I can hardly believe you don't know anything about it, Louise."

"There's nothing to know. Eric has never sold drugs. I know it for a fact. I guess he's tried marijuana, most young people have. But I'll bet you five dollars it was Verity who gave it to him."

"Call your son, Louise. Ask him how he pays rent on that apartment when he hasn't had a real job for three years. Ask him why he pays for everything in cash."

Louise's breath was deep and uneven. "I'm the one who provides him with money. Eric's just a victim of the recession, that's all. He's certainly *not* dealing drugs." She glared at Jonathan, who carefully adjusted the sleeves of his sport coat.

"Sure, Louise. You know, one reason I'm marrying a punk-rock singer is that, after being shackled with you *and* Eric, I thought we'd need somebody to bring up the tone of the family a little."

11

In the early evening of that same day, Cassandra and Rocco showed up at Jonathan and Apple's apartment in the Prudential Towers. It was almost dark, and from the thirtieth floor, Back Bay lay like a map in shades of blue beneath them. Jonathan's two-bedroom apartment was furnished in bright blue and steel gray, but all the lights were soft white and warm. Cassandra looked around. "Apple, are you sure you moved in today? I can't see a thing that's out of place."

"I like to travel light."

Jonathan looked at his fiancée. "I had a run-in with Louise this afternoon," he said, starting to prepare drinks for them all. "Verity, did you tell her she could have all of Mother's furniture?"

"I told her not to bother me," said Verity.

"That was a very stupid thing to do. Louise interpreted that as permission."

"Is this a family conference?" asked Verity. "If this is going to be a family conference, I'm going to have to do some coke."

"This is a family conference," said Jonathan, pouring himself a Scotch. He went to the window and looked out over the city. When he turned back he said: "We're the Hawkes now."

"Not me," Verity pointed out. "Technically, I mean."

Jonathan ignored her. "Before," he went on, deliberately, "we were just the children—Mother and Father were the principal generation. Now that's us."

"Don't forget Louise," said Cassandra.

"Does anybody else want a few lines?" asked Verity, looking up from her razor blade.

"Verity, *please*," said Cassandra.

Jonathan said, "I'd like to know if anyone else thinks the will business is suspicious. The fact that Father made it out only two days after he was married, that he died two days later of mixing pills and liquor."

Verity sniffed loudly. "I'd like to have a little confidential chat with that Atlantic City coroner who didn't see anything in it but an accident."

"So would I," Jonathan agreed.

"I'm sure Louise badgered Father into changing the will," Verity went on blithely.

Cassandra sat up straight, and interrupted: "Let's please not get on that track again. I want to talk about something else that happened today." She waited until she had everyone's attention, and then began, "I went in those rooms over the garage this afternoon."

"Why on earth?" asked Verity.

"I'll get to that in a minute. Did you know that Louise has started fixing it up? Everything uncovered and rearranged, like a little apartment."

"You think she's going to move in?" cried Verity. "Oh, God!"

"No," said Cassandra. "If she wanted to move in there, she wouldn't have sent all that furniture over to her own apartment. I think she's fixing it up for Eric."

"Worse," breathed Verity.

"Does she think we're blind? Or stupid?" said Jonathan.

"Obviously she thinks she can push us around," said Verity. "Personally, I don't care what she does, as long as she doesn't talk to me."

"Verity," said Jonathan, "how are you going to feel when Eric starts a drug-handling operation on the grounds?"

"It would certainly save me a few trips into town."

"Come off it, Verity," said Jonathan irritably.

"Don't worry," said Cassandra. "Louise isn't going to move anyone into that space. I'm seeing to that."

"What are you up to?" asked Jonathan.

"I spoke to the contractors today."

"What contractors?" asked Verity.

"The real reason I went over to look at those rooms over the garage," said Cassandra slowly, glancing with a smile first at Rocco, and then at Apple, "is that I'm converting it into a rehearsal studio for People Buying Things."

Verity clapped her hands and breathed, "Wonderful! Louise will be livid."

Apple and Rocco were open-mouthed with astonishment. "Cassandra," Rocco began.

"I want to do it," she said quickly, anticipating his objection. "You don't have a regular rehearsal space, and I've seen how much of your time and energy is wasted in setting one up. There won't be any neighbors to complain, you'll have a place to leave all your things where you know they'll be safe—there are a hundred reasons. Besides, in a few months, Apple will be family, and that's even more reason to see that the band goes somewhere."

"Do you need any help?" asked Jonathan. "I'd be happy to help out some."

"I can take care of the construction," said Cassandra crisply, "but if you want to put out for some new equipment and instruments and costumes, that's fine."

"Why are you two doing all this?" asked Apple, who seemed shocked but very pleased.

"I want to help too!" cried Verity. "I don't know how, but I'll do something."

"We appreciate this," said Apple, "but I think you're doing it all just to spite Louise." She looked from Verity to Jonathan to Cassandra. "Isn't that right?"

"Can you think of a better reason to do it?" Verity asked seriously.

Louise Larner's apartment was second-floor front of a converted town house on the sunny side of Marlborough Street, between Arlington and Berkeley. If Louise had ever leaned out of her bowed window, she might have seen the Public Gardens fifty yards away. The address was fashionable, and so was the building. The Hawke Agency managed it, and Louise's rent hadn't gone up a penny since she had first gone to work for Richard Hawke fifteen years previously.

The flat had one bedroom, a living room, an alcove that would have been termed a dining room in advertisements for the place, a kitchen, a bath, and a warren of closets. But all the rooms were tiny, and the ceilings low, so that the place seemed cramped. A dozen years ago, Louise had borrowed money from her future husband, and hired a decorator to do the place over. He had done it in his showiest, most uncomfortable manner. The apartment looked like a decorator's model, not a home, and in twelve years, Louise hadn't changed a single thing. She always left the front curtains open, even at night, for she liked the idea that passersby would look into the place, and wonder at its pristine beauty. The apartment never failed to give the impression that it had just been photographed for a Sunday supplement the day before. It bore unmistakably the designer's mark, but there was nothing of Louise in it. She had only her clothes, all hidden away in closets. When she was at home alone, Louise ate frozen dinners. Her freezer was filled, but the refrigerator and cabinets were empty.

One evening about ten days after she had moved her husband's bedroom furniture into her own apartment, Louise stood in her living room staring out at the street. She gnawed at her lower lip as she gazed through her own reflection in the dark window panes. By contrast with what Verity, Jonathan, and Cassandra possessed, Louise had received almost nothing at all. What irked most was that the house remained in possession of those three, who had no use for it, no appreciation of it, no moral *right* to it. After some time in such contemplations, she turned, swept across the room—which seemed tinier and more cramped than ever, with the ceiling bearing down upon her—took up the telephone receiver, and dialed rapidly.

"I'm sorry I couldn't come when you called, Louise," said Eugene Strable, later that evening. "I was in the middle of dinner. I take it this is important."

He followed her down the hall and into the living room of her apartment.

"I'm sorry to have bothered you," said Louise absently, touching a hand to the ornamental comb nestled in her loose chignon. Her gaze became steady. "But it was urgent."

One of the windows of the living room had been pried open, and the room was damp and chill. Wisps of evening fog visibly drifted in. Louise didn't seem to notice, and the lawyer made no remark.

"Would you like a drink?" she asked.

Eugene shook his head. Louise then seated herself at the desk near the cold and black hearth. Eugene sat at one end of the sofa, facing her.

"Are you in some sort of trouble?" he asked, when she had made no motion to begin the conversation.

Louise leaned forward, resting one elbow on the green desk blotter. She toyed with a silver letter opener. "How much did you know about Richard's affairs?"

"I knew as much as I needed to know, which, when it comes down to it, was not very much. Of course my firm represents the agency, Louise, but I didn't often work directly with Richard. We were friends of course, good friends, and he often came to me for advice."

Louise nodded impatiently through this speech; it was evident this was not new information to her.

"Did you know about the waterfront business?" she asked impetuously. "That's what I want to know."

"I knew something about it. He had mentioned it. I believe he had one or two of the younger lawyers in the firm doing title searches and things like that. Why?"

"Because," said Louise, "before he died, it was the *only* thing on his mind. For the last six months, that waterfront business took up *all* of his time. I ran the agency."

Eugene Strable looked askance at this, but said nothing.

"You know the new Marriott Hotel down on the waterfront?" Louise asked. "You know how successful it's been since it opened?"

"I do read the *Globe*, Louise. And their restaurant is quite decent," said the lawyer, with an impatient clearing of his throat. "The whole area is changing."

"Well," said Louise, "there's more in the works than most people know about."

"Well," said the lawyer, "the waterfront is only so big. And the city owns a lot of it, so that—"

Louise smiled. "The city is selling off their property."

"I didn't know that."

"No one does."

"And Richard intended to buy it?"

Louise nodded.

"And do what with it?"

Louise, as if reading down a list before her, ticked off: "The warehouses will be made into first-floor shops, second-floor restaurants, and upper-floor condos. Another hotel, at least five hundred rooms. A major convention center, bigger than Hynes. A Hyper-Market for every antique dealer in New England. An arts center with a nine-hundred seat theater, ten movie houses, and a Las Vegas-style cabaret. And two fifty-story apartment houses, with every apartment overlooking the bay."

Eugene, impressed, remarked, "That's big-league."

Louise nodded.

"Who's doing it?" the lawyer inquired.

Louise hesitated. "It's a big secret. But I'll tell you. It's all Hong Kong money. They're worried about being taken over by the Communists in nineteen ninety-seven, and so they're looking for places to invest. But they try to keep everything secret. And Richard was helping them do just that. Richard had a reputation for discretion."

"Well deserved," smiled the lawyer. "But what's going to happen now?"

"Now that Richard is dead? I'm going to handle it."

"Good," said the lawyer, nodding. "Sometimes there's a problem in transfer of power and responsibility. . . ."

"I was Richard's business partner before I was his wife," said Louise. "I've already talked to the people involved. They'll be working with me. Besides, they have to—Richard and I were investors."

"Investors! Louise, you're talking about a project that's at least two hundred million dollars."

"More," said Louise.

"Richard couldn't afford to invest in that. He couldn't have afforded one tenth of one percent—"

"Eugene," said Louise, interrupting him, "you know all that property I was left in Richard's will? The apartment buildings, the portfolio, and so on?"

"You were well provided for, I think," said the lawyer.

Louise shook her head. "None of that exists," said Louise soberly. "Everything was sold off. Even the building the agency is in was mortgaged to the hilt. Everything was invested in this venture."

The lawyer sat back. After a pause, he asked, "Everything?"

Louise nodded, and dropped the letter opener with a clatter. She leaned back. "If this went under, I wouldn't have a penny."

"But you've been talking as if this were a sure thing."

"All that money Richard and I put in went for one purpose—to grease palms. Eugene, you would not *believe* how many influential men there are who aren't above standing in dark alleys with their briefcases open in front of them, waiting for someone to come along and pour money in. Not to mention campaign contributions and testimonial dinners and the like. *That's* how big this project is."

The lawyer took a long breath. "Louise, are you sure you aren't in too deep?"

"Of course I am. But I intend to come out on top—on the very top!" She leaned forward suddenly. "But I need your help, Eugene."

"My advice? I'll be happy to give you whatever counsel—"

"Your advice, of course," Louise cut in. "But something more than just words."

"Louise, all my money is tied up."

"I'm not asking you to put anything in, Eugene. At least not personally," she corrected herself. "I want you to invest the Hawke family trust."

Eugene stared at her.

"I couldn't," he said after a moment.

"Why not? That's exactly what Richard was planning to do. He was executor of his wife's will, and he was going to put every penny of it in this project."

"And it would have been wrong," said the lawyer definitely. "It would be impossible to simply liquidate everything and turn it over to a consortium of real-estate developers. How could I explain that to Verity and Jonathan and Cassandra?"

"I would hope," said Louise carefully, "that you would be discreet enough so that you wouldn't have to do any explaining."

"Impossible," replied the lawyer. "For one thing, there wouldn't be any return on the money for several years, not until the damn thing gets built and rents start coming in. What would happen to their monthly incomes in the meantime? When that money stopped coming in, they'd start asking questions. And I'd have to answer them."

"That part is easy," said Louise. "You invest everything except just enough to produce that income. Then there are no questions." She shrugged, as if surprised the lawyer hadn't already thought of it.

"You've also got to remember that Verity turns twenty-nine in less than a year. She'll be entitled to a third of the capital then."

"All the more reason to get this business done quickly. When the time comes, there are ways of handling Verity. You forget, she's still married to Eric. If we need it, I can get Eric to put his signature to *anything*." The lawyer sat and thought for several minutes, his face betraying both the temptation he was allowing himself to feel at the prospect of such an immense fortune, and his fears. "Even if I could invest the trust in this deal, how would I benefit?"

"We'd work out some sort of commission."

The lawyer shook his head. "Partnership."

Louise looked up in surprise.

"You can't do it without me, Louise, and I'd be sticking my neck way, way out."

"We'll work it out," agreed Louise. "I'm not worried about the details. There's going to be so much money that percentages aren't going to matter much anyway. We've just got to look at this from the right perspective," she said delicately.

Eugene Strable sat silent, with his hands folded in his lap, as if waiting for her to elaborate on that perspective.

"Of course in all this," said Louise, "I'm thinking of Richard's children. I'm thinking only of Verity, Cassandra, and Jonathan. Verity is my daughter-in-law. I've seen the three of them grow up. And here's an opportunity for me to make them very very rich. . . ."

"And not hurt yourself in the process," commented the lawyer blandly. He glanced around the room, thinking. Louise did not disturb him. "I'd need accurate and concrete information about this business," he said at last. "I'd need details—a lot of them—

before I could even *think* about making a decision."

"I've arranged a meeting for tomorrow morning at eleven," Louise said quickly. "Upstairs at the agency. There'll be three men there. The first one's name is . . ."

Louise and Eugene Strable talked further into the evening. Louise declared that she wouldn't let him leave until he had made some sort of promise to her, and eventually the lawyer did just that. Louise walked him down to the front hallway of the apartment house. She stood with him in the opened door of the vestibule. The damp wind blew through her hair, and she stood with her arms crossed over her breast for warmth.

"You understand, don't you, Eugene, that Richard and I had already planned all this out before he died. It was one of the reasons we were in Atlantic City. The whole business was *his* idea. I'm just carrying out his last wishes."

"Oh, yes, Louise, I understand," Strable said. "I'll see you in the morning at eleven." As he turned to go down the stoop, he lifted the collar of his coat to hide the wry smile tugging at his mouth.

12

On a Saturday morning early in July, Jonathan pulled his Porsche into the horseshoe drive and angled smoothly into the space where his father used to park. Apple was beside him in the car, and in the back was a large wicker picnic basket. The owners of Menelaus Press were hosting the annual staff outing, and Cassandra had invited her brother and Apple to accompany her and Rocco to the private estate in Weston where the festivities were held each year.

Jonathan and Apple got out of the car and walked into the house. They both wore jeans and running shoes, but his starched checkered shirt was brown, and hers was red. Apple had removed her three ear hoops and replaced them with a tiny golden spur. She wore no makeup.

Inside, they found Verity lying on the living room sofa reading a magazine. The French doors were opened wide and a warm breeze blew the sheers about and played in her hair. When Jonathan and Apple spoke, Verity pulled her glasses down the bridge of her nose, and stared at them.

"Cassandra and Rocco are in the kitchen," Verity said. "They're dressed just like you. I feel like I've wandered onto the set for *State Fair*. How can you live in the modern world, and still look so revoltingly wholesome?"

"Verity, come with us today," said Apple.

Verity edged her glasses back up the bridge of her nose, sank lower into the sofa, and raised the magazine to obscure her face. "Thanks anyway, but I'd rather be tied face down on a hill of red ants."

Jonathan checked his watch. "It's eleven-thirty. What are you doing up?"

"Don't remind me of the time," said Verity. "Eugene Strable came over early, pulled Father's sailboat out right under my window, and decided to experiment with the entire repertoire of Black & Decker."

"Eugene Strable?"

Verity closed the magazine. "Apparently Louise gave him permission. She's going with him. Maybe she'll drown."

"Let's hope," said Jonathan. "But who gave *her* permission to lend out Father's boat?"

In the kitchen they found Rocco and Cassandra. Cassandra, her hair pulled back in a demure chignon, wore a full-length brown muslin skirt and a white blouse with puffed short sleeves. Rocco wore bleached farmer's overalls, a dark rust muslin shirt, and a wide-brimmed straw hat, set rakishly back on his head.

Ida was wrapping two pies in tin foil, but Apple cried, "Not yet!" She hurried over, closed her eyes, and breathed in the heady scent of apple, cinnamon, and vanilla.

"Are we about ready?" asked Cassandra. "Should we go in separate cars or take the station wagon?"

"I want to speak to Mr. Strable first," said Jonathan quickly. "Can we wait just a few minutes?"

"Don't be long," said Apple. "I'm starved."

"Jonathan," Cassandra said, "Mr. Strable asked me if it was all right to use the boat. I said yes, since he and Father used to go out all the time together, and it's always best that boats get *some* use. That was all right, wasn't it?"

"As long as it was you and not Louise," said Jonathan, as he went out the kitchen door. He made his way along the back of the house, to where Eugene Strable was hooking the boat to the bumper of his Cadillac.

The lawyer looked up. "Hello, Jonathan. Picnicking too?"

"Yes. We're about to leave, but I wanted to speak to you for a minute."

"I'm about to leave too. In fact Louise and I should have been off an hour ago, at least. She's around somewhere."

"This'll only take a minute."

"Certainly, then, what is it?"

"I wanted to ask you about a financial matter, about Mother's trust."

"What about it?"

"Why is it that we're getting so little, when she left so much?"

Eugene Strable sighed. "Jonathan, this seems to me to be the worst possible time for a discussion like this. Couldn't it wait? Why don't you make an appointment on Monday? Then we can sit down and I can answer all your questions. I've been looking forward to sailing today. I don't want to talk shop."

"I understand," said Jonathan, but he didn't retreat. The lawyer regarded him with a resigned expression.

"All right, Jonathan. Let's hear it. But if you're going to tell me you can't get by on your salary *and* thirty-six thousand dollars a year, you're going to have a hard time convincing me."

"I can get along on that, of course. I'd be fine on my salary alone, but I'm talking about investments."

"Investments?"

"That's right. I'd like to invest some money."

"All right, then. Live on your salary, and you've got that thirty-six-thousand dollars a year you say you don't need."

"I'm talking about a lot more money than that, Mr. Strable."

The lawyer seemed momentarily to have forgotten about the boat and his plans for sailing. He didn't ask Jonathan how much money he wanted, however, but inquired instead, "What kind of investments are you talking about?"

"I'm talking about seed money for a high-tech business that's about to be set up in Waltham," said Jonathan with an excitement he could no longer repress. "This guy I went to school with at Harvard, he was first in the physics department, and he's figured out this way to make the ultimate chip—"

"What?"

"You know, computer chips. He's got blueprints for one with storage space for a million pieces of information on it. The biggest one now has only sixty-four thousand, so if he can manufacture his he can make a fortune. But he needs seed money, and he came to me. If I can help set him up, I'd be one of the directors of the company, and I'd also get twenty-five percent of all the profit. It's a major opportunity, Mr. Strable."

"The only sound investment is real estate, Jonathan. That's what your father believed, and I believe it too."

Jonathan sighed. "I need three hundred and fifty thousand dollars. I'd like you, as executor of Mother's estate, to authorize it as an 'extraordinary expense.'"

"That's a third of a million dollars you're talking about!"

"Yes," said Jonathan. "And I intend to make it six times as much in the next three years. I've gone into this all in great detail with my friend."

"I can't let you have a third of a million dollars."

"It's *my* money. My portion of the estate alone makes that much in interest every year. If you want, I'll speak to Verity and Cassandra about it, and get their permission. What I can do is—"

"Don't bother," Eugene said. "I'm not going to authorize the money."

"Mr. Strable," said Jonathan with barely maintained patience. "The money, ultimately, is mine. This is not an irresponsible venture. I wouldn't be the only person putting up funds."

Eugene shook his head, looked at Jonathan, and said, "You don't give an old roommate a third of a million dollars because he's got this good idea, Jonathan! If you did, you'd be coming back to me in six months, saying you have to have another hundred thousand dollars because of unforeseen expenses, and then six months later it will turn out that something was wrong with your friend's idea and the thing doesn't work after all, or IBM decided to go into the same business and they beat you out. And all that money would be lost. The only safe investment is real estate, Jonathan."

"You sound just like Father. His idea of security was owning a block of Back Bay. Well, I'm not interested in that kind of security. I don't want to snap up apartment buildings for condominium conversion. I don't want to buy vacation houses on speculation. I'm much more interested in venture capital, and high-tech industries, and the *real* future of this country. I want to be part of all that, and I want to make money in it. And here's my chance, my first real chance at that, and I want that money." His face was set and determined. "I want your authorization, and that's that."

"I'm sorry, Jonathan, but you won't get a penny beyond what you're actually entitled to by the terms of the trust. I won't see you squander it on some cockamamie scheme. Now go on your picnic, Jonathan, and quit wasting my sailing time."

At the picnic, Jonathan made no attempt to disguise his anger and frustration. The four of them sat around a checkered tablecloth laid on the grass in the shade of a willow. The tree overhung a pond with geese and ducks. As Jonathan talked, they ate the chicken Ida had prepared, and drank champagne from a tin cooler. Apple crumbled bread and fed the noisy birds that gathered curiously around them.

"You wouldn't have minded, would you, Cassandra," said Jonathan in conclusion, "if I had taken that money out?"

"Of course not," said Cassandra. "It seems like a lot, but the money's there. It could even have been taken out of interest—it wouldn't have affected capital at all."

"That's right," said Jonathan, shrugging. "I wanted to prove I could make a little on my own. I wanted a chance to show that I had something going for me besides an inheritance. And Eugene Strable just screwed that."

"Did you explain it to him like that?" asked Apple.

"He didn't give me the chance. He was more interested in getting the boat out in the water."

"Jonathan," Apple said gently, "perhaps Mr. Strable is right. It sounds like a risky investment to me too. High-tech used to be a sure thing, but not any more."

"Christ, Apple! I don't need another lecture! Risky or not isn't the point! It would have been a chance to do something on my own, make a few decisions that actually mattered one way or another. Sometimes I feel like I'm trapped by that damned trust fund."

They were silent for a moment. Apple turned away from Jonathan and tossed the last of the bread to the ducks. "Poor little rich kid," she muttered as she stood and brushed the crumbs from her hands. "I'm going for a walk around the pond," she announced and strode off without waiting to see if anyone would join her.

Jonathan stared down at the checked tablecloth. Cassandra touched Rocco's arm. "Go talk business for a while. I want to speak to Jonathan." Rocco nodded, rose, and hurried off after Apple.

Cassandra turned to her brother. "You were short with her. It wasn't her fault."

"I know, I know," he said. "Strable just got on my nerves this morning. I mean it's not as if I were irresponsible or anything. It's not as if *any* of us had ever squandered any money at all."

"Do you think Father would have let you have the money?" asked Cassandra gently.

"No," replied Jonathan after a moment. "But he would have been wrong too."

Cassandra pondered a few moments and then suggested: "Why don't you get up a prospectus or whatever they call them? Do it all as businesslike as possible, and then go back to Mr. Strable. Let him have it evaluated by an investment firm. I bet if it turns out to be a good thing, he will come through with the money."

Jonathan eyed his sister. "That's pretty smart, you know. That's what I should have done in the first place. I just hope I haven't screwed everything up by going to him cold the way I did this morning."

"I don't think so," said Cassandra. "If it's a good investment, it's a good investment."

Jonathan still appeared troubled, and after a moment he said, "I think I may have jumped into something else a little too quickly, too."

"What?"

"I did something a couple of weeks ago, and now I think maybe I should have come to you and Verity first."

"Jonathan, what did you do?"

"I hired a private investigator."

Cassandra's brow wrinkled, but she said nothing.

"To look into Father's death," Jonathan explained. "He's down in Atlantic City right now. Was that a stupid thing to do?"

"No," said Cassandra quickly. "I told you once I thought it was a bad idea, but now I'm glad you did it. I think we should have done it sooner."

"Why do you say that?"

"I'm not sure, it's just a feeling. Instinct."

"Me too," said Jonathan. "Real instinct. You know, I used to distrust instinct. I was always told to make rational decisions. I don't think rational decisions take everything into account. Instinct is better." He laughed. "*That's* the kind of stuff I get hanging around Apple. Apple believes in instinct."

"Well," asked Cassandra, "has he found anything?"

"The P.I., you mean?" Jonathan grinned, amused by the jargon. "Nothing major, I guess. He would have called. But I'm going to speak to him this week. So I think I'd like to have a little conference soon. You and me and Verity. Whether our P.I. has found out anything or not. We should decide—together—how we're going to handle Louise. That woman just gets worse and worse."

Cassandra laughed. "Father always wanted us to be closer. And Louise is accomplishing that. Why don't the three of us get together next weekend, and plan strategy?"

"That sounds good. And why don't we go down to Truro? We'll be relaxed, and besides, I don't want Louise dropping in unannounced in the middle of it. It's the sort of thing she'd do if she suspected anything."

"I'll have the house opened this week. You're right. Louise is not likely to bother us there. And we'll also try to figure out a way to get that investment money out of Mr. Strable."

"Good," said Jonathan. "The poor little rich boy will get all his problems solved down at the beach."

13

"Dear Mr. Cirina," Cassandra wrote at the top of a small sheet of *Iphigenia* stationery, "I was very pleased to have the opportunity to read your cycle of poems, *Reckless Dust*, but I fear that its principal themes of necrophilia and decay make it unsuitable for an appearance in *Iphigenia*. Sincerely yours, Cassandra Hawke, Editor." She signed her name, typed a label with Mr. Cirina's address, placed the label on a large gray envelope, and shoved in a pile of pages at least an inch thick. She sealed the flap with tape, and tossed the envelope with a sigh into the wooden tray marked "Mail."

The room was hot. More than that, it was dark because of a power outage, and Cassandra had to turn her manual typewriter so that the dim light of the overcast day shone upon the paper in the bail. A fan with blue blades sat desolately on the corner of her desk, unmoving. Out on Brattle Street, the sidewalks were crowded with summer-term students at Harvard. Despite the fact that no signals were working, traffic moved as usual—Cambridge drivers tended to ignore them at the best of times, and the set of lights that had previously been right in front of the offices of the Menelaus Press had been removed a year before, since they were no more than a joke. Cassandra lifted her eyes above the leafy trees and roofs of surrounding buildings. The sky was darkened to a steely gray by thick unmoving clouds, and the still air was strong with the smell of impending summer rain. From down the hall she could hear Sarah's transistor radio playing a golden oldies station. The Beach Boys were singing "I Wish They All Could Be California Girls."

Cassandra picked up the clipped manuscript that lay at the top of a pile of unsolicited submissions at the corner of her desk. She went over to the window, leaned against the sill, and shifted so that the light fell upon the pages as she turned them. There were three poems, by Mr. Eugene Lefavre, called "Trash Bag Love,"

"Dancing in the Sink," and "Housewives in Cellophane"—each a monologue composed in rigid blank verse. She quickly typed out a rejection note for that one too.

From down the hall, Sarah's radio was now playing the Monkees' "I'm a Believer." Cassandra picked up a third manuscript, and went to the window with it. Outside, in the little garden before the building, most of the Menelaus employees sat with cups of coffee and pastries brought from the Blacksmith's House bakery around the corner. They had taken the excuse of the power outage to abandon their desks.

Cassandra glanced up at the sky again, and her thoughts drifted to the coming weekend with Jonathan and Verity at their Cape house in Truro. Verity had agreed to it with surprising alacrity, and taken elaborate precautions against Louise discovering any of their plans. Now that she knew about the investigator Jonathan had hired, Verity seemed eager to participate in family ventures. No one else, not even Apple, Rocco, or the servants were told of the investigator or the meeting Jonathan had called to discuss his findings. Cassandra and Verity themselves would open up the house late on Friday afternoon.

The telephone rang, startling Cassandra from her thoughts; she had forgotten that blackouts don't affect phone service.

It was Rocco on the other end, changing their plans for the evening. Lenny had at the last moment procured a play date for the band.

"Where are you playing?" With the receiver cradled against her ear, she went over and shut the door. Cutting the cross-ventilation would raise the temperature, but it would also keep out the noise of the Doors' "L.A. Woman."

She walked back to the window. As she talked to Rocco, she stared at the sky. "Rocco, you told me you weren't going to play the Basement anymore. You told me—"

As Rocco explained, she stuck her hand out the window to see if the rain had yet begun to fall. She felt a drop or two on her palm.

"I'll tell you why," Cassandra replied quickly. "Because the Basement's crowd is made up entirely of Northeastern students. They're drunk when they get there and their idea of a good time is to see who can throw up the farthest. Those people don't care who's playing, so long as it's loud enough so they don't have to talk to their dates."

Outside, the rain began to fall in earnest. The Menelaus employees all scurried inside through the front door, directly beneath Cassandra's window.

"I *know* what the take at the door is like there," said Cassandra. "And of course it's good, but it's an audience that doesn't carry any weight. The people who go to the Basement are people who don't want to have to stagger home more than two blocks. These aren't the people who'll follow you bar to bar. When you play at the Basement, you're not building. You'd be surprised how much this is like trying to establish a subscription basis for a little magazine—it's *just* like it, in fact. You've got to have your base. It makes me furious that Lenny would book you into a place like that for three nights. Three nights completely wasted, so far as I'm concerned."

The rain began suddenly to come down hard, and at such an angle that it splashed on the windowsill. With one hand, Cassandra lowered the windows as she listened to Rocco.

"No," she said at last, "of course I'm going to come. I'm not mad at you—I'm mad at Lenny. I think he's wasting your time. I think he's living hand to mouth on his commission. He'd book an English band in an Irish pub on St. Patrick's Day if it got him fifty dollars. . . . No, I don't know what time it is, the power's off here. I'm going home early today. I'll see you at ten. If I can get away a little earlier, I'll come over to your place first. Oh, by the way, I talked to the contractor. He said the job will take about a month and they'll start tearing the walls out next week. Okay? Good. See you at ten."

His reply was lost beneath a great roll of thunder. The sky outside had darkened, and now was nearly black. Suddenly it was lighted up with flashes of lightning, and a sharp crack of thunder told that it had struck very close. Cassandra hung up the telephone.

The windows were open at the top, and the room quickly filled with the fragrance of the rain. The rain beat upon the window-panes and thrashed the trees outside. The Menelaus sign swung creakily. And, just faintly underneath it all, she could hear Sarah's radio, playing The Byrds' "Turn, Turn, Turn."

That evening Cassandra went down the short narrow staircase of the Basement. She paid the two-dollar cover charge to a heavy-set man with close-cut black hair and a full black beard. He sat on a stool by the door with a small cash box resting on one wide thigh. He reached out for her hand, and was about to stamp it, but Cassandra declined. "Hey," he said, "what if you want to go outside and smoke some weed?"

Cassandra still declined. She stepped through a low doorway, and went a few steps over to the bar. She seated herself on a stool and ordered a glass of white wine. It was nearing ten o'clock and the bar was doing brisk business for a Tuesday night. With a practiced eye, Cassandra looked the place over, and saw that the lighting was ill-designed and entirely too bright—it served only to emphasize the dinginess of the place. A jukebox near the restroom doors was blaring Blondie's "Heart of Glass," unpardonably out of date. On the raised dais that served as a stage she saw that the band's equipment had been set up, but she didn't see any of the members of the group about. She did, however, see Lenny Able, the band's agent, standing halfway down the bar. As he waited for the bartender to mix his drink, Lenny looked at himself in the mirror behind the bar. He smoothed a hand over his fuzzy beard, and pushed his frizzy hair farther down over his forehead. He adjusted the open collar of his floral-patterned shirt. The gold chains around his neck gleamed under the bright light. Lenny took a satisfied breath and glanced away from his image only when the bartender placed his drink before him. Lenny paid and then made a pointed display of slapping down a generous tip. He did not leave until the bartender had seen the tip, taken it up, and acknowledged it with a nod.

Cassandra turned her head as Lenny passed by her. He did not see her. He went and stood by the doorman only a few feet behind Cassandra. Cassandra could make out most of their conversation. She was amused by Lenny's Mr. Gladhand routine. The doorman, who it turned out was also the manager of the place, merely grunted, always in the same tone, at anything

Lenny said. As she listened with half an ear to Lenny's inanities, she looked over the increasing crowd, wondering that so many, so young, could be so drunk so early in the evening.

"Don't bust my ass with shit like that," she heard the doorman say in a loud voice. Cassandra shifted a little until she could see him and Lenny in the mirror. She strained to catch more of their conversation.

"Hey, come on, Charlie, you known me a long time."

"So what? I say what groups play here."

"Hey," said Lenny affably. "I bring you my best acts. Class shit. Look here, People Buying Things is fucking packing 'em in." Lenny waved a hand to take in the bar behind him. "Fucking look around, man."

"It's two-for-one on beer, Able. That'd pull 'em if the Russians were dropping the bomb and this was ground zero."

"Yeah sure, but what about Friday? Friday when you got a five-dollar cover, you got to have some class shit to bring 'em in."

"Sure, sure, bring 'em back."

"Great. So terms, talk terms to me, man."

"You give me five hundred," said the doorman, "and you get full take at the door."

"Hey, no way, man, five hundred, that's robbery."

"Don't call me man," said the doorman. "Five hundred, take it or leave it."

"Hey, what if there's a blizzard or something?"

"This is July. Ain't gonna be no blizzard."

"Sure," said Lenny, after a moment's consideration, "give you five hundred. This band'll pull 'em in off the streets."

"Five hundred," repeated the doorman, "up front. Tomorrow morning, or I don't put it on the radio and in the papers."

"Hey, no way!" cried Lenny. "You'll get your fucking five, I can't front bills like that."

The doorman shrugged. "Then screw it. Hey, I'll get fucking Surgical Penis Clinic in here. I love those fucking girls. They tear the fucking place up."

"Hey, man, do it for four."

"No."

"Two-fifty up front, and two more as soon as it walks in the door on Friday night."

"Five up front. Hey, Able, move your fucking ass, you're blocking traffic."

Lenny scrunched against the wall to let in a group of six or seven already drunken members of a college fraternity.

"I can't give you five up front," said Lenny.

"Then fuck you," said the doorman. "Hey, you're supposed to be this band's fucking agent and manager. What kind of guts have you got behind them if you won't even put up a lousy fucking five hundred dollars? You don't think they can pull in a hundred lousy fraternity jocks from across the street on a fucking Friday night?"

"Sure! Sure I'm behind 'em two hundred percent. It's this up-front shit I don't want to deal with."

"Then fuck off, cheapskate, and leave me alone to make change."

Lenny glared at the doorman and manager of the club, and then walked off, muttering.

Cassandra finished off her drink and signaled for another. She wondered what she ought to do: tell Rocco and Apple what she'd overheard, silently offer to lend Lenny the five hundred dollars, deal with the manager of the place herself, or simply do nothing at all. She sipped at her second drink, still considering the business, when her attention was drawn to a table nearby. A college student stood up suddenly, knocking his chair over behind him. His friends around the table were laughing. The college student lurched to the side, and threw up into the lap of the girl who was sitting next to him.

It was then that Cassandra decided to say nothing at all. One night's profits, and radio and print exposure, did not weigh sufficiently against the uselessness of such an audience as this.

14

The Hawke summer house in Truro on Cape Cod was a modest structure built in the thirties, one-storied, gray-shingled, and weather-beaten. At one end of the house were four small bedrooms and two baths, at the other a living room, a dining room, and a kitchen. The front door opened onto a bare, grassless stretch of white sand sloping down to the rocky beach. A small dune rose up behind the house, just high enough to make the house invisible to walkers or drivers on the shell-paved private road that wandered along the coast here. The house's casual, comfortable furnishings and its low-key appearance masked its real value, since few properties on this part of the Cape could now boast two hundred yards of private beach—so much had been taken over in the creation of the National Seashore in the fifties.

On Friday afternoon, Cassandra took off from work early, picked up Verity, and arrived in time for late-afternoon sunbathing. The house had been opened at the beginning of June, but none of them had used it with any frequency. Cassandra and Jonathan had been too busy, and too disturbed by the death of their father; Verity had been too lazy to be bothered with the trip down. As soon as she had put away her clothes in bureau drawers fragrant with lavender, Verity announced with unaccustomed energy, "I'm going over to the grocery store."

She brought back lobsters, avocados, and a sampling of fresh fruit. "This place seems so empty with just us. I wish you had invited Rocco and Apple."

"No. This weekend is family, just family. Besides, People is doing a fill-in at Channel One tonight and tomorrow," said Cassandra. "It came up this afternoon when Amoebas in Bondage had to cancel. It's going to be broadcast live on ZBC radio. Unfortunately, the signal won't reach this far. I really wish we could hear them. They're playing with Solar Blood and Judy's Tiny Head."

Verity looked up with a grin. "You're really getting into all this, aren't you?"

Their dinner was relaxed and pleasant. Over the Atlantic the sky was a refulgent cobalt. Verity asked Cassandra about the Press and her projects there. And when Cassandra replied, Verity seemed genuinely interested.

Afterward, as Cassandra made coffee, Verity shaped four lines of coke on the glass coffee table. This time, without demur, Cassandra joined her sister, not admitting until afterward that it was her first time.

They sat at opposite ends of a bamboo couch with faded green cushions. Light from a fringed floor lamp burned low and cast the room in comfortable shadow. A cool, salt-sparked breeze drifted into the room from the ocean, and the steady, gentle lapping of the water was matched by the creaking of Cassandra's rocker, as she levered it with one foot on the bare wood floor.

"I'm glad we came here," said Verity at last.

"Me too," said Cassandra quickly. "I don't know, just when I think the family is falling apart, and I wonder if it's the result of Father's dying, something like this happens, and I know we're still in there together. For one whole weekend, we don't have to think about anything but a strong wind and a good tan."

"For one whole weekend," said Verity, "I'd like not even to *hear* Louise's name mentioned."

The mood was broken by the ringing of the telephone.

"Christ," breathed Verity, "why did Jonathan have to remember to connect it?"

Cassandra shrugged apologetically. "Because we always think of everything. It's a bad habit, I guess." She got up to answer.

"It's Jonathan," she said to Verity, then spoke into the telephone. "Are you coming down tonight? Or are you waiting till tomorrow?"

"I'll be down in the morning," Jonathan replied. "One of the taillights is out on the trailer, and I'm afraid to drive down there tonight. I'll come down early in the morning."

"You're in Brookline?"

"Yes, I came over to hook up the boat. I might as well spend the night here, since I'll be leaving so early."

Jonathan was calling from the darkened study at the front of the house. The only illumination was through the fanlight above the front door, patterning a soft glow on the marble floor of the hallway outside the study.

"Did you find out anything from that detective in Atlantic City?" Cassandra asked.

"Yes. A great deal. And I'll tell you tomorrow. I'm not going to say anything over the telephone."

"Verity and I want to know!" Cassandra protested.

"Tomorrow," said Jonathan, and hung up the telephone.

He did not hear the click of the extension phone upstairs being dropped into its cradle a moment later.

The next morning Cassandra was waked by the unexpected smell of frying sausage, perking coffee, and a third, sweet odor she couldn't immediately identify. She was puzzled, since Verity never rose before noon. She pulled on a pair of faded jeans and a blue cotton work shirt, which she knotted beneath her breasts. She stepped into her leather sandals and made her way down the hallway toward the kitchen. Passing a window that looked out toward the bay, she paused to watch two sandpipers hurrying across the beach. Just before she reached the doorway to the living room, she heard the sound of shattering glass.

Cassandra stopped short and her hands curled into fists at her sides as she saw Eric Larner step past the doorway. After a moment, he came back again with a broom and dustpan. He was not dressed for the beach, but wore white linen slacks with a green vest over a pale blue dress shirt. His tie was loosened, and he'd put on a chef's apron imprinted with homy sayings about barbecues.

When Eric turned to let the shards of glass slide into the garbage can, he gave a noise of surprise at seeing Cassandra standing in the living room, arms folded and mouth set.

"Good morning, Cassandra! I didn't hear you come in. Have you ever noticed how much better food smells by the ocean?"

Cassandra made no reply. Eric put aside the broom and dustpan, opened the oven door to check some sweet rolls inside, and nudged the sausages about in the skillet. "Why don't you go wake up Verity? This'll be ready in a few minutes. Shouldn't let sausages get cold."

"When did you get here, Eric?"

"Half an hour ago."

"I'm sorry," said Cassandra. "What I meant to ask was, *why* are you here?"

He smiled vaguely and, scraping the sausages loose from the bottom of the frying pan, said without looking at Cassandra, "Mother asked me to drop off a Purchase and Sale Agreement to one of her clients who lives down here. Anyway, since I was in the area, I thought I'd drop by and fix breakfast and maybe go for a swim later on."

"Verity said your car had been repossessed."

"Mother lent me hers."

"I didn't think the office had clients this far down on the Cape."

"Well," said Eric, still not looking at Cassandra, "actually Mr. Martin lives in Plymouth."

"Plymouth is an hour and a half from here. That's not 'in the area.' Plymouth's not even on the Cape."

Eric at last looked up. He smiled and touched his mustache. "Are you saying I shouldn't have come here? It was an impulse. Spur of the moment."

"And how did you even know we were here?"

At that moment, the Mercedes drew up into the driveway. "Here's Jonathan," said Eric, avoiding Cassandra's last question. Seconds later, Jonathan stepped through the screened door.

"Morning, Jonathan," Eric said.

"What the hell are you doing here?" Jonathan asked in amazement.

Cassandra turned and looked at her brother. "Eric dropped by, 'spur of the moment,' with eggs, sausages, sweet rolls, orange juice, and a new apron.

"Unfortunately," she added as she walked out the door that opened onto the beach, "I have no appetite."

Gulls' cries cut through the stillness of the late morning heat the birds careered and streaked across the clear azure sky. The sun was bright and hot—as bright and as hot as it ever gets in Massachusetts—and the breeze that rippled the surface of the water offered little relief to Cassandra and Verity. There were three or four small sailboats out in the luminous blue water, their white or green sails bellied full as they glided about. But it was only their father's boat, bearing Jonathan and Eric, that they attended to. Eric had all but begged his brother-in-law to take him out in the water. Jonathan finally agreed. Both Verity and Cassandra had without ceremony declined Jonathan's invitation to go along.

"Conniving bastard," said Verity. She was stretched on a blanket, propped up on one elbow with a drink in her other hand. Her pale body was heavily coated with oil, and her halter and bottom were the barest of excuses for a bathing suit—or as bare as anything that could be purchased in Boston. She had in fact dropped the halter, and had turned over onto her stomach. Cassandra, in a suit far more substantial than her sister's, lay on her back, with her eyes closed against the glare of the sun.

"What you think of Eric is not going to make any difference to his being here or not," Cassandra said.

"I still don't understand *why* he came," said Verity thoughtfully. "And what's worse is that he's been very pleasant all morning. Well, not pleasant exactly, but I haven't thought once how I'd like to slit his nose with my nail file."

"Louise sent him," said Cassandra definitely. "Somehow she found out we were here, and she sent him down as a spy. That's why he's being so nice. I'm dying to find out what that private investigator told Jonathan, but we certainly can't talk about it while Eric is skulking behind the doors."

"I'll get rid of him after lunch. Then we can talk."

"Just how do you intend to get rid of him? I think Louise has told him to dig in for the whole weekend."

"Either he drives back to Boston this afternoon, or I'll give a boy scout a buck fifty to murder him."

After a while, the wind died down. The sailboat floated idly about two hundred yards from shore. Eric's lime-green T-shirt could be seen as he slouched in the stern. Jonathan stood up, peeled off his shirt, dropped his shorts, and then stood holding onto the mast, clad only in his bathing suit. He said something to Eric and then dived into the water on the far side of the boat.

"Doesn't Eric swim?" asked Cassandra, who had watched all this.

"Not very well," said Verity.

In the boat Eric sat up and looked about. The other sailboats were farther down the coast now. He could scarcely make out the figures manning them. He slipped down into the middle of the boat and leaned over the side away from the shore. He watched as Jonathan made wide, smooth circles in the water about the craft, always coming closer until he buckled his lithe body and disappeared beneath the surface. But Eric could still see his shape moving in the shimmering blue darkness. Quietly, while Jonathan was well beneath the surface, Eric opened the toolbox at his side, felt for the heavy flat wrench he knew was on top, and lifted it out. He held it cradled and invisible in his arms. He glanced over his shoulder at his wife and sister-in-law on the beach. Neither was looking out at the boat. When Jonathan came around again and broke the surface for air, Eric grinned and motioned him over. Jonathan threw back his head questioningly, and stroked over to the side of the boat. Just as he began to speak, Eric slammed the smooth surface of the wrench down with a thud on the crown of Jonathan's head. Jonathan's body jerked as if a jolt of electricity had shot through it; he stared at Eric with a dazed expression and began to sink. Just before his bloody head disappeared beneath the water, Eric grasped Jonathan by the shoulders, holding him entirely beneath the water until his arms ached. Then he let go, sloshed the blood off his hands, and sank back in the boat with a long expiration of breath. Noticing, in a sudden panic, that there were flecks of blood on the head of the wrench, he hastily rinsed the tool in the water. Then he wiped it dry with the hem of his T-shirt and replaced it in the toolbox—he didn't want anyone later noticing that it was missing. He slammed the lid of the box shut, stood up so as deliberately to rock the boat, and began waving at Cassandra and Verity on the shore.

Seeing Eric waving to them, Verity raised her glass in an ironic toast. Cassandra ignored the distant greeting.

"For God's sake, Verity, wave back before he tips the boat over," breathed Cassandra. "Now he's waving both arms," she sighed.

"Why doesn't he just light a box of flares and be done with it?" breathed Verity. She put down her glasses and was about to raise her hand when they heard Eric's voice calling.

"I am *not* yelling back," said Verity.

Eric, however, was no longer calling or waving. He leaned over the edge of the far side of the boat, grappling with something in the water.

"Where's Jonathan?" said Cassandra, with quiet alarm.

Cassandra stood up, and walked quickly toward the water. "Jonathan!" she called.

On the boat, Eric tried to stand, but lost his footing and fell into the water. He raised a hand above the surface and waved it frantically.

Cassandra broke into a full run and splashed into the bay. Verity was standing now, with her arms crossed over her bare breasts, her eyes riveted on the boat for some sign of her brother in the water. Cassandra swam swiftly out toward the boat.

Verity walked to the edge of the water. She watched as Cassandra climbed into the boat, and pulled Eric in after her. Then she gasped as she saw them lean over the other side and pull into the vessel Jonathan's limp body. Verity trembled in the heat and her oiled flesh prickled. The surf seemed like icy water lapping over her feet.

Jonathan Hawke was dead before Cassandra could get the boat back to shore. While Verity looked on in shock, she and Eric lifted Jonathan's body and carried it into the house. Verity had already called the police.

Later, two policemen looked at the body, and heard Eric's brief description of the accident. Two paramedics hoisted Jonathan Hawke's corpse, shrouded by a white blanket on a stretcher, into the back of an emergency van.

The county coroner arrived in his own car, made a hasty examination, and pronounced Jonathan officially dead. He ascribed the cause of death to accidental drowning. Jonathan had, from Eric's account, banged his head on the bottom of the boat when he miscalculated his ascent through the water. Eric had attempted to pull him out of the water, but in vain.

Two more policemen arrived, and the sergeant sat at the dining table with a small spiral notebook open before him. Cassandra and Verity, in caftans, sat on opposite ends of the wicker sofa. Eric sat in the rocker, wearing Jonathan's robe, his hair disheveled and stringy about his face. Eric, pale and now and then trembling, said nothing. His eyes remained on the policeman as the officer made a small series of notes.

The policeman looked up as he jotted. "Your brother was only twenty-seven, huh?" he mused. "That's tough."

"Yes," remarked Verity grimly, "pretty tough."

The policeman looked at the sisters. "You'll take care of the arrangements? I'll give you the name and number of the morgue in Hyannis. Your mother and father—"

Cassandra shook her head. "Mother's been dead a long time. Father died in March."

"I'm sorry," said the policeman quickly. He looked as if he were afraid of saying anything else at all. He gathered up his notebook, pen, hat, and jacket. He stood and mumbled, "There's not much to say in a case like this. You'd be surprised how many people slam their heads against the bottom of a boat. You'd think—"

"Thank you, officer," said Cassandra, with a firm, dismissive smile.

The policeman left. Eric turned and looked at Verity and Cassandra.

Both women regarded him steadily until he became uncomfortable. He stood, looking distractedly about. "Well," he said at last, "I guess I should call Mother and tell her what's happened."

"Yes," said Cassandra grimly, "I guess you'd better do that."

Eric looked up with an expression of injury. "I can't swim, damn it! All right, and if I could swim, he wouldn't be dead, I know that—but I can't swim. I'm afraid of water."

Verity looked away from him and stared out the door. Cassandra watched Eric and he became even more distressed.

"I realize," said Cassandra at last, "that it probably wasn't possible for you to jump in and bring him to shore, but why didn't you at least reach over and pull his head up above water?"

"I tried! I tried! Didn't you see me? I tried so hard I fell in the water myself. Shit! I thought I was going to drown, it was horrible." He waved his hands in great agitation at the very memory of his ordeal.

"I don't want to hear any more about it," said Verity quietly. "Eric, go put some clothes on and get out of here. Leave us alone."

Eric pulled into a rest stop in Eastham and telephoned his

mother. Louise picked up the telephone on the first ring. She listened in silence as Eric told her of Jonathan's death.

"What did the police say?" she asked at the end.

"Nothing," returned Eric. "They just asked questions. And they wrote down my answers."

"That's all?"

"That's all."

"So Jonathan hit his head on the bottom of the boat, right?" she asked.

"Right."

"And you tried to save him but you couldn't, because you don't swim very well."

"Right. Aren't you even going to thank me?"

"Thank you for what?"

"For a job well done," said Eric spitefully. "I just wish it had been you out on that fucking boat instead of me."

"The question is, did Jonathan talk to Verity and Cassandra? Did he tell them anything?"

"No," said Eric. "I didn't let him out of my sight all morning."

"Good," replied Louise. "Now, did you find out the name of that man he hired in Atlantic City?"

"No."

"Damn!" exclaimed Louise. "Why not?"

"How was I supposed to find out?" cried Eric, aggrieved. "I wasn't supposed to know anything about his hiring a detective. Was I supposed to say, right out of the blue, 'Hey, Jonathan, you don't happen to know the name of a private detective in Atlantic City, do you? A friend of mine was asking'?"

"Don't get smart with me, Eric. Do you think Verity and Cassandra know who the man is?"

"I don't know that either. And hey, I did your dirty work this morning—your *really* dirty work. I'm going to let *you* find out about the detective."

"Don't stop for a drink on your way back," said Louise, ignoring his last remark. "Or for anything else either. The last time you had a wreck in my car, my insurance rates doubled. I'd hate for something like that to happen again."

15

After Eric left the Cape house, Verity and Cassandra sat together as the air in the living room grew increasingly warm and stuffy. Neither spoke, and both seemed overcome with a strange lethargy. When it seemed impossible to breathe anymore, Cassandra stirred herself. She moved silently through the house, securing the windows and draping the dust covers back over the furniture. Verity's chair was last, and Cassandra said, "Stand up, Verity." Startled, Verity rose to her feet, but when Cassandra had put the sheet over the chair, Verity didn't seem to know where to go or what to do. Cassandra took Jonathan's travel bag and filled it with the toiletries and clothing he had brought down. She made up his bed, then went to her room and changed. On the trip back to Brookline, Verity nestled in the corner of the air-conditioned car, her arms tightly crossed over her breast, and slept.

As they neared Boston, Verity struggled into wakefulness. "Jonathan won trophies for swimming," was the first thing she said. "How could he have drowned?"

"I don't know," said Cassandra grimly. It was obvious that she too had been thinking of nothing else. "He hit his head, I guess."

"Right," said Verity. "Another accident."

"Another?" questioned Cassandra.

"Like Father's, in Atlantic City."

"No," said Cassandra doubtfully, "I don't think so. I mean, we were right there, we saw what . . ." She trailed off, but Verity didn't argue. "Do you really think Eric . . . ?"

"I think we ought to talk to that private detective Jonathan hired, that's what I think," said Verity.

"About what?"

"About what he found out in Atlantic City."

"I don't know his name," said Cassandra.

"Neither do I," said Verity, shaking her head. "And I don't know how to find out either."

They were surprised and not displeased to find that Louise

was not at the house in Brookline. The news of Jonathan's death had preceded them, however, and the servants offered shocked condolences. Eugene Strable telephoned the house as did Jonathan's immediate supervisor at Commonwealth & Providential. They were not otherwise disturbed. Verity retired to her room, saying she had never been so weary in her life. Cassandra went into the library and shut the door. She first dialed the number of Rocco's apartment, but got no answer. Then she tried getting through to Apple at the Prudential Towers apartment. Her mind wandered and she allowed the telephone to ring fifteen or twenty times before she suddenly slammed the receiver into the cradle. She called Channel One, where People Buying Things was to perform that evening, but the woman who answered said the place was empty except for the cleaning staff. Off and on, all afternoon, Cassandra alternated calling the two apartments, but never with success.

Late in the afternoon, she drove into Boston. She let herself into Rocco's apartment, but he wasn't there. She walked over to the Prudential Towers, and let herself into Jonathan's place with the key her brother always left at the Brookline house in case of emergency. As she patiently waited for Apple to return, she sat on the sofa and stared out the wall of plate-glass windows at the Boston skyline. The late-afternoon light filling the room gradually faded to a brilliant orange and pink sunset. Finally an azure twilight signaled the rapid fall of evening. Cassandra remained in the dark. The lighted dial of a digital clock on Jonathan's desk slowly and brightly counted off the seconds. Cassandra watched it intently, not realizing what she was doing. When it snapped to 8:15, she got up and walked out of the apartment.

Channel One was located beyond South Station, across a little man-made inlet of Boston Harbor. Cassandra was apprehensive as she drove over the creaking girder bridge and found herself on a set of dirty narrow streets between vast closed-up warehouses. Occasional dark figures lurched out of the shadowed doorways. As she waited for a light to change, a man wearing a torn white T-shirt and blue work pants emerged from the narrow space between two brick buildings and crooked his head to look in at her. His watery eyes glinted in the streetlight, and he stepped off the curb toward her. Cassandra slammed the car into gear and shot across the intersection through the still-red light. She slowed two blocks farther on when she began to see a larger number of people moving along the sidewalks—young, apparently sober, and in small unthreatening groups. At the end of the block she was relieved to see the lighted sign marking Channel One. The parking lot was crowded even at this early hour. She pulled into a space by a wall of a warehouse abutting the single-storied frame building housing the bar. On the other side of the parking lot was a tall chain-link fence bordering the inlet; across the way was the postal annex with the blue-and-white trucks pulled up in front of a dozen loading bays. Beyond that was a field of train tracks ending at South Station. The Prudential Towers rose up distant behind. Everything looked bleak, industrial, and oily.

Cassandra got out of the car and looked around. She did not see the van belonging to Bert and Ian—their principal contribution to the maintenance of People Buying Things. An intermittent flow of people passed in through the heavy double steel doors of the bar. Cassandra felt safe. Four cars down in the lot were three women dressed like parochial-school girls—complete with bobbed hair and barettes on one side, middy blouses, tartan pleated skirts, white anklet socks, and Mary Jane shoes. They passed a joint among themselves and slowly gyrated in beat to the music from their car radio.

Cassandra got back into her car and waited in the same dazed state that she had maintained in Jonathan's apartment. At last the van, with Rocco driving, swung into the lot and angled into a space near the front doors. Cassandra watched as Apple and Rocco climbed out of the front seats, and Bert and Ian pushed open the back doors of the van and hopped down onto the pavement. The three parochial-school girls moved nearby and watched with stoned interest.

As soon as Bert and Ian began unloading equipment, Cassandra got out of the car. Apple saw her first, smiled, and touched Rocco's arm.

He smiled. "Couldn't stay away, hunh?"

Cassandra smiled back. "Apple," she said, "could I speak to you for a minute?"

"Is something wrong?" Rocco asked.

Cassandra did not reply.

Apple went over to her.

"Let's sit inside," said Cassandra. Puzzled, Apple got into the front seat.

Rocco, Bert, and Ian continued unloading the van. In a few minutes, Apple lowered the window of Cassandra's car, and called Rocco over. Holding extension cords wrapped around his arms like a skein of wool, he leaned against the next car and peered inside. "Girl talk?" he said.

Apple looked at him out the window. The tears in her eyes were stained yellow by the sodium arc lamp overhead. "Jonathan's dead," she said. "He drowned this morning down on the Cape."

Cassandra got out of the car and looked over the roof at Rocco.

"You're not joking," he said softly, drawing the extension cords tight between his hands.

"No," said Cassandra. "He was out in the boat with Eric, and he evidently hit his head on the bottom of the boat, got caught in some seaweed, and drowned. Verity and I saw it."

"Why didn't Eric do something?"

"He didn't know how to swim well enough," Cassandra replied. "And he panicked."

Rocco looked at Apple. "You can't go on tonight. I'll tell Bert and Ian to pack everything up."

"Of course I'm going on," said Apple, looking straight ahead.

Rocco looked across at Cassandra. Cassandra nodded. "I certainly wouldn't have told you this now if I had thought you'd cancel the performance. You had a right to know, and a right to find out as soon as possible. But I certainly don't think you should cancel. This is being broadcast live, and you simply can't pass up the chance."

"Don't tell Bert and Ian either," said Apple. "They'll get thrown."

"And you won't?"

"No," said Apple grimly, "absolutely not."

"It's going to throw me, then," said Rocco. "I can't believe this—"

"That audience tonight is going to get its money's worth," Apple said sternly, "and you and I are going to make damn sure they walk out of there talking about us and nobody else. You understand?"

He nodded. Apple threw open the door of the car. "I'll go help set up," she said softly. She got out, and walked to the doors of the bar.

When she had disappeared inside, Cassandra said to Rocco, "Is she going to be all right?"

"Yes."

Cassandra slammed shut the door of the car, locking it. Rocco took her into his arms and Cassandra leaned her head against his shoulder. He held her tightly a moment and then pulled away. He pushed a wave of hair back from her forehead.

"What are you going to do now?" he asked.

"I'm going inside to watch the show, of course."

At the back of Channel One, alone against a black-painted wall on the dark side of one of the three bars, Cassandra stood with her third drink. About ten feet away was a large crescent of spectators, beyond them the dance floor, and against the far end of the room, the stage, raised about four feet from the floor. A large light panel, operated by two women, was to Cassandra's left. Radio technicians from WZBC had set up their equipment to the right of the stage. The recorded music was suddenly shut off, and the radio announcer, who turned out to be one of the parochial-school girls, came on with the list of bands playing that evening. At the end she said:

"Solar Blood couldn't be with us tonight, but we're lucky to be able to replace them with this first band. You've probably all heard them over at Betsy's Pit, and at the Rat, and last Thursday they did a really fabulous set at Spit! I know 'cause I was there. Their first number is called 'Velvet Glove,' and *it turns me on*. Everybody get up and dance, 'cause it's PEOPLE BUYING THINGS!"

Bert and Ian ran onto the stage and took their positions. Lights flashed and swept the stage. Two loud chords brought Rocco on, and on a third chord Apple leapt onto the stage. She grabbed the microphone. Standing at the edge of the stage, she raised an arm

and brought it defiantly down for the opening beat of the song.
Rocco's drums made a tempest of noise behind her as the stage
was suddenly bathed in crimson light. Apple dropped to a crouch
as Bert and Ian joined the drums. Holding the microphone close
to her lips, she shot her free arm out over the heads of the dancers.
In a deep, guttural voice, she sang:

> Lead me, feed me, throw away that velvet glove;
> Drain me, stain me, I'm ready for your wounding love.
> Bait me, hate me, let me crawl whenever you call;
> Shove me, love me, hang me on the bathroom wall.
> Thank me, plank me, bathe my face in acid rain;
> Crave me, shave me, wrap me up in cellophane.

Apple gyrated along the lip of the stage, emphasizing each line
with a stabbing gesture of her hand and a toss of her head. Rocco
joined her on the chorus:

> Bed me, wed me, love you more and more each day;
> Thrill me, kill me, guess you know I'm here to stay;
> Taste me, waste me, guess I'll never go away.

Cassandra took a swallow of her drink, her eyes never leaving
Apple. She watched for the slightest, subtlest of movements to
signal that Apple's concentration was anywhere but on her performance. Cassandra saw none. She moved forward, and pressed
between the spectators until she stood on the edge of the dance
floor. Apple saw her, caught her eye, and sang the second verse as
if to Cassandra alone:

> Slap me, trap me, strap me to the freezer door;
> Blame me, tame me, fuck me on the cement floor.
> Gag me, drag me, trample on my innocence;
> Tame me, maim me, chain me to that 'lectric fence.
> Trick me, stick me, kick me into pleasure's void;
> Punch me, crunch me, pain preserved on Polaroid.

Cassandra backed away through the crowd. She put down her

glass and walked toward the exit. Behind her, she heard Apple and Rocco's amplified voices on the chorus:

> Bed me, wed me, love you more and more each day;
> Thrill me, kill me, guess you know I'm here to stay;
> Taste me, waste me, guess I'll never go away.

Eugene Strable lay on his back on the bed, staring at the ceiling. Louise had turned on the air conditioner hours before, and now the room was chilled. She pulled the pale coral sheet higher about them.

The lawyer turned to look at the clock on the bureau. "I should be getting home."

"Not yet," Louise whispered.

"Jeannette asks lots of questions," said Eugene, "and I should start thinking of a few answers."

"You'll think of something very convincing," said Louise confidently.

"Yes," said Eugene, "I'm good at that sort of thing." He turned and looked at her. "I didn't plan this, you know, when I came over to tell you about Jonathan."

"Of course not," said Louise. A shadow crossed her face at the mention of her dead stepson's name. "But I needed you." She brushed her lips across his stubbled cheek. "I don't feel guilty. I hope you don't either."

"Grief is strange," he remarked softly.

"Always," returned Louise solemnly.

He again looked at the clock. "I've really got to go." He made a move to rise from the bed, but Louise prevented him.

"A few minutes more. Please. I don't want to be alone yet."

He settled back into the bed. Louise cuddled closer, snaking her arm about his neck. She placed her mouth on the pillow near his ear, and whispered, "I know I probably shouldn't be asking this right now. . . ."

"What?"

"How does Jonathan's death affect everything?"

"Don't you know?"

He glanced over at her. She nodded softly against the pillow.

Her black hair lay thick and tumbled over the coral case.

"Tell me anyway," said Louise.

"Next February," said the lawyer, "Verity comes into half of the trust instead of a third. That's the only difference. Eric will have a considerably richer wife."

Louise nodded again. "And what about . . ."

"The investments we've made?"

"Yes," said Louise hesitantly.

"Everything's the same," said the lawyer.

"Good," whispered Louise.

"Now that you've found out what you wanted to know," said the lawyer, "may I go?"

"No," said Louise, shaking her head, "not yet." She pulled closer to him and rubbed her soft, perfumed cheek against the beard-roughened side of his face.

16

The funeral services for Jonathan Hawke took place in the same chapel in Brookline where his father's, and his mother's seventeen years before, had been held. The affair was well attended, but at Cassandra's insistence the graveside services at Mount Auburn Cemetery were limited to the family, which to the ever-deepening regret of the sisters did of course include Louise and Eric—plus Rocco DiRico, Miriam Apple, and Eugene Strable.

All in black, the small knot of mourners were gathered to one side of the open grave. At the end of the required prayers the minister expressed in an appropriately colloquial manner his sorrow at the passing of a man so young and promising as Jonathan. In one corner of the family plot, demarcated by a low cast-iron fence, was a mound of flowers that the workmen, waiting out of sight behind a white marble mausoleum nearby, would pile on top of the filled-in grave, once the coffin had been lowered and the mourners dispersed. After the brief benediction, the words of which were blown away on a sudden breeze, Verity and Cassandra, together holding the small beribboned spade, scattered black moist soil atop the mahogany casket. The minister shook hands with Verity and Cassandra, and then went over to speak to Eugene Strable and Louise. Verity broke off three white rosebuds from the large spray with the banner reading "Family" across it. She gave one to Cassandra and one to Apple, and kept the third for herself.

"Come back to the house," said Cassandra to Apple. She touched Rocco's arm gently, "You too. I'd like to have you there. It's funny," she said, glancing at the workmen who had moved closer now, "Eric and I lifted Jonathan's body out of the water, and carried him into the house. But now is the first time I've actually realized that he's dead."

"We'll go back with you," said Apple. She kissed Verity and Cassandra on the cheek and then walked with Rocco down the slope to her car, last in line behind two rented limousines and Eugene Strable's new cream Cadillac.

Eric, at his mother's elbow, seemed bored. He was leaning forward and peering into the open grave at the top of the coffin, still suspended with canvas straps, with the single spadeful of rich earth scattered over its dark wooden surface. Louise nudged him, and he moved over to stand by Verity.

"Can I come back with you?" he asked Verity.

"Back where?" asked Cassandra. Verity stared blankly into space and made no reply at all.

"To the house."

Cassandra adjusted the collar of her black silk dress. "No," she said shortly, "you may not."

Louise's mouth tightened. She pulled off her short black gloves and slapped them together into the palm of one hand. "Maybe you don't want either of us at the house today? Is that what you mean?"

Verity looked all around her, as if the conversation held no interest or meaning for her.

Cassandra sighed. "Louise, I don't care where you go or what you do when you leave the cemetery. This is very trying for us, and in any case, I don't want a scene before Jonathan's grave has even been filled. If you want to go to the house then fine, if not then that's fine too. I don't care."

Verity jerked out of her stupor, as if Cassandra's speech had been her cue, and she had almost missed it. "Neither do I," she said shortly.

Louise stiffened. She lifted the netting on her black picture hat, and tossed it over the wide brim. She glowered at her stepdaughters, then snapped her head back to Eric. "You come with me, Eric. If Verity and Cassandra want to start fighting in front of a corpse, it's none of *our* business."

"Good God," breathed Eric. "I just wish everybody would make up their mind what I'm supposed to do." He stalked down the slope and threw himself into the back of the second limousine, jerking the door shut with a bang.

Louise gave Cassandra and Verity a look of reproval and then walked back to where Eugene Strable was still in conversation with the minister. She spoke briefly to the lawyer, shook hands with the minister again, and then headed for the limousine. Her sharp-heeled shoes stabbed the ground, and the black netting of her hat flapped about her face.

Verity and Cassandra followed shortly. In the first limousine, Verity leaned into the corner of the backseat. As the driver snaked along the curving lanes of Mount Auburn, she laid her dark glasses aside on the seat, and massaged the bridge of her nose. Cassandra glanced out the back window at the second limousine bearing Louise and Eric, unmoving silhouettes in the rear, and then shifted her eyes to Verity.

"I think you should make an appointment to see Mr. Strable tomorrow."

"What for?"

"To have him file divorce papers on Eric."

Verity laughed a brief harsh laugh, and dropped her hand from her nose. "You mean you actually want me to divorce my very own stepbrother?" She unsnapped her black silk clutch bag, carefully placed the white rosebud inside, and snapped it shut again. "I don't have the energy for a divorce. Maybe this winter. February seems like it would be a good month for a divorce. Besides," she said, looking up, "if I got rid of Eric, what would I do for a dealer?"

"Honestly, Verity, you're making ridiculous excuses. Eric will sell you whatever you want as long as you're willing to pay top dollar. Do you think he cares whether you're married to him or not as long as you've got the cash in small bills?"

"Yes," said Verity soberly, "I do think he cares. He's very petty and vindictive. The only reason I get such high-quality stuff from him is that he thinks he's buttering me up for a reconciliation. It's the only way he knows to be nice. And I like keeping him in suspense."

"Wouldn't it be simpler to get another dealer?"

"I could never find anybody as reliable as Eric. Every other dealer I've ever had has got himself wasted, or turned cheat. Eric's just a phone call away, day or night. His coke is always quality. Which reminds me . . ." She unsnapped her bag again and took out her gold matchbox and silver straw.

Cassandra frowned. "Must you do that here?"

Verity looked up and smiled into the eyes of the driver, reflected in the rearview mirror. "Grief takes many forms. Besides, limo drivers have seen everything." She pushed open the end of the box, inserted the straw, and inhaled deeply once. Her eyes teared as she replaced the simple paraphernalia. She rested back and sighed in contentment. "You know what I like best? The numbness at the back of my throat."

"You know what you have, Verity?" said Cassandra after a moment.

Verity sniffed and frowned. "A blocked nasal passage. Damn."

Cassandra sighed. "You have a marriage in name only that is based on a cocaine habit."

"And Eric's greed, don't forget that." She blinked several times in rapid succession. "My eyeballs just went numb."

They rode on in silence for a while. Cassandra watched the road through the front window. She saw the driver glance around with a puzzled expression. Cassandra turned and looked out the back window. "Verity, look."

"What is it?" said Verity, not bothering to turn.

"Louise and Eric just turned off down toward Harvard Square. I wonder where they're going?"

"Who cares?" returned Verity. "Maybe they had an attack of good manners, and decided not to come back to the house after all."

*

Louise's limousine moved through Cambridge and crossed the Charles River into Back Bay. She directed the driver onto Exeter Street, and then into the parking garage beneath the apartment towers of Prudential Center. Louise and Eric got out at the elevators, and instructed the driver to find a space and wait for them.

"I thought everybody was going back to Brookline," said Eric.

"Everybody is," snapped Louise. "That's why we're *here.*"

The guard on duty in the lower lobby knew Louise. Three years before, the apartment building had been turned over to the Hawke agency for assistance in conversion to a condominium. He had, moreover, heard of Jonathan's death, and when he saw Louise in black, he offered his condolences. "You're going up?" he asked.

Louise nodded.

"You want me to send somebody up with a master key?"

"I have one," said Louise. She and Eric got into the elevator.

"Where'd you get that key?" Eric asked, when the doors were closed.

"Jonathan always kept one in the front hall in Brookline. I picked it up before the funeral."

Eric loosened his tie and leaned against the back wall of the elevator. "I still don't know why you dragged me here. We should have gone to Brookline. I'm starving."

They got off on the thirtieth floor, and Louise let them into the apartment. Leading Eric through the rooms, she unpinned and removed her hat. She tossed it onto Jonathan's bed, then pulled open the louvered doors of his closet.

She turned to Eric. "Forget about the shoes, of course, but all the sport coats should fit. Jonathan was longer in the legs than you, so we'll have to alter all the pants. Look at all these ties! And every time I saw him he was wearing that dingy old Harvard thing."

"Ma!" Eric protested. "Is that why we're here?! I don't want to wear a dead man's clothes!"

"For God's sake, Eric, take the whine out of your voice. You're twenty-eight years old." She yanked a tweed jacket from its hanger. "These coats are the best wool. Look at the labels: Louis, Saks, Barney's. Wait, here's two silk suits for summer. More men ought to wear silk. Here's some vicuna." She went to the dresser and began pulling open drawers. "These sweaters are cashmere and wool. The shirts all come from Brooks Brothers. You've never had clothes like these, and if you don't take them, Verity and Cassandra will come by here and send everything out to Goodwill."

"All right, Ma," said Eric with a leer. "I guess I earned them. Just like you earned that house in Brookline, right, Ma? Or *thought* you earned it."

"Eric," said Louise severely, "there are things that aren't to be joked about, or even talked about, at any time. Not even when you and I are alone together—do you understand?"

"I understand," said Eric, shrugging. "I just want to know what you intend to do about—"

"Do about what?"

"Do about Verity and Cassandra."

"I don't understand," said Louise, a little uneasily.

"Well," said Eric blandly, "Richard and Jonathan are dead, right? And Verity and Cassandra are still alive. That's all I mean."

"I have no idea in the world what you are talking about, Eric," said Louise. "I don't intend to do anything. After all, you're married to Verity, aren't you? And in eight months, Verity is going to have a great deal of money. And Cassandra's only twenty-five or something, she's not old enough to—"

"To what?" Eric prompted.

"To cause trouble."

"But what if she does?"

"She won't," said Louise. "I'll see to that."

"What about that detective Jonathan hired?"

"Jonathan obviously didn't tell Verity and Cassandra who the man was," said Louise. "Or they would have said something. You know how snide Verity can be. She wouldn't have let *that* opportunity get past her."

"So everything's all right for now?" said Eric. "No more accidents for a while?"

Louise turned away from her son. "Just look on this as recycling," she said, as she leaned into the closet. She pulled half a dozen sport coats from their hangers and tossed them on the bed. "Try everything on. There's no point in taking anything that doesn't fit." She thrust a handful of ties at her son. "Charity begins at home."

As Eric began trying on the jackets, Louise went through the bureau. "Do you need any cologne?" she asked.

"Why not?"

She selected three bottles of brand-name scent and put them aside. She went through Eric's jewelry case, and picked out the cuff links and rings that were unmarked.

"What if Apple notices somebody's been through Jonathan's things?" said Eric, extending his arms to measure the length of a shirt sleeve.

"That's perfect," said Louise. "And don't worry: women never remember men's clothes the way men remember women's. All men's clothes look pretty much alike. The only thing that distinguishes them is quality. This stuff is quality."

"I don't know," said Eric doubtfully. "Did you chain the door?"

Louise went to do it.

When she returned, she went methodically through the closet, pulling out what she'd missed on the first go-round. Rummaging through the laundry bag, she extracted in triumph a handsome pair of gray wool slacks. "These go with everything!"

"Ma, will you go see if there's something to eat? I can't go on with this unless I have something to eat."

"All right, but you keep trying things on."

She returned from the kitchen in a few minutes with a large glass of milk and a package of Pepperidge Farm Milanos. "This was all I saw."

Eric grabbed the cookies and devoured several greedily. He then swallowed off half the milk, and licked his lips.

"All right," Louise asked, "what fits and what doesn't?" Eric pointed at the smaller of two piles on the bed. Louise began hanging these up again. After half an hour or so, there was a large pile of clothing on the bed, but everything else looked as if it hadn't been touched.

"How are we supposed to get all this stuff downstairs?" asked Eric.

Louise's mouth twitched. She walked out of the room, and

returned a few moments later carrying a large, dusty suitcase. "Vuitton," she said. "Bet it hasn't been used in years."

She packed the clothes in the bag, and Eric lugged it out into the living room. Together they set the bedroom to rights, and then took the elevator down to the basement.

The limousine was brought around, and Louise gave the driver Eric's address in Cambridge.

"I wish we could have taken all that luggage," sighed Louise. "It's a beautiful set."

As they crossed the river back into Cambridge, Eric started to ask his mother something, stopped himself, began again, and again stopped.

"Are you having some kind of spasm?" Louise said. "If you have something to say, then say it."

"Can you give me a check?"

"I gave you a check two weeks ago."

"The economy's soft."

Louise draped her veil up over the brim of her hat and pulled off her gloves. She leaned forward toward her son. "Eric, darling, I am sick up to here," she said, touching her chin with a flick of a ruby fingernail, "of hearing this sort of thing from you. I go out of my way to do things for you, to provide you with a wardrobe any young man in this city would be proud of, for instance. There is nothing I wouldn't do for you, but sometimes I think I am too generous for your own good. Let me remind you that you are married to a very rich young woman. You know what happens when Verity turns twenty-nine?"

"She gets a third of the trust fund."

"No. Now that Jonathan's dead, she'll get *half.* That's at least four million dollars. I don't need to tell you that is considerably more money than *I* have. There's no reason in the world you should come to me, when your wife has that kind of wealth. I'm serious. As of now, I stop subsidizing you."

Silence fell between them. After a few moments, Eric said, "You keep going on about how rich Verity is going to be, but you haven't told me how . . ."

"How what?"

"To get Verity to give me some money."

Louise seemed to have been waiting for this.

"Get her pregnant," she said without hesitation.

Eric looked at his mother as if she'd slapped him. His eyes narrowed suspiciously and he tilted his head as he said, "How am I supposed to do that? She won't even let me touch her. We haven't slept together since before she went out to Kansas City."

"Seduce her, for Christ's sake. Be nice to her, tell her you're still in love with her, get her drunk, I don't care! Just get her into bed."

Eric threw up his hands. "So Verity gets pregnant. So what? Where does that get me? There's no guarantee she'd take me back. And even if she did, I don't want a kid. Neither does she."

"Of course she doesn't. She'll get an abortion."

"Then what—"

"Then you sue her for a divorce. Do you know what a judge in this city—this *Catholic* city—is going to do when he finds out that your spoiled rich wife went out and willfully destroyed your baby, your only chance at a reconciliation, the baby you've always wanted, even after you said you'd keep it if she didn't want it?"

"With my luck, she'd go through with having the kid. *Then* where would I be?"

"She won't go through with it, and we both know it." Louise touched a hand to her breasts and said mockingly, "And you'll be devastated. You'll be a mere shell of your former self, a broken man overwhelmed by the tragedy of your insensitive wife's selfish cruelty." Louise recovered her tone. "Newspapers'll love it. You'll walk away from that courtroom with enough to keep you on the sunny side of Easy Street for the rest of your life."

Eric remained doubtful. "Nice plan, but lots could go wrong."

"Like what?"

"Like what if she won't have anything to do with me, no matter *how* nice I am to her? *Then* what do I do?"

Louise shrugged, and lowered her veil again. "Drug her," she advised quietly.

PART THREE

The Clever Daughter

17

Shortly before his death, Jonathan had turned over to Cassandra twenty thousand dollars of his own money, to fund the conversion of the space above the garage into a rehearsal studio for People Buying Things. Cassandra herself had hired the carpenter-contractors, men who had restored and reworked the eighteenth-century building in which the Menelaus Press had its offices. These young men had presented several alternative plans for the job, which Cassandra, Rocco, Jonathan, and Apple went over in detail. As soon as a plan was chosen, the men went to work. Jonathan had died just as the work was getting well under way. By the end Cassandra had had to add another fifteen thousand to her brother's original contribution, but the thing was done right.

The garage had been converted into an apartment during the early 1950s; now the workmen took down all the interior walls except those defining the kitchen and bath. The space was soundproofed, rewired, and weatherized. A stage was built at one end, and along one long wall were accommodations for storage of instruments, costumes, and personal effects. Worktables had been set up at the end of the room away from the stage, with filing cabinets for the band's records, a rehearsal piano, and comfortable furniture for guests, potential backers, and the band itself. "If you ever make money," Cassandra explained, "this place is all set up to turn itself right into your very own recording studio."

The workmen drove in the last nail, swept up the last wood shavings, and soaped away the last black marks on the walls one

Friday afternoon in August. Rocco began bringing over instruments and music on Saturday morning. Cassandra helped him unload the car, and when everything had been brought in, he looked around and said, "I can't believe you did this for us."

"Jonathan and I did it," returned Cassandra. "Because we wanted to."

He threw his arms over her shoulders, leaned forward, and smiled. "Shouldn't we have a dedication ceremony?"

Cassandra bit lightly at her lower lip and breathed out as she turned her face to one side and closed her eyes. Rocco trailed his lips down her neck. She drew her breath in again as he closed a hand over her breast and bit lightly at her bare shoulder. Cassandra slid her hands about his neck and pulled one leg up to press herself closer against his nakedness. Slowly and gently Rocco entered her. Cassandra groaned aloud, her body buckling slightly against his thrusts. Her fingers twined in his hair as he covered her mouth with his, grazing his tongue across her teeth and probing deeply into her wet mouth. Cassandra, moving with him, drew up her other leg. Rocco leaned up to brace himself on his elbows and drove more deeply into her, his mouth never leaving her lips. Sweat began to glisten on their bodies as the sound of flesh smacking against flesh echoed against the walls of the empty room. Rocco's muscles tightened and Cassandra pulled her mouth free of his. She pressed her face against his neck and cried out as they reached orgasm together. He remained tense for several moments while her body buckled and shook against his. Then a long spasm racked her legs and stomach, and after that she was still. Rocco held her even tighter, and together, they slowly relaxed. Cassandra lowered her legs. Rocco kissed her again as he slid off to one side, his arm beneath her neck, cradling her against his shoulder. He pressed one of his knees between her legs. With the back of his hand he tenderly wiped the beads of sweat from her cheeks, and then pushed damp tangles of hair from her forehead.

They lay on a blanket in the long wide open space above the garage on the Hawke property. Their clothes were discarded about the blanket on all sides of them. Although the afternoon was cool, the windows along one wall had been raised a few inches and a light breeze pushed at the blinds drawn against the light. The air felt suddenly chill against Cassandra's body and she shivered as the sweat began to dry on her flesh. Rocco leaned across her and yanked up her side of the blanket and pulled it over her. Cassandra rested her face against his chest.

As she lay snuggled in his arms, Rocco asked, "Shouldn't I close some of the windows? Aren't you cold?"

"I like being cold. At least when I've got somebody to warm me up." She lifted up her chin and he leaned down and kissed her.

"And the floor doesn't bother you either? It's not too hard?"

"No," she replied. "See?" She slid out of his arms, and lay flat on the blanket. She held out her arms to him, and he slipped on top of her. They began to make love once more.

The door of the rehearsal studio opened. The soundproofing was so effective that they had not heard footsteps on the hollow wooden stairs.

Cassandra looked over, and gasped, "Louise!"

Rocco stopped moving atop her and looked at Cassandra in confusion. "What . . . ?" He followed Cassandra's line of vision and was mildly startled to see the widow Hawke. He rolled off Cassandra and lay on his back, one arm behind his head. He made no move to cover himself, though Cassandra instinctively pulled up the blanket to conceal her nakedness.

Louise's hair had been permed into a mass of black waves that fell heavily about her shoulders. She flipped it off one shoulder as she came into the rehearsal room. Several wide bands of silver on one wrist clinked as she fingered the large gold heart-shaped pendant resting just above her exposed cleavage. She looked at Cassandra and Rocco with sarcastic disdain. She sighed and touched the collar of her snugly fitted black silk pantsuit.

"I just came," said Louise, glancing up and down the length of Rocco's exposed body, "to look the place over."

"Louise, what do you want?" Cassandra demanded.

She stepped farther into the room. Her eyes drifted about the space. "This was such a nice apartment, perfect for a single. It was cozy. Now it looks sterile. It looks like a room above a garage."

"That's exactly what it is. Didn't you notice the two cars and the boat downstairs?"

Louise peered into the kitchen and the bath. "Eric would have been very comfortable in here," she mused, then turned quickly and smiled a brittle smile at Cassandra, "before the conversion, I mean. I would have thought you and Verity would have liked to help him out. You know what kind of financial state he's in. He hasn't been able to find any work, and his landlord raised his rent by thirty percent this past year. I don't know what—"

"Louise," said Cassandra, "please go away."

Ignoring this, Louise wandered toward the stage end of the room. "The problem with a conversion like this—and I imagine it didn't put you back less than thirty thousand—is that it'll cost you more than that much to reconvert."

"Why should I want to reconvert?" asked Cassandra.

"This place," said Louise, glancing at Rocco, "makes a great love nest, but what happens when the bird flies away? You're stuck with a rehearsal studio."

Rocco started to speak, but Cassandra put a hand on his arm. He clapped his mouth shut.

"Louise," said Cassandra with warning in her voice. "If you have something to say, say it."

Louise stood at the edge of the stage. She suddenly turned around, and leaned back against the edge. "I did come over here to talk to you about something, but ..." She looked disapprovingly at Rocco.

He started to sit up. If he felt any embarrassment at being caught naked in front of a middle-aged woman who was distinctly overdressed for Saturday morning, he effectively concealed it. "I'll run over to the house."

"Put something on first," said Louise.

"Stay put," said Cassandra.

He leaned back, propped on his elbows. Cassandra draped a corner of the blanket across the middle part of his body.

"I came over here to tell you what I think of your little investment here and about the way you've been acting these last months."

"I don't care what you think," said Cassandra mildly.

"I'm going to tell you anyway. I wouldn't be doing my duty as your guardian if I didn't."

"You are not my guardian," Cassandra pointed out.

"Maybe not legally," said Louise. "But morally. I'm your father's widow. As your father's widow, I have some responsibility toward you and Verity. I wouldn't say anything now, except that I think you've gone off the deep end."

Cassandra laughed.

"Laugh," said Louise, nodding her head, "but the fact is, since your father's death, you've been acting like a sex-starved teenager running around with these rock 'n' roll singers, and that's a fact. I know it's hard to cope with the death of a parent, and grief comes in all shapes and sizes. But it's time to snap out of it. You're not a teenager."

"She's not sex-starved either," interjected Rocco.

"And you, young man. At your age, you ought to have a responsible job."

Rocco lay back and smiled. "I'm an assistant buyer at Filene's. Third-floor men's department."

"Have you got it all off your chest, Louise?" asked Cassandra.

"Certainly not. This *place*," she said, looking around with distaste.

"What about it?"

"What are the neighbors going to think when they see this rabble floating in and out of here? What will they think has become of Richard Hawke's well-brought-up daughters? They'll think you've gone wild, that's what they'll think. Verity lying around the house all day, swilling down liquor like there's no tomorrow, smoking pot all the time—"

"Verity hates grass," said Cassandra.

"—and *you* with this rock 'n' roll band. You weren't raised to act this way. This is a disgrace, a disgrace to the family!"

Cassandra asked curiously, "Louise, did you really think that Verity and I would have let Eric move in here?"

"I'm sure you would have," Louise replied complacently.

"No," said Cassandra, "I'm sure we wouldn't have."

"Verity has been seeing a great deal of Eric lately. A reconciliation is just around the corner."

"Verity sees Eric twice a week," said Cassandra flatly, "on business. Do you want to know what kind of business?"

"Cover that man up," said Louise, ignoring Cassandra's offer to explain the real relationship between her son and daughter-in-law. The blanket had slipped off Rocco.

"If you're offended, Louise, then leave."

"I'm ashamed for your father's sake. I'm glad he's not alive to see such a thing." Louise glared at Rocco balefully.

"I can imagine," said Cassandra.

"Imagine what?"

"Imagine that you're glad he's not alive."

Louise's eyes flared, but she made no reply. She pushed away from the stage, and stalked across the floor. She went down the stairs and out the door, slamming it forcefully behind her.

"Well," said Rocco with a smile, "she certainly does make her entrances and exits."

Cassandra laughed. "What time is it?"

Rocco reached over and peered at his watch, lying atop his undershirt. "Nearly noon, why?"

"What time are the others coming over?"

"One, they said. But Bert and Ian are always late."

"Then we have time," said Cassandra, pressing his shoulders against the floor.

18

Later that same afternoon Apple brought over in her car all the band's music, notes, business records, publicity files, and some of the costumes they wore on stage. Rocco unloaded the car while the two women arranged the papers. Bert and Ian showed up at two with the collected hardware of the band—the instruments, amplifiers, cords, and speakers—much of it secondhand when the band was formed, now quite old and frayed. Bert, Ian, and Rocco set up the stage. By three they were ready to practice.

"Stay and listen," said Apple to Cassandra. "Help us inaugurate this place."

Rocco laughed. "We've already done that."

Apple clucked her tongue. "Hit it!" she cried, and she flew into their newest showpiece, "Nan Reagan's Humiliation."

Cassandra sat sideways in a heavily upholstered chair at the far end of the room, with one leg slung over the chair's arm. The music was loud, and until she had sensed the presence of someone behind her, she did not turn around. Lenny Able, the band's manager, stood just behind her chair, looking all around the studio and nodding approval at what he saw.

He stepped closer to the stage, past Cassandra's chair, without even acknowledging her presence. Apple stopped singing, then Rocco left off his percussion. Bert and Ian trailed off together.

"Hey," Lenny exclaimed, his eyes still roving over the room, "don't stop for me. Man . . . ," he shrugged, laughing and running one hand through his frizzy hair. Then, raising his chin and staring at the soundproofed ceiling, he scratched his equally frizzy beard. "This is perfect, perfect." He came right up to the stage. "Top quality," he mumbled. "*Very* top quality."

"Thank you," said Apple coldly. "It suits us."

"Hey, I guess it does. Listen," he said, turning in a circle and looking over the room again, "this place is a perfect rehearsal space. No rent, no neighbors to complain. Hey, you know I'm managing the Instant Spellers now too, and they just got thrown out of that loft they had over in Chinatown, they *really* need a place to rehearse. Maybe we could work something out."

"Work something out?" echoed Rocco.

"Yeah, I mean, you guys can't rehearse all the time. You can't let this place go to waste, I mean, if it was coordinated and everything, you could have three or four bands in here rehearsing all the time, and you'd never even see each other."

Apple looked across the room, and caught Cassandra's eye. Cassandra slowly sat up in the chair, but she said nothing.

"Hey, what's the matter?" said Lenny, looking at the four impassive faces on the stage. "What's with the mime show here? Don't you like my idea?"

"Your idea stinks," said Bert.

"All your ideas stink," said Ian.

"Hey, don't say that," Lenny protested, arching his head sideways and taking on an expression of persecution, "I do a lot for you guys. I get you more play dates than you can handle. You guys work as much as any new band in Boston."

"We work in more dives than any other band in Boston," said Rocco.

"We play more third-on-the-bill's than any other band in Boston," said Apple.

Lenny's expression of persecution deepened. His eyes narrowed. He climbed up onto the stage, so that he wouldn't be so far below them. "You guys are upset about something. I can tell. You can talk to me. Tell me what's eating your ass. Hey, man, we don't have to share this space if you don't want, the Instant Spellers can practice in Jerry's mom's house. So, hey, what's wrong?"

"There's nothing wrong," said Apple. "You're fired, that's all."

Lenny's mouth fell open. A momentary look of surprise streaked his face before one of suspicion replaced it. "What the fuck is this?" he muttered.

"This is," said Apple, "your final notice. We don't want you for our agent, or our manager. You were a mistake from the beginning, and it's a wonder we've got as far as we have. You can find some other band to bleed your ten percent out of."

"Fifteen," said Lenny absently. "My rates went up last week. Man, I got people crawling at my door. I got club owners call me up say, 'Hey, Lenny, get me some bands for week after next.' I got bands come up to me, say, 'Hey, Lenny, take us on,' 'cause they know I can get 'em in any club in town. Man, I got you guys in *everywhere.*"

"You didn't get us in the Paradise," Rocco pointed out.

"Hey, man, that's for headliners pure and simple. That's not your speed. They wouldn't let you in the front door. They don't even want Boston bands in there, gotta come from L.A. or New York."

"Apparently," said Apple, "you don't read the entertainment section of the *Globe.* We're playing at the Paradise tonight. We're second on the bill, with Blackmarket Babies at the top."

"Who arranged that?" cried Lenny.

"Apple and I did," said Rocco. "You weren't doing your job. We heard their second band canceled out, so we called up the manager and brought over the tape. He said sure, and put the ad in the

Globe. It was too late to catch the *Phoenix.* That's the kind of thing *you* should have been doing, but you weren't. So if we're going to have to do it, then we're keeping that ten—I mean fifteen percent for ourselves."

"This is a really fucked-up thing to do to me!" he shouted. "I brought you up the fucking ropes, I—"

"You're not the injured party, Lenny," said Apple slowly. "We are, because of your incompetence over the last two years. So get out. Now."

"You piss me off, Apple, you know that? I'm going to fix it so you guys never get another gig in this town again. I've got the club owners in the palm of my hand. They do what I say. They book who I say fucking book."

"The stairs work going down too," said Rocco. "Go try 'em."

"Hey, fucking Rocco man, you piss me off too!"

Rocco, clenching his drumsticks, stood and took two menacing steps toward Lenny. Lenny retreated immediately, and nearly stumbled off the stage. He hopped down and stalked across the room.

Cassandra held out to him a copy of the *Globe,* folded back to the entertainment section. "Here's the ad," she said.

He swiped at the paper and knocked it out of her hand. He stomped down the steps. After he'd flung open the door of the studio, he turned and screamed up, "You're all a bunch of fucking salamis, you know that!" He slammed the door behind him.

Apple and Rocco glanced at one another and burst into laughter. Cassandra reached down to retrieve the paper, and when she looked up again she was smiling too.

"Well?" Apple asked her. "Did we do it right? I've never fired anybody before."

"Perfect," said Cassandra.

After Jonathan's death, Apple had intended to move back into the Commonwealth Avenue apartment with Rocco, but Cassandra objected to this plan. She suggested that Rocco move instead into the Prudential Towers. Apple made no sense out of this, but Cassandra explained. "It's a condominium. After Jonathan's death, the deed to it came to Verity and me, and since the payments are only a few hundred dollars a month, we've decided to keep it as an investment. We're not going to live there, and we'd just as soon have somebody taking care of it for us. And since there's room for two, and you and Rocco were planning to live together anyway, you might as well stay there and save the rent. You know what it will mean, don't you?"

Rocco and Apple shook their heads in a little bewilderment, as if Cassandra were already too far ahead of them.

"It will mean," said Cassandra, "that with the money you're saving on rent, at least one of you will be able to quit work and go full-time on band business. Manipulation."

"You certainly are taking our lives in your hands, aren't you?" Apple asked, laughing.

"It's probably what I'm best at," returned Cassandra. "Not minding my own business."

"Listen," said Rocco, "if you can get one of us out of work, then that's a hell of a lot more than *we've* been able to accomplish."

Apple sighed. "Oh, I guess it ought to be you, Rocco."

"Why?"

"I make more money than you."

Rocco grinned. "I don't mind. I'll sacrifice my employment for the good of the band."

"Only if you promise to do my laundry."

He agreed with a nod, and the plan was set into motion. He gave up the Commonwealth Avenue apartment, and moved into the second bedroom of Jonathan's Prudential Towers place.

Cassandra's involvement with the band became more intense. Frequently she stayed over at Rocco and Apple's, seeing Rocco, but at the same time helping to plan strategy for People Buying Things. She often sat in on their rehearsals in the studio over the garage. She went to many of their gigs, and learned, as a result of natural curiosity and her involvement, as much as there was to know about the financial side of the Boston rock scene.

For a time, Rocco acted as the band's agent and manager, but he soon discovered that his self-promotion was taken less seriously than it warranted. Club owners didn't want to deal with a member of the band, they wanted to talk to an agent. Often agents and club owners worked out a deal that was mutually advantageous to themselves, at the expense of the band and the club's customers. No club owner wanted to allow the bands in on those secrets. Rocco complained that because of their self-management they were being kept out of some clubs.

Cassandra, Rocco, Apple, and Verity were sitting in the Prudential Towers apartment one Sunday afternoon, after they had all gone out to brunch at the Copley Plaza. Verity had insisted on champagne, and the four were a little looped. As always, the subject of their conversation was the band, its problems and its future.

"Get an agent in New York," suggested Cassandra. "Somebody high-powered."

"Fat chance," said Rocco. "Do you know how few good agents there are, even in New York? Besides, we're a Boston group."

"Wouldn't a high-powered agent on the telephone carry more weight up here than you would, certainly more than Lenny ever did?" Cassandra argued.

"Yes," said Apple, "but we still don't know one."

"What about Ben James?" suggested Verity.

"Who?" asked Rocco.

"An old friend of Verity's," said Cassandra meaningfully. "But Ben's not an agent, he's an accountant."

"But lots of his clients are rock people, and people in the business. He'd at least be able to supply us with a few contacts. I'll call him now." She began rummaging through her bag for her address book.

"Wait till tomorrow," said Rocco. "Don't call on Sunday."

"Today's better," said Verity. "I imagine it's pretty hard to get through to him at his office. And I have his home phone. Somewhere." She found her book, and picking out the number, began to dial.

"I've never seen you with such energy," said Cassandra admiringly.

Verity shrugged, a little sheepishly. "I don't often get the chance to be of use to anybody."

Ben James asked first to listen to the band's tape. The tape was sent by express mail the following day, with a letter written by

Cassandra, describing the group and its strengths. James telephoned a few days later, and said he was flying to Boston the following week on other business, and would take the opportunity to hear the band play in person. He couldn't promise anything, he warned, and he was primarily a financial manager—but he'd see what he could do.

Cassandra took the matter in hand. She and Verity met James at the airport, and brought him to the house for drinks, where he was introduced to Apple and Rocco. Ida, who had grown fond of the members of the band, prepared one of her best dinners, and afterward, Rocco and Apple excused themselves to set things up in the rehearsal studio. Cassandra left Verity and Ben James alone in the living room.

"I was sorry to hear about your brother," said Ben.

"Thanks," Verity replied. "And thanks for the flowers."

"You've had a rough year of it."

"Yes," said Verity, agreeing with a sigh. "It has been rough."

"Need some comforting?"

"Sure," she smiled. "Right now or later? My place or yours? Standing up or lying down?"

James laughed. "I also came by to hear the band."

"Right," said Verity. "Do you want a drink?"

"If you're having one."

Verity hesitated. "I was thinking of having something else," she said.

"Oh, yes?" asked James curiously.

"Would you be upset if I had some coke? Just a little?"

"I'd be upset if you didn't offer me any," said James, shrugging.

Verity smiled broadly and reached into her pocket.

"Here," said Ben gallantly, taking from her the gold matchbox, the mirror, and the razor blade. "Allow me."

Twenty minutes later, Ben James and Verity wandered over to the garage. Cassandra had arranged the furniture very comfortably, and the band had changed into their simplest costumes. The stage was lighted with soft amber spots; the opposite end of the room was in near darkness. The band played a polished twenty-minute set. At the end of it, Ben James stood up and clapped. He came up to the stage and said, "All right, give me three more, things that come at the ends of your range, you know what I mean?"

He went back to his seat, and accepted more cocaine from Verity. Rocco and Apple conferred briefly on the stage, and in only a few moments, started up again.

Bert and Ian began an introduction that was quick and spirited, with the feel of banjo music to it. And to everyone's surprise—Cassandra's, particularly—it was Rocco who sang, in a crooning falsetto, an old music-hall song called "Frigidaire Fanny, the Flame from the Argentine." It was old-fashioned, charming, and altogether pleasing. Apple then performed a surprisingly straightforward and melancholy rendition of "Ten Cents a Dance." At the end of these, Apple bowed, thanked their small audience, and remarked, "We did *not* write those songs. The last is something Rocco and I have been working on for a few days, and it's not entirely set, but it's called "Braces" and—as they say —it goes something like this. . . ."

Rocco began a metallic clatter on the cymbals, Bert came in on the keyboard, and Ian wasn't far behind. Apple grinned and sang:

> Metalmouth, metalmouth,
>   Taste my silver;
> Metalmouth, metalmouth,
>   Lick my gold;
> Metalmouth, metalmouth,
>   Weigh my kisses;
> Metalmouth, metalmouth,
>   Rim my mind.
>
> Braces, you got braces,
>   Now you hang heavy in my mind;
> Braces, you got braces,
>   How you take possession of my soul.

The agent's audition was a complete success. Ben James agreed to do all he could to help the band. Afterward, when he, the Hawke sisters, and the band had gone back to the house for drinks and more cocaine, he took Cassandra aside, and said straightforwardly: "It was the combination of the studio, the location, the lighting, the cocaine, and the songs. I know I ought to be judging them simply on the basis of the music, but when it comes down to it, that's never the only factor. Sometimes it's not even the most important one. One thing I really liked about this band was its sense of professionalism. The whole thing was done *right*, and that goes a long way in my book."

Cassandra was very pleased by this, for her intuition had proved correct.

Ben James looked at Cassandra closely, and said in a low voice, "You take care of these people, all right? You tell 'em what to do. I'll get them an agent, and a tax man, and all that business, but they still are going to need somebody close to them to tell them what to do. And I think that should be *you*. You've done a good job so far."

Cassandra flushed, and replied, "Of course, let me give you my numbers. Call anytime. The band is very important to me."

"One piece of advice . . ."

"Yes?"

"Whatever they do, make sure they do it right. I'll get going on things from my end. And I'll depend on you to keep things straight up here. One other thing: they all have to be ready to get up and go. If their agent wants them in New York or Washington tomorrow night, I want you to make sure that they get there. Fuck their jobs, if they've got them. We're going to make sure they don't need 'em for long."

Cassandra realized suddenly to what extent she was already involved in all of this. She didn't shrink, but took the opportunity to explain to Ben James the financial structure of the group. "Jonathan was engaged to Apple, and before he died, he put aside twenty thousand to set up the studio for them. While we were working on the conversion, he died and I finished it up. I help them here and there, not real support, just making sure they don't waste all their time in trying to figure out how they're going to eat. It's not that—" She paused reflectively.

Ben James finished for her. "You're not supporting them, no. This is an investment, believe me. When I get back to New York,

I'll have my lawyers draw up a set of contracts, one for you, one for me, and they can sign. That way everybody'll be protected."

Cassandra nodded her assent to this.

Ben James was as good as his word. An agent arrived in Boston three days later, met the band, listened to them play, and remarked, "I intend to make a fortune off you people." He flew back to New York, and contracts arrived four days later. The agent was to receive fifteen percent of all revenues; and Cassandra became the group's official manager, at another fifteen percent.

"I told him to put down ten for me," she said to Rocco and Apple. "I guess he forgot."

"He didn't forget," said Apple. "He spoke to us, and cleared it all, and we told him to make your take fifteen as well. None of this would have happened without you."

"And Verity's cocaine."

"Next time I see Eric," said Rocco, "I'm going to shake his hand."

Things began to move quickly for People Buying Things. Their new agent showed up with a photographer and took shots of the band rehearsing, in actual performance, and then, with Cassandra's help, arranged portrait shots using the Brookline mansion as background. These photographs and press releases began appearing almost immediately in the *Globe*, the *Herald*, and the *Phoenix*, as well as the local rock periodicals. Bert and Ian's visibility in the gay community got the photographs and releases into the numerous bar throwaways in town.

Cassandra commissioned an illustrator who had once worked on an issue of *Iphigenia* to design an insignia for the band. He came up with a logo of the Art Deco initials *PBT* surmounted by a broad red dollar sign, with three vertical crossbars bearing the name of the band. It was painted onto Rocco's bass drum, and used on all the posters and fliers. Cassandra had many hundreds of T-shirts printed up with the insignia, and allowed them to be sold below cost in record and trendy clothing stores.

Using her personal funds, Cassandra backed the production of a flexi-disc—a record pressed onto one side of a six-inch square of thin cardboard—and had it distributed in the monthly edition of *Charts*, the Boston equivalent of *Billboard*. Copies of the disc were also given away at bars and in record shops. "Velvet Glove" gained immediate attention. It was played widely in gay discos, and then picked up a little later by WERS and WZBC, the Boston radio stations specializing in new rock music. Unasked, Verity came up with funds to produce a forty-five of the song, with "Nan Reagan's Humiliation" on the reverse side. In four weeks, by the beginning of November, the single was a number four seller in Boston, and a number twelve in New York.

Their new agent insured that the one-night stint at Paradise was repeated. Before long, People Buying Things was headlining on Monday or Tuesday nights, no mean thing for a local band without an LP. Ben James fiercely sold the group to the program manager of Channel 68, an independent Boston television station. As a result, a performance of the group at Channel One was taped for airing in mid-December in a featured time slot.

What the agent couldn't immediately negotiate was a major record contract. "If you people had come to me two years ago," he told Cassandra over the telephone, "there wouldn't have been any problem. But the bottom's fallen out of the market since then, everybody's scattering for cover, and the record companies don't know *what* they want. What we got to do is convince 'em that they want People Buying Things."

"How do we do that?" asked Cassandra.

"I want to send your people on a tour."

"Where?"

"New York, Columbus, Chicago, St. Louis—St. Louis is big right now, God knows why—back to New York, New Haven, and places in between."

"That's expensive."

"I know it is," said the agent. "And there's got to be some front money to get things going. But I think it'll get paid back, and paid back quick. Once they get started the thing'll be self-propelling."

"How much will it take?" asked Cassandra.

"Three thousand will get 'em out there. Five thousand'll do it right."

Cassandra paused a moment.

"Well?" prompted the agent.

"We'll do it right," replied Cassandra firmly.

19

Eric turned full around on his chair and peered through the smoky amber and blue lights of the Paradise. He and Verity sat at a table that had been reserved for them at stageside. All the other tables in the place were now occupied and surrounded by a ring of standing spectators, who in turn were surrounded by those leaning against the bars. Three red spots swept continually over the crowd, and occasionally the green beams of a laser would come on, aimed at mirrors or at the enormous glitterball above the stage. In beat with the driving recorded music, luminescent bands of lime-green light struck across the ceiling in precise cross-hatching. Two television cameramen stood in conversation with Rocco, their shoulder video cameras resting on the stage. A third cameraman roamed through the audience taping for images to be edited into the final cut of the performance.

The mood of the audience was up.

Eric swiveled back and took a swallow of his third Scotch and water. He watched Verity, who wore a new pair of silver-framed glasses with cat-eye slits. Otherwise her outfit was conservative compared to most of those surrounding her. Eric wore one of Jonathan's Izod pullovers and a pair of his tan slacks. Verity was unabashedly attending to an argument at the next table. She and Eric had each done four lines of cocaine in the car before coming inside.

"Some of these people," he said in a low voice as he leaned across the table, "give me the creeps."

"You're looking in a mirror, Eric."

"No. Look over there at that woman by the deejay booth."

"The one in the three-piece suit?"

"Not that one," said Eric irritably, "the bald one with the dangly earrings. She's got the masthead from the *Boston Globe* stencilled across her scalp. And the other one with the dyed hair, whatever color *that* is—"

Verity raised her glasses to peer across at the two women. "Puce," she pronounced. "Puce," she repeated, and lowered her glasses again.

"What kind of woman has puce hair? What kind of woman has the name of a daily newspaper tattooed on her head?"

"One who is very sure of herself. The kind of woman who wouldn't give you the time of day."

Verity took a sip of her bourbon and turned her attention to the stage. Eric continued to look around, pointing out members of the audience to Verity, with disparaging comments on their appearance and behavior. Verity waved to her sister, when she caught Cassandra's eye, as she stood at the far side of the stage. Apple appeared over Cassandra's shoulder, and both smiled and nodded.

Eric relentlessly pursued his diatribe against the audience.

Verity finished her drink and set the glass down hard. "Eric," she said in a hard voice, "the only reason you're upset is that I've brought you to a place where not everyone is in Newbury Street drag like yourself. Remember, *you're* the one who asked me to take *you* out. And you also said you didn't care where we went so long as we were together. So shut up."

"When I said we should go somewhere together, I wasn't talking about a place like this."

"The only reason I agreed at all was so that I could pick up my four grams."

"Shhh!"

Verity continued to speak at a normal volume.

"Any other dealer in the city would be *happy* to make the trip out to Brookline to deliver to me, considering the amount of money I drop on coke each week."

"Will you shut up?" cried Eric, glancing around them with furtive desperation.

"Christ!" sighed Verity. "Do you really imagine that there is *any*body in this room, and I'm counting the cop on the door, who hasn't used cocaine, and doesn't have his own personal dealer?"

"Shut up, goddamnit! You never know who hangs out at these places. The narcs have got plants everywhere!"

"Give me the four grams then," said Verity matter-of-factly.

She opened her purse and took out six crisp one-hundred-dollar bills, and pushed them across the table.

"For God's sake!" gasped Eric, and snatched them up. He pushed the bills into his pants pocket.

"Where's the coke?"

He breathed hard through his nose, and pressed a glass vial against her leg beneath the table. She reached down, took it up, held it up before her eyes, and then dropped it into her purse. The roving cameraman came by and focused on her just as she was snapping the pocketbook shut. She smiled broadly.

"You're making me a nervous wreck," whispered Eric.

"Good. Then maybe you'll shut up. I want to hear the band tonight. I'm an investor now."

"All right, but we're so close they're going to blow us away. I hate loud noise. And as soon as they've finished, we'll go someplace quiet, okay? You and I have got things to talk about."

"We do not," said Verity flatly. "And I intend to stay here tonight until they shoot that last dog."

The recorded music left off abruptly. The red spots moved off the audience and focused on the stage. Verity was suddenly aware that Bert and Ian were in their customary places. She could see Rocco and Apple standing in the shadows to the left of the stage. Cassandra was edging along the crowd toward the light-and-sound booth. A man Verity recognized from watching television raced up to one of the microphones, and experimented with the sound.

Verity flinched. Eric had grabbed her hand.

"What are you doing?" she asked.

"Hey, we really do have stuff to talk about tonight. I mean, seeing you for the past couple of months has really made me realize what a bad mistake we made in breaking up, I mean it, Verity. Listen—"

"You always get maudlin when you mix coke and liquor. You shouldn't do it."

"Aw, Verity, come on."

The lights had gone out, except for a single white spot on the announcer, large enough to include Verity's and Eric's heads in its circumference. Verity smiled into the blinding light. "Eric," she said through barely opened lips, "everyone in this bar can see us. Three video cameras are aimed at that man who is standing three feet away from us." She maintained a low civil voice as she spoke, and her smile was vague. She picked up her glass, and casually spilled the ice onto the table. "If you don't let go of my hand, I am going to smash this glass against the side of your head."

Eric tightened his grip and started to speak just as the announcer's voice boomed through Paradise. "And now, ladies and gentlemen, Paradise, in connection with Channel Sixty-eight, is proud to give you the hottest, the newest, the rockingest group to hit the boards of *any* Boston stage: PEOPLE—BUYING—THINGS!!!" To riotous applause the announcer trotted offstage. Rocco flew on and slid behind his drum set. Apple was right behind him, and raising her left foot in a high arc, kicked the microphone off the stand and into her grip. The band immediately launched into the introduction to "Braces." When Apple opened her mouth to sing, the audience applauded—for her teeth had been painted a shining silver that caught, broke apart, and reflected the spotlight in the same manner as the glitter-ball hanging above her head.

The audience stamped their feet, applauded, whistled, and screamed their approval.

Verity gritted her teeth. She wrapped her fingers about Eric's wrist and dug her sharp nails into his flesh. She dug hard and deep enough to break the skin. Eric released her suddenly. His yelp was lost in the noise cascading about them. He stared at his wrist, with the four tiny crescent lacerations welling drops of bright blood. He glared at his wife and his lips formed an unheard *Bitch* before he stood and pushed his way through the crowd.

Verity lost sight of him almost immediately. She signaled the waiter for another bourbon, and then turned back to watch the performance.

While Verity and Eric were at the Paradise, Louise and Eugene Strable sat at opposite ends of the velvet-covered couch in Louise's apartment living room. She was curled into one corner, her slippered feet drawn up under her, a glass of Scotch and ice in her hand. "Eugene," she said lovingly, "you're so jumpy tonight, what's wrong?"

She sighed when he did not immediately respond. She picked at an imaginary speck of lint on the slacks of her navy-blue pant-suit, hoping that the jangling of her gold charm bracelet would attract his attention when her words did not.

Eugene got up suddenly, and went to pour himself another drink. His suit jacket was draped over one of the dining chairs in the alcove. His tie had been loosened, but his vest remained but-toned. He made a noise to suggest irritation as he recapped the sherry and replaced the decanter. He stood for a few moments in the curve of the bay window, and looked out onto Marlborough Street. Moonlight filtered brightly through the golden autumn trees, and a breeze stirred a scattering of fallen leaves along the sidewalk.

"Eugene," Louise insisted from the sofa, "what is *wrong* with you?"

He turned and looked at her, but did not come nearer.

"Jeannette found out," he said bluntly.

"Found out about what?" asked Louise, in apparently genuine surprise.

"About us. What do you think?"

After a moment, Louise said, "You mean she didn't already know?"

"Of course not. How would she know?"

"A smart woman always knows," said Louise sententiously.

The lawyer shrugged. "Jeannette's always so tied up with her charity and committee work—never thought there was any real world but her own."

"Then how did she find out?"

"I'm not sure—I think someone may have said something to her."

"I bet it was Cassandra," said Louise harshly. "That little tramp."

"I don't think so," said the lawyer mildly. "And it really doesn't matter now anyway. Jeannette has proof."

"Proof?" Louise cried, putting her drink on the end table. "What sort of proof? Has she been following you?" She got up from the sofa and went to the window and peered out into the night. "Is that her standing across the street? Has she been looking in my windows?" Louise jerked the cord that drew the draperies closed. Eugene Strable moved out of her way.

"She hired a detective."

"You mean we've been *followed?*" Louise struck her fisted hand against the back of a wing-backed chair. The bracelet clattered loudly against the upholstery tacks. "This is so *awful*, Eugene. I'm not going to stand for it. Is there some man out there now with binoculars and a notebook? Because if there is, I feel like giving him something to put down in his notebook."

"Jeannette hired a woman. I don't even know what she looks like. She must have been pretty clever."

"Some woman's been trailing all over town after you?"

The lawyer laughed ironically. "Most nights she must have followed me here. Maybe she *is* out there now."

Although the curtains had been drawn, Louise moved uneasily away from the bay window. "Is there going to be trouble?" she asked. "Do you think that detective got any photographs? You know, with a telescopic lens or something?"

"Photographs of what? Of us sitting on the sofa with drinks in our hand? You know we always go in the bedroom for . . . Well, you know we've never done anything unseemly in here."

Louise poured herself another drink, occupying herself several moments with fresh ice cubes, and opening another bottle of Scotch. She seemed to regain her composure as she did so.

"So," she said, turning to the lawyer, "what was the point for Jeannette? Now that she knows, what's she going to do? Did she ask you to 'give me up' for the sake of the children?"

Eugene looked puzzled. "We don't have any children. Jeannette wants a divorce."

Louise took a long swallow of her drink.

"Do *you* want one?" she asked.

Eugene didn't answer at first. He looked closely at Louise, and said, "If I got a divorce, you and I could get married."

"Well, yes," said Louise absently, "of course we could. . . ."

Eugene prodded her. "Don't you think that would be a good idea?"

"Of course I do. I love you so much. There's nothing in the world I want more than to be your wife. . . ."

"But? I hear a *but*."

"But I'm still in mourning right now, that's all."

Eugene laughed. "For Richard? Louise, we went to bed three weeks after he was buried."

Louise pouted. "I mean, Eugene, that right now I am still regarded as a recent widow. That's all. You've made me forget all about Richard."

"But you don't want to get married yet?"

"I don't think it would look right."

"Even if Jeannette started proceedings now, the divorce probably wouldn't come through for another year. By then Richard will have been dead for almost two years."

"Oh, well," said Louise, a little vaguely, "then of course I'd marry you."

He had seated himself on the sofa again, and she curled up beside him.

"No, no, no," she whispered, "I'm not going to lose *you*. Good for Jeannette. She'll get a divorce, and you and I can get married."

"Jeannette is going to take me to the cleaners. That's what she says."

Louise drew back, and said, in a brisk voice, "How much does she know about your finances?"

"Some. Not everything."

"Good," said Louise. "Then start putting things aside. Lawyers know how to do all that kind of thing. You know what you might do?"

"What?"

"You might transfer some things to me. Deeds of gift, or whatever they're called. I mean, if we're going to be married afterward . . ."

"Louise . . ."

"What?"

"Let me ask you something."

"Of course, darling."

"What do you *really* think? About this divorce?"

"Eugene, the one thing in the world that will make me happy is to be married to you."

"Even if means that you're no longer Mrs. Richard Hawke?"

A shadow crossed Louise's face. "I'd even give *that* up for you."

"Are you sure?"

"There's only one thing I don't want to give up," she said.

"What's that?"

"*I want that house.*"

Eugene pulled back from her. "Why?" he asked in surprise. "It's monstrous. Twenty rooms, at least, and three acres of grounds to keep up. It costs a fortune just to heat the thing. Do you have any idea what the *taxes* are on a piece of real estate like that?"

"I don't care, Eugene. I want it. It's exactly the house I've *always* wanted, ever since I first laid eyes on it. I hate this apartment. I hate every apartment I've ever been in. *I want that house.* Richard couldn't leave it to me, but when you and I are married, we'll be able to afford it, won't we?"

The lawyer looked at her quizzically. "It belongs to Verity and Cassandra," he said.

"We'll buy it from them. They don't need anything that big."

"We wouldn't either!"

"Oh, but it will be perfect for you and me, just perfect!" She snuggled closer to him.

"Louise, even if we had the house, it would still be too expensive to manage properly."

"Oh, no ..." She unbuttoned his shirt, and thrust her fingers inside, massaging the wiry gray hair of his chest. "The house is *so* big and those two don't care about it anyway. Verity's on cocaine all the time, and Cassandra's always out somewhere with that awful band. It seems to me the place should be put to some better use. You and I could give wonderful parties. I have always liked Jeannette, but, Eugene, she was *never* a very good hostess. She *never* helped your career."

Eugene silently digested this criticism of his wife.

Louise looked around her apartment and grimaced. "You can't do *anything* in a cramped place like this. It's like being caged."

Eugene laughed a small mirthless laugh. He looked Louise in the eye. "Oh, well, you may not be able to have a party for fifty in here comfortably, but a party for just two ..."

Louise didn't reply. She pulled his shirt open and brushed her lips across his flesh. She glanced upward, and smiled. "If you don't want to think about that house, don't. I'll take care of things. You know, Eugene, I *like* having something I can fight for."

20

The servants had been given the day off at Thanksgiving. The holiday afternoon was lowering, raw, and wet. Gusts of rain blew away and scattered the few leaves that remained on the trees. Rocco and Cassandra prepared an early dinner in the kitchen, while Verity was entrusted with the preparation of drinks. Apple wandered back and forth, sometimes helping with some chore, sometimes chatting with Verity in the living room.

They ate dinner late in the afternoon, sitting in the dining room with candles and a fire, while the continuing rain spattered loudly against the windows. Not only the weather, but the absence of Jonathan, rendered the meal a melancholy affair. Later, when Verity had lighted all the candles in the living room in an attempt to stave off some of the damp exterior gloom, they all sat down before the fire blazing in the hearth.

While Verity was pouring brandies, Eric, unannounced and uninvited, rapped on the panes of the French doors. For several moments everyone stared at him shivering in the chill and the wet, until he impatiently rattled the knob, and called out dimly, "Why the fuck doesn't somebody open the fucking door?"

Rocco got up and unlocked the door. Eric jumped inside, shaking water off himself like a wet dog. He glanced through the open dining room door and saw the remnants of dinner on the table. "Why didn't you invite me?" he asked querulously. "I ended up having a sandwich at Howard Johnson's. It was depressing."

Verity was kneeling at the marble coffee table, drawing out lines of coke.

"Sorry," she said without looking up. "None of this was planned. It was just thrown together. Maybe next year, Eric."

"Yeah," he sulked, "sure. A lousy chicken sandwich. Whole place was full of pimps. If anybody ever asks where pimps eat Thanksgiving dinner, you tell them, 'Howard Johnson's on Route Nine.'"

Verity held the razor blade poised. She looked up and said, "Eric, it's time for you to go. Good night."

"I just got here," he protested in a whine.

"Then stop complaining, take your coat off, and help me cut this coke. Come dry off by the fire, you're dripping on the rug."

He tossed his wet pea coat over the back of a chair, and stepped around the couch. He knelt across the table from Verity, with his back to the fire. Cassandra picked up his coat and carried it to the hall closet.

"Are you hungry?" asked Apple politely.

"No," he said, taking the razor blade from his wife.

"There's plenty left," offered Rocco.

"How many lines do we need?" he asked.

Cassandra, Apple, and Rocco declined on account of full stomachs.

"Well," Verity sighed, looking up at Eric. "I guess it's just you and me. Thrown together—again—by circumstance." Passing the straw back and forth in an unvarying rhythm they cleared the table of coke. They spent several moments of watery-eyed sniffing until Verity was slightly out of breath.

Cassandra, Apple, and Rocco watched the coke business with some amusement.

"Eric," Cassandra asked, "why didn't you go to your mother's today?"

His mouth creased sharply downward. "She didn't invite me either."

"Couldn't you have thrown yourself on her?" Verity asked.

"I tried," admitted Eric. "She told me not to come over, she was busy."

They were silent for a while, staring into the fire. The rain began to come down harder as the daylight dwindled quickly past twilight into darkness. Verity put on music, and, after a bit, Cassandra said, "Verity, would you and Eric mind doing me a favor?"

"What?"

"Go in the kitchen and get out five champagne glasses."

"Sure. Have we got anything to go in them?"

"It's in the fridge."

In a few minutes they had returned. The tray was set down on the coffee table, and Eric held out the bottle. "Who likes to do this?" he asked, holding the neck of the bottle pointed away from him.

Rocco took the champagne, and pried out the cork. It popped loudly, and flew into a dark corner of the room. The champagne bubbled over, and he poured out the five glasses.

"What are we celebrating?" asked Verity.

Cassandra stood and moved by the fire to face them all. She raised her glass toward Rocco and Apple.

"The first leg of the road tour was signed, sealed, and set, yesterday afternoon. The play dates beyond that will be confirmed next week. People Buying Things plays second on the bill at CBGB's in New York on New Year's Eve."

Verity gulped her champagne, and exclaimed, "This calls for more coke!"

Apple, still sitting on the couch, was flushed with pleasure.

Rocco stood up and kissed Cassandra lightly on one cheek.

Eric yawned and refilled his glass.

Cassandra raised her glass: "To the success of People Buying Things!"

Glasses were raised and there was a general murmur of reinforcing sentiments. From the hallway, a voice, loud and crystal clear, intoned: "Let me add my congratulations as well."

There, in the darkness, stood Louise Hawke, enveloped in her sable. Her hair was no blacker than her coat, and the firelight was reflected in her glittering eyes.

"Hello, Mother," said Eric politely.

"I'm so glad someone invited you somewhere, Eric darling," Louise said languidly. "You always seem to end up alone at holidays."

Louise came forth out of the darkness of the hallway and took a chair across from the fire. Verity, very slowly, removed the evidence of the cocaine. "Would you like some champagne?" Rocco asked.

"I have nothing to celebrate," said Louise dolorously. A queen, whose realm had just been snatched away by a revolution, might have spoken in the same tone.

"What's wrong, Louise?" asked Cassandra suspiciously.

"There was a fire," she whispered.

No one said anything. Louise looked sharply at her son.

"Where?" Eric asked suddenly. "Where was it?"

"My apartment," Louise replied, almost inaudibly.

"Your apartment?" exclaimed Verity, with real surprise.

"That's terrible," said Apple. "I once got burned out, and it was horrible."

"Was it an accident?" Cassandra asked. "Or was it set?"

"Set? Who'd set a fire in my apartment?"

Cassandra said nothing.

"What happened, Mother?" Eric moved beside her.

"I was in the kitchen fixing myself a little Thanksgiving dinner, when I went in the other room for a minute. Suddenly there was this huge explosion, and the kitchen just blew apart! I was lucky to get out alive!"

"A gas explosion?" asked Apple.

"It caught fire," said Louise breathlessly, "and started spreading before I knew what was happening. I got my credit cards and my checkbook and that's about all."

"And your sable," Verity pointed out.

Louise touched the fur. "I was wearing it, lucky thing."

"You were wearing a sable coat while you were fixing dinner?" Verity exclaimed.

Louise paused a moment. "The furnace wasn't working. I was cold." Then she sat up and exclaimed, "I have just been burned out of the only home I've known for seventeen years, so what difference does it make what I was wearing when the fire started? I'm just happy to be alive." She sighed, leaned back in the chair, and massaged her forehead with the tips of her fingers.

"How much was damaged?" asked Cassandra.

"The kitchen is gone," said Louise softly. "Everything else has smoke and water damage."

"How long is it going to take to fix back up?" asked Verity.

"I don't know," she sighed. "I don't even want to think about it."

"You *have* to think about it, Ma!" Eric exclaimed. Louise looked up suddenly. "*Mother*," Eric corrected himself. "I mean, where are you going to stay? Hey," he went on, feeling the effects of the coke, "you can stay with me."

Louise sat up straight and stared at Eric as if he were insane, or as if he were an actor in an important role who had just forgotten his lines and was making up new ones.

"I thought," said Louise, glancing at her stepdaughters, "that I would ask Verity and Cassandra if I might stay *here*, at least for the time being. They have a great deal more room than you do, Eric."

"Here?" echoed Cassandra.

"Of course," said Louise. "This seems the natural place—my husband's home. I'll just slip into the master bedroom, it's empty."

"It certainly *is* empty," said Verity. "You took all the furniture away. Now I suppose it's all been ruined in the fire."

"Actually, no," said Louise. "The bedroom door was closed, so everything in there was protected. I know what! I'll just send the movers over tomorrow and have them bring it all back. That'll please you two, I know, won't it?"

"This was a terrible thing to have happen to you, wasn't it, Louise?" remarked Cassandra blandly.

"It was," agreed Louise. "And disaster is *so* exhausting. I think I'll go upstairs and lie down for a bit. I'll just stay in one of the guest rooms tonight. I don't want any of you to give me another thought!" She stood, shook her hair back, and disappeared into the darkness of the hallway.

"It really is an awful thing to happen," said Apple.

"Awful isn't the word," said Verity, slapping the container of coke back onto the coffee table. "Now she'll be here night and day, in and out, upstairs and downstairs, and in my lady's chamber."

"I meant it was awful she got burned out of her apartment," Apple corrected.

Verity laughed. "Don't try to tell me that Louise didn't take a blow torch to that kitchen. I can just see her, in those spikes and that sable, zapping the toaster with a flame gun!"

"That's not true!" Eric snapped.

Verity turned around to him. "Where'd you find her a torch, Eric?" she asked quickly.

"I—" He clamped his mouth shut. He looked around at the

others. "I'm getting out of here," he said, standing up unsteadily. "I was crazy to come here in the first place."

"I put your coat in the hall closet," said Cassandra.

He stalked out of the living room, and a moment later the sound of doors slamming echoed through the rooms of the house.

"We need to talk about the insurance on my apartment," said Louise to Eugene Strable later that evening. Rocco and Apple had left much earlier, and Verity and Cassandra were out at a film. Louise led the lawyer to the study, and seated herself behind her late husband's desk.

He looked at her apprehensively. "Are you sure," he asked in a low, earnest voice, "that you want an investigation into the cause of that fire?"

"There's already been a preliminary report," said Louise. "It was a combination grease fire and electrical shortage, or something. It could have happened to anybody."

"Oh."

"So I might as well get the money that's coming to me."

"Are you going to fix the apartment up again?"

"Of course."

"And move back in?"

"Not on your life," she said flatly. "I intend on remaining right here in Brookline. Those two girls are going to have a pretty difficult time getting rid of *me*."

"Then why do up the apartment again?"

"I might as well make some money off it. I'll sublet it, for eight hundred a month, and stay on here. Or maybe I'll give it to Eric. He could use a decent place to live. I wanted that garage for him, but Cassandra went and turned it into a damned studio for those punks."

Eugene ignored this. "We'll have to sit down and itemize what was lost and its worth."

Louise slid open the middle drawer of the desk, and extracted a sealed business-size envelope. She handed it to Eugene. "I've already done that."

The lawyer's brow creased in question as he slipped the envelope into an inside pocket of his jacket.

"It gave me something to do while I was waiting for you to show up," remarked Louise. "Christ, you aren't thinking I torched the place too, are you?"

"I didn't say a word," he said gently. "Has someone accused you of it?"

"Cassandra and Verity think so. They actually said it in front of strangers tonight after I went upstairs."

"Strangers?"

"That Italian, and that awful woman Jonathan was engaged to."

"They're hardly strangers around here."

"They're *going* to be," said Louise firmly.

"How do you know they accused you?" asked the lawyer.

"Eric told me. Eric," said his mother with a proud smile, "has finally learned who's on his side, and who isn't."

21

The following day, the moving men brought back Margaret Hawke's bedroom furniture from the smoke-damaged apartment on Marlborough Street. When Louise appeared at the house in Brookline late in the afternoon, she had four suitcases filled with clothes. "Not as much was damaged as I thought," she explained to Verity, who met her at the top of the stairs.

"That's good," said Verity. "I know you'll be happy to be back in your own cozy apartment after having to camp out here. Do you think everything'll be cleaned up by the end of the week?"

Louise looked hard at her daughter-in-law, and said, "There's another couple of bags down in the car. Could you help me with them, please?"

"I've just done my nails," said Verity, fanning her unpainted fingers before Louise and turning around. "They're still wet."

During the next few weeks, Louise's presence wasn't as all-pervasive and overpowering as Verity and Cassandra had feared it would be. She was up early and out of the house usually just as Cassandra was coming downstairs to breakfast. She didn't return in the evening until six or seven, and was always careful to telephone Ida ahead of time to let her know whether to prepare dinner or not. She seemed to go out of her way not to antagonize her step-daughters. Still, there was a strain in Louise's demeanor, as if her pleasantness were an ill-fitting garment that chafed, but was still necessary to the occasion.

If Louise wasn't around the house very much, her son certainly made up for the slack. He appeared nearly every day, usually at a time when he very well knew that Louise was at the agency, or conveniently close to a meal. Verity sometimes sent him away, but more often, because he provided her with a few lines of coke, she lazily allowed him to hang about. They listened to music, or watched movies on television, or went out to the garage to listen to People Buying Things rehearse. Eric seemed always eager to be in his wife's good graces, and tried desperately never to cross her. It amused Verity to trip Eric up at every opportunity, and pick small fights with him. She knew that he was acting under his mother's orders to engineer a reconciliation, and she wondered at the opacity of the two, who didn't understand that she would *never* consider setting up her marriage with Eric again, not for all the cocaine in the Miami airport.

Cassandra had very little time to worry about Louise and Eric. *Iphigenia*, in addition to changing its format, had just switched from being a quarterly to a monthly, so that her work at the office more than doubled in a short time. She couldn't really complain of this, for it had been her management that had made the magazine successful enough to warrant the expansion. Most evenings she spent with People Buying Things, attending rehearsals over the garage, appearing at one club after another in and around Boston, or conferring with the publicist Ben James had recommended for the group. The proposed six-week, nine-city East coast and Midwest tour required a staggering amount of planning, detailing, conferring, and confirming. For each city, Cassandra and the publicist had to time the proper rhythm for the release of posters, fliers, flexi-discs, and photographs. They set up interviews with local alternative publications, called television stations, wrote letters, and began to fill up an enormous chart of all that was to be required of the band during those hurried six weeks.

Rocco said to her, "I can't believe you're doing so much for us."

She shrugged. "I love it. I always thought I hated the telephone, hated talking to strangers, but right now I don't even *think* about picking up the telephone and calling the program managers of every cable station in St. Louis."

"I wish you were coming with us. I'm going to miss you. And who's going to tell us what we're supposed to do?"

"I wish I could go too, but I can't and that's why I've made up that chart."

"I just hope all this planning is worthwhile, that the tour works."

Cassandra looked at him with astonishment on her face. She had never once entertained the thought that the tour might prove unsuccessful. She had never felt so sure of anything in her life as she was that Rocco and Apple's band would return triumphant to Boston.

As Christmas approached, Verity made a concerted effort to get into the spirit of the season. With Eric's help she purchased a tall, perfectly shaped blue spruce, which they raised in the corner of the living room. Two days before Christmas, they went up to the attic and brought down all of the holiday decorations and trimmed the tree. They cut holly from the garden and placed it above all the picture frames, and laid pine branches across the mantel. On the front door they hung a large wreath of hemlock. Louise oohed and aahed appropriately, and suggested they place electric amber candles in all the windows that could be seen from the road. Verity politely said no to this suggestion—the wreath on the door was sufficient to express the holiday spirit within.

Christmas Day proved a brighter affair than either Cassandra or Verity had anticipated. The servants had been given the day off, so Cassandra fixed a small but elegant meal of Cornish game hens, chestnuts, and endive. She had planned for just herself, Verity, and Louise. Louise had wanted to call Eric over, but Cassandra said evenly, "If Eric comes then I'll invite Rocco and Apple as well." This was an empty threat, since Apple and Rocco were spending the early part of the day with Apple's sister's family in Providence.

Louise paused a moment, and then said, "Eric is always much happier at a deli anyway. . . ."

Eric, Rocco, and Apple came a little later in the afternoon, and gifts were exchanged. Louise gave Verity and Cassandra hand-painted silk scarves she had purchased in a shop in Quincy Market. Verity had two gifts for Louise, one marked "For My Mother-in-Law" and the other "For my Wicked Stepmother." Louise's laugh came a little harsh when she read the tags aloud. Eric's gift Verity had marked, "For my Stepbrother."

When all the gifts had been exchanged, and everyone was sitting back in a pile of torn paper, ribbons, bows, and discarded boxes, Cassandra went to the mantel and from beneath one of the pine branches drew out a bulky envelope. She handed it to Rocco and Apple with a smile. "This is for both of you."

They glanced at one another. Apple took the envelope and opened it. Inside was a sheaf of printed papers with typing.

"Is that a deed to something?" Louise asked suspiciously.

"No!" cried Apple.

"What is it?" said Rocco impatiently, reaching for the document.

"It's a contract," said Cassandra.

"For what?" demanded Rocco.

"To play at the Orpheum," said Apple in astonishment, handing the contract over to him.

"On Valentine's night," said Cassandra, "the night you return to Boston from the tour. Ben James and I thought we'd arrange a little homecoming gift."

"The Orpheum!" said Rocco. "You know how many people that place holds?"

"You'll sell out," said Cassandra confidently. "Tickets go on sale tomorrow."

The band played that night at Exit 13 in Framingham, and Cassandra went along with them. She didn't get back until nearly four, and because the following day was a holiday at work, she slept late. She had showered, dressed, and was on her way downstairs, when she heard strange mechanical noises issuing from Verity's bedroom through the cracked door. Cassandra pushed it gently open.

She was surprised to see her sister awake at this hour. The room was cool and smelled of the snow that had begun to fall that morning. The curtains had been pulled back and the windows were opened slightly from the tops.

Verity was stretched on her back across the rumpled bed covers, staring at the ceiling through her dark glasses. Right by her ear was a tiny cassette player, emitting a series of haphazard groans. Her black-velvet sleeping mask lay on the floor at the side of the bed.

"What in the world are you listening to?" Cassandra seated herself on the corner of the bed.

"Shhh!"

Verity listened for several seconds more, with a smile on her face. Her fingers toyed idly with the slender green ribbons sewn through the lacy collar of her full-length nightgown. Then she sat up quickly, played her fingers across the tabs at the bottom of the recorder, and rewound the cassette.

"Is that a new group?" Cassandra asked. She picked up the mask from the carpet, and put it on the night table. "Did Apple give you the tape?"

"No," she said, "it's not a group. It's a recording of the Gene and Lou Show. I taped it last night."

"I thought you hated television," said Cassandra.

"It wasn't on television," said Verity. She flicked another button and the tape began playing again, but for many moments there was only silence.

"Gene and Lou?" said Cassandra, still with a puzzled voice. Then she exclaimed: "Eugene and Louise? Eugene *Strable?*"

Verity smiled broadly. "You got it."

The silence on the tape was broken by a *swoosh*, as of a door opening across a thick carpet, followed by the muffled voice of a man—quite obviously the family lawyer. Then they heard Louise reply, though still they couldn't make out the words. Jewelry clattered on a table, and then there was a loud creaking of springs, as if someone had sat heavily on the side of a bed.

"You put it under the bed!" whispered Cassandra, in awe.

Verity nodded, and held her finger to her lips.

Cassandra shook her head, still in disbelief.

"Here she comes!" whispered Verity.

There was another loud crashing of springs, followed by a succession of rattles and hisses.

Ouch. Gene, be careful! And don't throw it on the floor.

Verity explained, "He's taking off her clothes."

"I don't believe you did this," said Cassandra. "Turn it up."

Verity did so. There was a loud sizzle.

"Somebody's zipper," said Verity.

Louise...

Ummm?

I feel uncomfortable in this house. Especially in this room. Richard was a very close friend of mine.

There's no reason to be nervous. Cassandra's off somewhere with that band, and Verity's sitting in the ladies' room of some sleazy bar shoving a hundred dollars' worth of that awful stuff up her nose. So it's just you and me and every inch of this mattress.

Louise...

There was a long pause.

"How did you have the nerve to do it?" whispered Cassandra.

"Shhh! Here come the sound effects."

More creaking of springs, which kept up for five minutes or so; and under that constant creaking forced breathing and moans—obviously from Louise—then a shrill squeak, then more moans. For several minutes they got nothing from Eugene Strable, then quite unexpectedly there came a hoarse grunt that was like nothing so much as a difficult throat-clearing. Much long slow breathing, a very little bed creaking, and, after a bit, a louder creak, footsteps, and at last, the sound of running water.

"Seven minutes and twenty seconds," said Verity, checking a digital clock on the bedside table. She ran the tape forward, then turned it on again to a rhythmic rumble. "Louise snores," she added before stopping the tape and rewinding it. "Aren't these new models marvelous? They're so small and quiet. Ninety minutes on a side, and you can't hear it when they click off."

"How did you do it? Louise said you were out at a singles bar."

"Easiest thing in the world," Verity shrugged. "Eugene was here, ostensibly on business with the real-estate office, but what lawyer makes house calls on Christmas night? And Louise kept prodding Eric to take me out somewhere. I knew something was up, so on my way out, I walked in Louise's bedroom, put it under her bed, and turned it on. I figured they'd be up there going at it by the time I had pulled out of the driveway. I was right. After the tape ran out, it turned off automatically. This morning after they left, I got it out again. The only problem is that most of the tape is Louise snoring."

Cassandra stared at her sister. "Louise is certainly maintaining her usual level of bad taste. Muscling in here on the strength of being our father's widow, and then sneaking married men up to her dead husband's bedroom." Cassandra shook her head in amazement. "And if we confronted her with it, she'd get all huffy, and complain that we were spying."

"I wonder what Mr. Strable sees in her," mused Verity. "I wonder if she's got something we don't see. I mean, my God, Father *married* her."

"Well," said Cassandra, "Louise is very attractive in a heavily made up, I'll-bet-you've-never-seen-*this*-outfit-before sort of way."

"Jeannette Strable is so elegant, though," mused Verity. "Very much the way Mother was. The way Louise never *could* be."

"Maybe Eugene Strable—maybe *Father*—got tired of all that refinement, and that's why they went over to Louise. Sexual slumming, in a way. I suppose," Cassandra went on, "she must have a kind of physical electricity to her."

"So does a cattle prod." Verity lay back on her pillows. "I'd just like to know if she was sleeping with Eugene before Father died." She pressed a button that ejected the cassette into the palm of her hand. Verity then went on, quickly, as if a thought had suddenly come to her, "It's not likely Louise went after Eugene Strable just for sex, just to have an affair. Not after all the years they've known each other. There's got to be another reason. I think she's playing a deeper game than he suspects."

Cassandra looked mystified. "What sort of game? Louise is not what you'd call subtle. What would she want from Eugene?"

"I'm not sure," said Verity, "but I wouldn't be surprised if it had something to do with the administration of our trust fund."

People Buying Things drove to New York City on the morning

of New Year's Eve. Late that afternoon, after work, Cassandra took the air shuttle down in order to be present at their opening night at CBGB's. The band, without an LP cut and still with only limited exposure, was still considered to be unestablished. The gig at an important club on a major holiday was considered to be a coup, and Ben James confided to Cassandra that he had called in a couple of favors in order to arrange it.

Verity had thought about going, but called up her sister at noon to say the trip would be too much of a bother. She'd rather sleep and read. Cassandra said in a serious voice, "You don't get out enough. I think you're at home too much."

Verity laughed. "You're getting to sound like Louise. You want to try the marital reconciliation speech too?"

Verity napped in the afternoon, and came downstairs just as twilight was settling in, but before the lights in the house had been turned on. Below the stairs, there was an amber penumbra of light shining out of the telephone niche. She heard Louise on the telephone.

"Wonderful, Eugene! . . . Ummm, all right . . . Say, eight. Have you made reservations? . . . See you at eight, then."

Louise hung up, snapped off the lamp, and stepped out humming "Auld Lang Syne." She came face to face with Verity. "How long have you been standing there?" she asked, her voice oozing a forced cheer.

"Half an hour. I heard every word."

Verity wandered down the hall toward the kitchen. Louise followed her.

"Want a drink?" Verity asked.

"It's not even five o'clock," said Louise. "Besides, it's New Year's Eve, and if you start drinking now, you'll be completely sloshed by midnight."

"If I'm lucky, I'll be sloshed by seven. You're going out, I take it, with Eugene, at eight?"

"Yes," replied Louise uncomfortably. "You *were* listening."

Verity poured bourbon into a glass with a single ice cube in it.

"I'm glad Eugene and Jeannette are taking you out," said Verity mildly. "It must be difficult for a widow to get back into the swing of things."

Louise regarded her stepdaughter closely. "Yes," she said at last, "it is."

"Where are you and Eugene and Jeannette going?"

"To the Café Budapest."

"Give Jeannette my love," said Verity. "I don't think I've even seen her since Father's funeral. One of these days I should go over and visit her. Catch up on the news."

After a pause, Louise asked cautiously, "What news?"

"Oh, *news* news," returned Verity vaguely.

"Pour me a finger of that bourbon, please," said Louise. "I think I will join you."

Verity smiled, and took out another glass. As she poured the liquor, Louise asked, "And what do *you* have planned for this night of nights?"

"I'm going to stay in and read the five novels Barbara Cartland wrote last week."

"You shouldn't stay in by yourself. You should go out! *Everybody* goes out on New Year's Eve."

"I can't think of a better reason for staying at home."

"Eric's not doing anything either," said Louise thoughtfully. She looked at Verity. "I know, because I spoke to him earlier."

Verity sipped at her drink, smiling at Louise over the rim of the glass.

"Why don't you call him up?" said Louise, taking the smile for encouragement.

"Because the only thing I can think of that would be worse than being crushed to death by seventeen thousand drunken celebrators would be to spend an evening with your son."

"Your husband," Louise corrected. "He could keep you company. Nobody should be alone on New Year's Eve. You'll get depressed. *He'll* get depressed. Do it for him, if not for yourself."

"Louise, sometimes I think you are Looney Tunes on the loose."

"Why?" said Louise, with offended dignity.

"Because you *still* imagine that there is a chance for a reconciliation between Eric and me."

"I see you together all the time!" cried Louise. "Every time I come in the front door, he's down in the living room with you listening to music. And sometimes," she went on significantly, "you two are upstairs in the bedroom, with the door closed. It looks like there's been a reconciliation already."

"There hasn't been," said Verity. "And there won't be."

"You have no way of knowing that. I'm further away from it. I can see the ways things have been going better than you can. I'll bet it won't be too long before Eric gives up his apartment."

"And moves in here?"

Louise nodded solemnly.

Verity considered this a few moments, then she shook her head. "I don't think so, Louise," she said softly. She poured more bourbon, dropped in another ice cube, find started out of the kitchen.

"I don't think so," she said again, looking back over her shoulder. The door swung shut behind her.

Five minutes later, Louise picked up the telephone extension in the kitchen, and punched out Eric's number. "Eric," she said, "listen to me. Verity didn't go to New York after all. I'm leaving here at eight o'clock tonight, and when I go Verity'll be here by herself. You show up at eight-thirty sharp. Don't give her a chance to change her mind and go out somewhere. Bring a bottle of good champagne. . . . I *know* they've already got champagne over here, but that doesn't matter. What matters is that you will have thought to bring it. Bring *two* bottles while you're at it. Flowers too, and not something you pick up from a street vendor either. Go to a florist—a good one. You— . . . What?! Well, cancel! I don't care if you've got a date with Brooke Shields and her damned mother together—cancel it! You be here at eight-thirty with the champagne and flowers and a smile on your face, and you seduce her. She's ripe for it, I can tell. *Everybody's* up for it on New Year's Eve, for Christ's sake, and Verity's no exception. Tonight is *perfect*, Eric, and I'd better see your car still in the driveway when I get back, or you will never get a penny out of me again."

She banged the receiver down in the cradle.

Verity, with a second drink in hand, wandered listlessly about the house, still trying to decide whether or not to go out. Passing through the hallway, she noted a large manila envelope on the marble half-table below the mirror; it was marked *Jonathan's Mail* in Apple's script. Idly, Verity carried the package into the study, turned on the light, and spilled out the contents. She looked cursorily at the forty or so envelopes there, immediately tossed out the fliers and charity requests, and separated the personal letters from the bills. She opened the three personal letters and read them through, wondering if she would cry or not, thinking of Jonathan. She managed not to. Then she started to open the bills, but was stopped with amazement at the very first. She looked carefully at the masthead, at the breakdown of the services that had been provided Jonathan, and then she picked up the telephone and dialed a New York number.

"Could I speak to Mr. Norman, please," she said to the woman who answered.

The young woman was only the answering service, and Mr. Norman had already gone home for the day.

"Give me his home phone, then," said Verity calmly. "Mr. Norman was doing some work for my brother, Jonathan Hawke."

The young woman at the answering service refused to comply.

"Because of the information he got, my brother was murdered," said Verity calmly. "I *have* to find out what Mr. Norman told him."

A moment later, Verity wrote down the detective's home telephone number, and promised never to tell where she had gotten it.

22

After dinner together at the Café Budapest, sans Jeannette, Eugene Strable and Louise Hawke attended a ball at the Copley Plaza Hotel. The lawyer had been reluctant to appear in so public a place in Louise's sole company, but Louise had insisted with such vigor that he could not easily refuse. They were seated at a small table next to a window overlooking brightly lighted Copley Square. Absently fingering a pearl stud on his dress shirt, and with a troubled expression, Eugene stared down into the concrete plaza crowded with revelers. Louise's face was turned toward the much more fashionable crowd inside the ballroom. She tapped one slippered foot in time with the orchestra playing a medley of Glenn Miller favorites. Her black hair was pulled severely back into a French twist. An ivory cameo on a velvet ribbon bound her neck, and she wore a sleeveless black velvet gown with a butterfly bodice. Her black evening gloves rested beside the paper party hats, horns, and streamers neatly lined on the edge of the table. An opened bottle of Veuve Clicquot nestled in a silver ice bucket.

Louise touched Eugene's elbow to get his attention. He turned and smiled wanly.

"Could you pour some more champagne, please?" she asked.

He did so, and they raised their glasses in a silent toast.

"What's wrong?" said Louise, lowering her glass.

"Nothing."

"This is New Year's Eve," Louise persisted, "and you are *not* celebrating. What are you thinking about?"

"My divorce."

Louise tapped a painted nail against the base of her glass.

"I received notice this morning that Jeannette has instituted proceedings."

"She doesn't let the grass grow under her feet, does she?"

"Her lawyer called me up. He said to be prepared."

"Prepared for what?"

"Prepared for a soaking. She wants everything. And with her 'evidence of my misconduct,' she can probably get it."

Louise paused and considered this. She said in a low voice, "Does she know anything about the waterfront investment?"

"No, of course not. Not even my secretary knows about it— why do you think I asked *you* to type all the documents?"

"Well, if Jeannette doesn't know anything, you'll be fine. Let her take everything. You and I are going to make more money on this deal than anybody with a clean heart has a right to make."

"I hope so," said Strable glumly, staring out the window again.

"*Now* what's the matter?"

He looked up at her. "I'm not so sure this whole business was such a good idea, putting *all* that money in this thing."

"Why do you say that now?"

"I'm saying it," Strable went on, "because Verity's twenty-ninth birthday is only six weeks away."

"So what?"

"So she's supposed to get half the capital of that trust fund then. And all that capital is invested in this ... this scheme. If Verity says, 'I don't want to be in that, give me cash,' then I don't know *what* we're going to do."

"Eugene, we've already been over this. Let *me* take care of Verity."

"How will you do that?"

"I have a little plan."

"What kind of 'little plan'?"

"Verity and my little plan are probably out at some very romantic bar together right this very minute," said Louise, with a self-satisfied smile. "Now come on, they're playing 'Stardust' and I've made a vow to dance holes in my shoes tonight. . . ."

Verity and Eric were only a couple of blocks away from the Copley Plaza, at Jason's on Clarendon Street. At nine o'clock, Eric had appeared at the door of the Brookline mansion bearing champagne, flowers, and two grams of cocaine. He wore Jonathan's altered trousers, Jonathan's gray alpaca sweater, and Jonathan's sport coat, with the sleeves shortened an inch. While he was drawing out lines of coke in the living room, Verity put the flowers in water and opened the champagne. They did four lines of coke, drank half the bottle of champagne, and did two more lines.

"Let's go out," suggested Eric.

"All right," agreed Verity. "Someplace where they serve food. I'm not hungry now, but when the coke wears off, I will be."

He suggested Jason's, and there they were. The kitchen had closed fifteen minutes before their arrival. Verity made him order another bottle of champagne, and a basket of dry breads. She wore a wine-red forties evening dress with several strands of silver chain around her neck and wrist, and had fastened to her waist a gardenia from the bouquet Eric had brought.

Jason's was a singles bar for the upwardly mobile. In the parking lot overlooking the expressway, Verity's classic Lotus was dwarfed by all the New Yorkers and Continentals. The young crowd inside was dressed in its sharpest, newest, most expensive styles. The deejay's selections were a blend of forties big-band music and familiar rock. Hundreds of white balloons were encased in loose netting at the ceiling, waiting to be released at the stroke of midnight. Multicolored streamers trailed from the netting to the carpeted floor. By eleven o'clock, Jason's was jammed. Lines had formed in front of the doors of both restrooms. Raucous laughter and good-natured drunken conversation rose and crested about Verity and Eric at their small round table near the edge of the dance floor.

Eric poured out the last of the champagne. "Do you want more?" he asked hesitantly.

"Of course," Verity replied.

"Uh," he said, "this stuff is forty dollars a bottle. I'm sort of—"

"Ask the bartender if he'll barter for coke," she suggested.

"I can't do that!"

Verity laughed, and opened her pocketbook. She took out three twenties, and gave them to Eric. He took them and smiled. "Hey, I'm really glad we came out tonight, aren't you?"

Verity looked at him, and said, "Eric, I think there's something I ought to tell you."

"What?"

She motioned him to lean forward over the table. He did so, and turned his head. Verity spoke in a low voice, directly in his ear.

"Darling," she said, "I know that your coming over to the house with champagne, and flowers, and coke, was all part of Louise's five-year plan for our reconciliation. I might as well tell you now: it won't work. I let you in not because of the champagne and flowers, not because it's New Year's Eve, not because it's the first time in five years I've seen you decently dressed, but because you never come over without bringing along some coke. And the reason I came out tonight is that I have a little something to celebrate."

"What's that?" asked Eric.

"You'll find out soon enough," said Verity, with a grim smile.

"It has something to do with me?"

"Possibly," said Verity. "I don't know yet. But I'll find out first thing tomorrow morning."

"I don't understand what you're talking about."

"You don't need to," said Verity. "Just go get the champagne."

At half past three in the morning, Eric pulled Verity's Lotus into a space in front of the house. The radio was on and playing loudly as Verity nodded her head in time with the song.

"This station hasn't played People Buying Things once," she complained, and hiccupped. "Not once," she repeated with emphasis.

"You've only been listening for twenty minutes. Probably they were playing it earlier. Anyway, how can you tell? All that new stuff sounds alike."

"You're absolutely—" She hiccupped several times. She took a deep breath, held it, and then exhaled slowly. "Father always said to hold your breath for ten minutes and walk backward to stop hiccupping."

"Ten seconds," said Eric, killing the ignition. "Not ten minutes."

Verity jerked sideways and looked at him seriously. She knitted her brow. "What are you doing here anyway?"

"I drove you home," he said slowly. "Here we are." He pointed at the door of the house, ten feet away.

"I mean," said Verity carefully, "how are *you* going to get home? I don't want to drive you—"

"I wouldn't let you, not in your condition."

"—I'll give you money for a taxi, that's what . . ."

Eric got out of the car, went around, and helped Verity out. She rummaged for her keys, but had some difficulty in fitting them into the lock. Eric took the keys from her and assisted. The door swung open onto darkness. Verity stumbled into the hallway. She struggled out of her coat, and threw it and her clutch bag onto a chair. "I'm exhausted," she announced, switching on a light above the hall mirror. She glanced one moment at her reflection, winced both at her appearance and the brightness of the light, and switched it off again.

"You're so beautiful," whispered Eric, standing behind her.

"Not at this point," she returned ruefully.

"Can we sit up and talk for a while?" he asked as she stumbled past the living room door. "I'll draw out some more coke."

Verity continued toward the stairs. "No, I'm going to sleep. My nose and the rest of me are done for tonight. Take a twenty out of my bag and call a taxi. Good night, Eric," she said, mounting the stairs. "Thanks for a splendid evening."

She was very nearly to the top, when Eric ran up the stairs behind her. He grabbed her arm, squeezing both her wrist and the silver bracelets around it. She turned and peered at him in the darkness. "Eric, I told you—"

"We had such a good time tonight," he pleaded. "It was the best time we've had in years." He paused. "Verity, I still love you."

Verity sighed deeply. "It *was* a pleasant evening, Eric. But you just ruined it." She tried to pull away and continue to the top of the stairs. He held her still.

"Just one more thing. Just one more thing and I won't say any more."

Verity didn't reply, but she turned to look down into his face.

"I want to kiss you," he whispered. "I just want to kiss you once."

"You already did, at midnight."

"That was in a crowd. Everybody was kissing. I want to kiss you here in the dark, on the stairs."

Verity fell unsteadily against the wall, sinking down a little. "God, I'm tired. All right, one kiss, Eric. Then it's beddy-bye."

Eric came up two steps so that they were even. He slipped his arms about her and they kissed. He moaned deeply and pressed closer to her. The moment became extended until Verity at last jerked her head back and hiccupped several times in rapid succession. She slipped her hands between his encircling arms, and pushed him away.

"Beddy-bye," she murmured, with sleepy insistence.

"Didn't you feel that?" he asked.

"If I hadn't hiccupped, I would have fallen asleep."

He leaned forward, overcoming the pressure of her hands against his chest. He pressed his mouth over hers.

She turned her face aside. "Eric, you promised."

"I want you, Verity." His voice was low and his eyes bored into hers.

"No," she said, with a sudden cold sobriety.

"Just tonight. Just this once." He pulled her tighter against himself, pressing his crotch against her thigh. "Old times' sake. Auld lang syne. Feel how bad I want you."

"Get out," she whispered. "Let me go."

"I need you. I want to be inside you and make love to you, I want—"

She had continued to push against him. He released her waist and grabbed her wrists.

"Please," he whispered, and began to press her against the wall, and then down.

"I hate it when you whimper," she said frostily. "I hate it when you whine and beg. . . ."

He flung her wrists free with such violence that she lost her balance and slid down the staircase wall. Eric lifted his arm, and brought the back of his hand across her face. Verity tumbled sideways on the stairs. One of her stockings caught on a carpet nail and was ripped open. Eric stepped hurriedly down several stairs, and then fell forward so that he was sprawled atop her. She hiccupped again. He raised himself, and with one hand ripped open the front of her dress. She struggled but he slapped her again, harder. He tore the dress almost down to its hem. She tried to struggle out from under him, but couldn't catch her footing on the steps. His hand clawed at her underpants and ripped them down.

"No, no," Verity muttered. She could feel warm blood on her lips. "Eric, please . . ."

He deftly undid his pants and drove into her with such sudden violence that Verity cried out in shock as much as in pain. He clamped his hand over her mouth, smearing the blood across her lips. He slammed his hips relentlessly between her legs, and every thrust was accompanied by a ladder of sharp pain as her body crashed rhythmically into the edges of the steps on which she lay. After a short while a guttural sound began to build in his throat. The veins of his neck strained against his sweat-filmed skin. He bared his clenched teeth, shut his eyes tightly, and reached orgasm with a long, attenuated gasp as his body buckled atop her. He pressed her shoulders against the edge of one of the stair steps until it seemed to Verity that her spine would break.

Verity lifted her head and opened her mouth wide. She sank her teeth into the palm of his right hand, not breaking the skin but with such force that he yelped and yanked back, stumbling to the side, and cracking one of the balusters there.

The hard breathing of both was the only sound in the darkened stairwell. Verity put her hands beneath her and began to push herself up the stairs. "You pig," she whispered huskily. "You groveling pig."

She crept over to the banister, and pulled herself painfully up. Eric rose, too, reached out as if to assist her. She slapped his hand away. She stumbled up the stairs and down the hallway to her bedroom. She slammed the door behind her.

Eric crept after her, and knocked at her door. "Verity, are you all right in there?" he called.

He heard running water from within. He went back and sat in the darkness at the top of the stairs.

He looked up a moment later at the sound of a door being opened. Louise, in a flowing black robe, her hair loose about her shoulders, stood in the doorway of the master bedroom.

"Eric?" she said softly. "Is that you?"

He stood up, and leaned against the banister. "Who the fuck do you think it is?" he demanded in a husky, savage voice.

"Shut up!" she hissed. "What did you do to her out here?"

"You were in there the whole time," he snapped. "You heard everything."

Louise started to come out into the hallway, but paused as Verity's bedroom door opened. Wearing jeans and a plaid shirt, Verity stood backlighted by the harsh light from her bathroom.

"Oh, Verity," said Louise, "I'm glad it's you and Eric. I was afraid burglars might have gotten in. New Year's Eve is one of their favorite—"

"Eric," Verity said, cutting Louise off, "give me the car keys."

"Is there anything *wrong?*" asked Louise solicitously.

"Yes, there is," said Verity, brushing back her hair, and leaning against the doorjamb for support.

"Where are you going at this time of night?" asked Louise suspiciously.

"To the hospital," returned Verity, snatching the keys out of Eric's hand. "I'm bleeding."

23

Six hours later, from her bed at Beth Israel Hospital, Verity telephoned Eugene Strable at home. "I'm in Room Four-oh-six. Get over here. Right now." She hung up, without answering any of the questions he began to babble.

He was there within twenty minutes, with a very worried expression on his face.

"Verity," he said, "I am so sorry to see you here. What happened to you?"

Verity glanced at the lawyer sharply. Without makeup and with her hair combed back from her face, she appeared a young girl. Her lower lip was swollen a purplish red where Eric had struck her. "I think you must know."

"How could I know? You just called me."

"Well, if you don't know, then it doesn't matter. What does matter is that I've decided to file for a divorce. Today. I'm going to start this new year off right."

"Verity . . ."

"I feel certain," said Verity coldly, "that you've talked to Louise. So you know what happened. Or at any rate you heard Louise's version of what happened."

"Yes, we spoke this morning."

"I don't care what Louise said. I don't care *what* story she made up. I don't even want to hear it. I called you over here to find out whether you will start divorce proceedings today."

"This is too sudden, you're—"

"I know that you're close to Louise," Verity went on with an ironic smile, "and perhaps I really should have some other lawyer handle this. But I thought you would be the ideal person to convince Louise to let all this go through as quickly as possible. And Eric will do exactly what she tells him to. But if you don't want to bother with it," she concluded grimly, "I will get someone who will."

"It's impossible to—"

"*I don't want to hear it!*" shouted Verity. "If you don't have something back here for me to sign by three o'clock, I'm calling another lawyer. Do you understand?"

Strable looked around the room. He went to the window and glanced out at the scant early-morning traffic on Brookline Avenue. Most everyone was at home recovering from the previous night's excesses. Strable turned and said, "On what grounds?"

"I don't care. Whatever's easiest. Incompatibility. Mental cruelty. That's your business, not mine."

"Eric could fight you."

"He won't. I guarantee it."

"Are you sure? He might very well—"

"He won't." Verity was determined not to allow the lawyer to argue with her.

"What about settlements?"

Verity snorted. "What's *he* got that I would want?"

Strable shook his head. "Eric may want a settlement from *you.*"

"We'll work that out later. I just want you to start today."

"These things take time. I mean, just my secretary—"

"Today," repeated Verity. "By three o'clock. Or I find another lawyer. For good."

Strable nodded. "I suppose the details could be put off until you're feeling a little better."

"I'll feel better when I've signed some papers," snapped Verity.

Strable looked around the room again. "Well," he said helplessly, "is there anything I can get for you while you're here?"

"You'd better get going," said Verity. "If you're going to get back here by three. There are a couple of other things I want done, but we'll talk about them when you come back."

He looked at her with a kind of melancholy reproof for the course she was taking, and said, "Good-bye, Verity." He walked toward the door.

"Good-bye," said Verity, "and you might as well send Louise on in."

Strable looked back in surprise at the young woman in the hospital bed, but he said nothing.

He pushed open the door, and Verity caught a flashing glimpse of fur and black beads. A moment later the door was jerked open, and Louise Hawke swept inside the private room. Beneath her open sable she wore a black silk dress with a half-dozen strands of seed pearls about her neck. They rattled in her excitement. In one hand she convulsively clutched a shiny black bugle-beaded bag.

"I hope you were eavesdropping," said Verity, "so that I don't have to repeat everything."

"I heard enough," said Louise, with set lips. She dropped her beaded bag on the rumpled sheets of Verity's bed. "You can't divorce Eric."

"I can," replied Verity simply.

"You have no grounds."

"Eric raped me last night," said Verity. "On the stairs. You ought to know—you heard it. You were in your room, and you heard me cry out."

"I didn't hear anything!"

"He ruptured my vaginal wall."

"It wasn't a rape. You two had a date. You went out together, and you got stinking drunk. You were so drunk you couldn't even wait until you got to your bedroom before you threw yourself on him."

"Eric raped me on the stairs," said Verity. "I have bruises all up and down my back and my legs, not to mention this swollen lip, to prove it."

"You *can't* prove it," said Louise savagely, "because it didn't happen. You seduced him. Besides, you're still married to him. You were both drunk, and you decided to do it on the stairs, and you cut your lip yourself—that's all it was. You'll never get a divorce out of that."

Verity shook her head, and began to grin. But she winced at the pain in her swollen lip. She said, "Louise, sit down."

A crease of puzzlement crossed Louise's brow. She looked behind her for a chair, and silently seated herself. She waited impatiently for Verity to speak, and looked as if she were preparing herself to accept a compromise or, better yet, a capitulation.

Verity spoke slowly because of her swollen lip. "I want to explain something to you. And for two minutes, I don't want you to interrupt." Louise opened her mouth, as if to speak, but then shut it again. Verity began, "I'm going to sue him for divorce on account of incompatibility or mental cruelty or some other innocuous charge."

"You'll never get it," whispered Louise, under her breath.

"If Eric chooses to contest the divorce on those grounds, then I will bring into evidence the fact that I was raped, and that I was hospitalized because of the injuries I suffered in that rape. I will also testify that you, his mother, heard my cries for help, and did nothing to interfere."

"That's a lie!"

Verity shook her head slowly. "You were in your room, ten feet away from the top step. You were out in the hallway when I came out of the bathroom bleeding."

"I didn't hear anything!"

"Still," said Verity, "you were right there. I was raped right outside your bedroom door, and you didn't do anything to stop it."

"No one will believe it," said Louise with a solemn shake of her head.

"Perhaps not," said Verity, "but I'll testify to it, and you'll get your name in all the papers. And all of Boston can think what it wants to think about you and your son."

"It won't work," Louise warned.

"Maybe not," repeated Verity. "But if it doesn't, then I will simply testify that Eric is a dealer, and has been selling drugs for the past seven years."

Louise rose up out of her chair in anger.

"And just who is it that buys it? Who keeps him in business?" she cried accusingly. "*You're* the one who buys it."

Verity shrugged. "I'll tell the court he got me hooked on it. I'll get the divorce, and Eric will go to jail. If I were you, Louise, I'd tell Eric to go along with 'mental cruelty.'"

"This is blackmail! This whole mess is your fault, nobody else's!"

"It *is* my fault," mused Verity. "You're right. And you know why? Because I never took you seriously. I always thought, Oh,

God, here's Louise, this piece of hopped-up trash that Father works with, what's she going to try next? But I never took you seriously. I never really thought you could do any harm—until Father died. And then, there you were, torching your own apartment so you could move into our house. Fucking Eugene Strable because Eugene Strable is executor of Mother's will. And I'm sure it was you who put Eric up to getting me drunk and raping me on the staircase, while you knelt with your ear pressed against your bedroom door, listening."

"I was not, I—" Louise began.

Verity took a deep breath, and said in a low, contemptuous voice, "Shut up, Louise, just shut up. What Eric did is only part of the reason I'm divorcing him." She looked at Louise and smiled. "As you know—or as you may not know—a wife can't testify against her husband in a murder trial. At least not in Massachusetts."

Louise stiffened. "What the hell are you talking about?"

"I'm talking about Jonathan," said Verity slowly. "And I'm also talking about Father. As soon as I sign the divorce papers, I'm going to find a criminal lawyer. And to begin with, I'm going to have Father and Jonathan's bodies exhumed."

"You're out of your mind," said Louise in a low voice. "You're a lunatic."

Verity smiled. "Did you know that Jonathan hired a detective? About a month before he was killed. The detective found out something, and Jonathan was about to tell us what it was, when he had that boating . . . she paused and smiled again, ". . . *accident* with Eric. So we didn't find out what the detective told him, and we didn't even know the detective's name. But guess what?"

"What?" asked Louise.

"Last night I found out that detective's name, and his telephone number. I called last night but he wasn't in. I called first thing this morning, and I woke him up with a hangover. But he still told me what I wanted to know."

"What?" said Louise.

"I found out you bought supplies at a hobby shop in Atlantic City—supplies for a chemistry set. Supplies that—mixed together—make a pretty lethal poison. Now of course I'm not saying you *did* mix the supplies together, or anything like that, but I think we really ought to have Father's body exhumed. This is all very unpleasant, of course, and there's bound to be publicity, and of course it's going to cost me a great deal of money—but I don't care. What else is money for?"

Louise was livid. She convulsively grasped the arms of the chair.

"Not one word you say is true!" she said at last, in a strangled voice.

"I have no interest in arguing about all this with you. I've made up my mind," returned Verity calmly.

Louise got weakly to her feet, shaking with anger and terror.

Verity smiled. "I'm going to drag you and Eric through every gutter in this city," she said blandly. "Now get out. Visiting hours are over."

Louise signed her name, threw down the pen, and ripped the check out of the book. She held it up and waved it at her son. Eric sat across the desk from her in the study of the Hawke mansion in Brookline. He reached forward and snatched the check away. His eyes widened when he saw the amount his mother had filled in.

"Take that to the bank tomorrow morning first thing, and get it converted to traveler's checks, and then catch the ten o'clock shuttle at Logan."

"I can't leave tomorrow, I've got to meet some people—"

"I want you out of town tomorrow by noon, *do you understand?*"

"How long do I have to stay?" Eric asked meekly.

"Until I tell you it's all right to come back. Call me at the office, person-to-person. Never call me here."

"Is she all right?"

"She is *not* all right. You ruptured the walls of her vagina, gave her a fat lip, and left bruises over her entire body. Not to mention that's she's probably suffering from cocaine withdrawal in that hospital."

"You don't get addicted to coke," protested Eric. "And that's the only thing Verity ever did. Just coke."

"She looks like hell. Even Eugene was shocked, and I'd warned him what to expect."

"Make him talk her out of it," said Eric.

"It's beyond that now," said Louise sourly. "I don't think you realize just how much trouble you have gotten us into."

"Tell Strable to try some more."

"He won't do it. Besides, he's got to stay on her good side."

"Verity doesn't have a good side," complained Eric.

"I wouldn't either," said Louise, "if I had just been raped on a staircase."

"*You* told me—" he began, anger twisting his voice.

"I told you to *seduce* her!" cried Louise. "I did *not* tell you to rip her clothes off and throw her down the stairs and jump on top of her!"

"That's not what happened! We were both drunk. It was New Year's Eve. We—"

"I don't want to hear it. It doesn't matter anyway. There's never going to be a reconciliation. The only important thing is for you to get out of town. I don't even want her to *see* you."

"She's going to beg to see me, Ma. When she runs out of coke and she doesn't know anybody who can supply her."

Louise snapped her checkbook shut, but her expression was thoughtful.

"Verity's not going to go through with the divorce, Ma. She needs me too much."

"She doesn't need you, Eric, she needs what you sell her. How much of that awful stuff do you have?"

"Coke?" Eric shifted uncomfortably in the chair. "Some. Not much."

"*How* much?" demanded Louise again.

"Maybe twenty grams of coke, and a couple of grams of angel dust."

"Give all of it to me," said Louise. "If Verity wants her cocaine, then she can damn well come to me for it."

Later that afternoon, Eric delivered the cocaine and the angel dust to his mother at the Brookline house. "Which is which?" she asked, and he explained.

"But Ma," he cautioned, "angel dust is real bad news. Even just a little."

"And the other stuff is not?" Louise demanded caustically. "And what do you mean exactly: bad news?"

"Unpredictable. You never know how much it takes to get you off, or to kill you. And it doesn't mix well, either. Doesn't mix with anything, in fact. It's mostly for teenagers whose bodies can take anything."

Louise considered this a moment. Then she said to Eric, "Write a note."

He sat down at the desk in the study, and waited for Louise to dictate.

"I'm really sorry about last night. I'm going to get out of your way for a few days. I hope this will tide you over while I'm gone. It's the best."

"That's all?" he asked, writing the words.

"Apologies, Eric," Louise added, then watched closely as he signed.

Eric looked at his mother for further instructions.

"Now get out," said Louise. "And make damned sure you call me once a day." She took his place behind the desk, and lined up the vials of cocaine and angel dust before her. Eric closed the door softly behind him as he left, and Louise didn't even look up.

24

Eugene Strable returned to the hospital shortly after two that afternoon, with papers for Verity to sign. She had the lawyer sit beside the bed while she read over each of the pages carefully, asking questions when she came across something she did not understand. Once or twice he spoke, as if to make a plea on Eric's behalf, but one glance from Verity shut him up. At last Verity held out her hand for a pen. He gave her one, and she signed wherever her signature was required. She handed the papers to the lawyer. "Mr. Strable," she said, "I want this to go through as quickly as possible. I don't want *any* delays."

"You know what the Massachusetts court system is like, Verity. You know how long it could—"

"Then use some pull," she said sharply. "I don't *care* how you do it or what it costs, I just want it done."

"Sometimes," said the lawyer, "pull is of no use. Divorce court . . ."

Verity smiled. "I know. You're getting a divorce from Jeannette too, aren't you?"

"How did you know that?"

Verity shrugged, and went on, as if she were talking about something else altogether. "The strangest thing happened to me a few weeks ago."

"What?" the lawyer asked mechanically.

"I lost my tape recorder. I couldn't find it anywhere. I had to look all over the house. And you know where I found it?"

"I don't know, Verity. What has this got to do with—"

"It was the strangest thing. I found it under Louise's bed." She stopped to take a breath. "God knows how it got there. Somebody had even turned it on the night before. That tape ran for ninety minutes."

The lawyer stared at the young woman in the hospital bed as if he had never seen her before.

"What's on the tape?" asked Strable. "Did you play it?"

Verity nodded, and then said, "Eugene," calling him by his first name for the first time in her life. "I want that divorce."

"But Louise—" he began to protest.

"I don't care about Louise!" snapped Verity. "And you'd better not either. You don't rake three percent off the top of her income, do you? Administrator of the Hawke family trust—it's a cushy position, and if I were you, I'd try to hold on to it. I would not hesitate five minutes to petition the court to have you removed."

"On what grounds?"

"Moral turpitude. Engaging in illicit sexual relations with the stepmother of the parties involved."

Eugene Strable looked at Verity closely. "There's no need to threaten me, Verity. I would have pushed the divorce through. Eric is no good, I know that as well as anybody."

Verity smiled. "As long as we understand one another, Eugene."

"I just want you to know, as a real friend, that this whole business is going to cause everybody a vast amount of trouble and unhappiness."

"Believe me, Eugene," said Verity with a grim smile, "this divorce is just the beginning of the trouble and unhappiness I'm going to cause Louise."

"What do you mean?"

"Did she tell you what we talked about this morning?"

"You talked about the divorce. What else?"

"She didn't tell you then," said Verity thoughtfully. She looked up at the lawyer. "If I were you, Eugene, I'd watch out. Louise has really been playing with fire—and she's liable to end up burned to a crisp."

Verity was released from the hospital at six o'clock that evening. She drove back to the house herself, and was pleased to find it dark and empty. Louise was nowhere about, and the servants had been given New Year's Day off. She went to the kitchen and prepared a large salad for herself, which she accompanied with a glass of Scotch and ice, and two of the painkillers her doctor had prescribed for her. She still felt discomfort and her thighs ached, but soon the liquor and the pills and the comfort of being at home took over and she felt much better. She poured more Scotch and went upstairs. She paused on the stairs, staring at the place where Eric had raped her. She could see, on the runner, a dark stain of her own blood. She set her mouth in anger, and went on up to her room. She removed her clothes, and, ignoring the advice of her physician, climbed into the bathtub. Placing the drink on the tiles beside her, she soaked in hot water to wash away the smell of hospital soaps and disinfectants. Half an hour later, she got out, put on a robe, and went downstairs to replenish her drink. She started to pour, reconsidered, and then brought the whole bottle upstairs with her.

She put the Scotch on the bedside table, gathered throw pillows from around the room, and tossed them onto the bed. After snapping on the television, she was about to throw herself down into their midst when she noticed, on the top of the dresser, a small vial of white powder. She went over and picked it up wonderingly—Verity never left her cocaine out. She read the note beneath it, and then crumpled it with contempt. She rummaged in the top drawer of the dresser for her golden spoon. Not bothering to draw out lines, she simply inhaled two nostrilsful of the stuff, and collapsed onto the bed.

She stared at the television, idly changing the channels by remote control, never watching anything for more than five minutes before she moved on to something else. She had poured herself another drink, but finished only half of it before her eyes closed, and she dozed off to a documentary on the marine birds of Newfoundland.

When the telephone rang Verity groaned and turned onto her side. Her arm dangled down to the floor, and her fingers searched the carpet for the instrument. She found it and knocked the receiver out of the cradle. She did not pick it up. The voice on the other end was tinny and distant.

"Hello . . . Verity? . . . Hello . . . Louise, is that you?"

Verity opened her eyes, and slowly rose on her elbows, staring blearily about the empty room. The tinny voice continued. Verity rolled over and picked up the receiver.

"Cassandra?" she said weakly.

"Are you all right? Why didn't you answer?"

"I dropped the phone. You woke me up."

"But are you all right?"

"I'm fine. I was just asleep. Are you still in, um, New York?"

"Yes. I'm calling from the hotel. Let me give you the number."

"No, don't bother, I don't have any paper. Or a pen. How'd it go last night?"

"Great. They had them playing until four in the morning!"

"That's wonderful. You must—" Verity sucked her breath in as a sharp jab of pain shot through her abdomen. She shifted onto her back and with her free hand took the bottle of pills from the bedside table, deftly flipping off the lid.

"What's wrong?"

"I stubbed my toe." She spilled out four of the capsules onto the sheet.

"You don't sound like yourself."

"Oh, you just woke me up, that's all." She started to put back two of the capsules, but then shrugged, and simply recapped the bottle.

"How's Louise?"

"Up to her old tricks, and some new ones. But I'll tell you about them later," said Verity grimly. She tossed all four capsules into her mouth, and washed them down with Scotch.

"Don't let her get to you. Any news?"

"A little," said Verity. "This morning I talked to the detective that Jonathan hired."

"You did! How did you find out who he was?"

"God, Cassandra, I'm in no condition to go into all that now. But it's important. When are you coming back?"

"One of the early shuttles tomorrow. I'm not sure which."

"Wake me up when you get here."

"All right. You sound done in. How was your New Year's Eve?"

"Crowded with incident. But you're right, I should have gone to New York with you."

"Are you staying in tonight?"

Verity didn't answer. A wave of euphoria swept over her entire body.

"Verity?"

"Sorry. Listen, I'm half asleep now. I'll see you when you get in tomorrow, okay? And I'll tell you everything the detective said."

"All right. Sorry to wake you."

"No problem. Good-bye, Cassandra."

"Good-bye."

Verity hung up the receiver. She sat up on the bed, threaded her fingers through her hair several times, and smiled contentedly. She ran through the channels on the television swiftly, stopping at some film from the forties that looked vaguely familiar. She looked all around the room absently, and saw the cocaine on her dresser. She got up, went over, and snorted two more large spoonfuls.

She started to climb back onto the bed, but lost her balance and fell against the bedside table, bruising her thigh. She hardly felt it. She grabbed for the wobbling bottle of Scotch, but only managed to knock it to the floor. Half of it spilled out onto the carpet, immediately filling the room with its odor.

"Oh, Goddamn . . . ," she breathed. She reached clumsily down and picked up the bottle, holding it up to the light to see how much remained inside. She poured out another drink into her glass, fell onto the bed, and stared blearily at the television. She lifted the glass to her lips, and spilled some of the Scotch onto the lapels of her robe. "Shit," she said, "what's wrong with me tonight?"

The movie made no sense. She couldn't follow any of the plot. The dialogue seemed random and pointless. She decided simply to watch the costumes. She spilled more of her drink, and in order not to bother with that anymore, she simply swallowed off everything that remained in her glass. She reached to set the glass down on the table, but it missed the edge and tumbled to the floor. Verity leaned over the edge of the bed, and watched it roll away. She waved a hand at it in dismissal and fell back into the pillows. Her breath came in heavier intakes but she wasn't aware of it. She stared at a peculiarly shaped shadow across a portion of the ceiling. It changed shape and texture with the blue-gray flickering of the television screen. The effort to keep her eyes raised became too much for Verity; her lids began to droop. She stared straight ahead at the window and the bright misshapen moon rising over the top of the firs in the back garden. Soon her eyes closed and she fell into a deep, dreamless sleep. Her breath came heavier and only erratically. She lay absolutely still. She breathed harshly for several seconds, and then a cough seemed to be strangled in her throat. Her breath slowed and finally stopped altogether. Verity's dried lips parted as her jaw went slack and then, slowly, on either side of her, her fingers uncurled out of damp fists.

25

It was the maid, Serena, who discovered Verity's body in the bedroom early the following morning. Cassandra arrived from the airport just in time to see the ambulance pull away without siren or flashing lights.

Two days later, Rocco and Apple—still on tour—flew up from Philadelphia for the funeral services. Louise came with Eugene Strable. Eric was conspicuous by his absence. Louise offered the vague excuse that he was job hunting out of town, and she had no way of finding him. Cassandra did not question this.

Cassandra was alone. In less than a year she had lost her father, her brother, and her sister. She pondered going to the police, yet still she could not bring herself to believe that the woman Richard Hawke had married was responsible in any way for the three deaths. Cassandra in fact could not imagine that she was personally acquainted with a murderer. And while Cassandra wondered what she should do, Louise remained with her in the Brookline mansion. And Louise's comfort was worse than no comfort at all. Cassandra and her stepmother spoke no more than civilities to one another. Whether on purpose or by accident Cassandra wasn't sure, but their meals seemed never to coincide. Eugene Strable often came over in the evenings, and sometimes he stayed the night—though he at least had the decency to conceal his automobile behind the garage.

During the first few weeks of January, Cassandra came to see how great a temporizing and calming influence Verity had been. Her laissez-faire attitude toward Louise and Louise's laughable plans had kept Cassandra in good humor. Verity, in her way, had been a bulwark against the grief that Cassandra felt for the deaths of her father and her brother. Now that prop had disappeared, and Cassandra felt herself abandoned. On the last day of January, Cassandra packed a suitcase and a couple of cardboard boxes, and moved into the Prudential Towers apartment. She was tired of avoiding Louise, knowing that any chance word might provoke an argument. She was even more anxious to leave the house on account of memories of her sister. Cassandra still couldn't walk into the living room without expecting to see Verity sprawled on the chintz-covered sofa.

That night, Cassandra telephoned Rocco in St. Louis, asked about the performance, and told him that she had moved out of the Brookline mansion.

"Good," he sighed. "Apple wanted me to ask you to do that anyway. And I was going to."

"Why?" asked Cassandra, puzzled.

There was a pause. "Let me put Apple on," said Rocco. "She wants to talk to you."

"Hi," said Apple, just a moment later.

"What is all this about?" Cassandra asked. "You're both being mysterious."

"There's no mystery. I just don't think you should stay in that house with Louise Larner."

"Why not?" said Cassandra. "Other than the fact that Louise is Louise, and always will be."

"Cassandra," said Apple carefully, "your father is dead. Jonathan is dead. Verity is dead."

"I'm well aware of those facts," said Cassandra, a little harshly.

"What happens if you die? Who gets your trust money? Who gets your house?"

"Louise," said Cassandra. "But that's—"

She didn't finish the sentence.

"That's what?" prompted Apple. "Coincidence? I don't think so."

"You think Louise has actually been killing us off, one by one?" laughed Cassandra. "That's crazy. You don't set out to systematically kill off a whole family. People notice."

"Well," said Apple, "in this case, people *haven't* noticed. Even *you* haven't noticed. The problem is, you're too genteel."

"What does that mean?"

"It means that when you look at Louise, all you see is a woman who has bad taste. You're looking at a woman who says the wrong thing at the wrong time. You're thinking, 'Oh, God, she's overdressed for this occasion.' And what you *should* be thinking is, 'She killed my father. She killed my brother. She killed my sister. And if I don't watch out, she's going to kill me.' Rocco and I have been talking about this lately. I thought it was just me who was thinking like this—and I didn't want to run off and go accusing anyone of murder. And the same with Rocco. But once we got together, we realized we ought to say something. Besides, there's something you don't know."

"What?" asked Cassandra warily.

"You know that private investigator that Jonathan hired?"

"Yes," said Cassandra. "Verity found out who he was—she may even have talked to him—but then she died before—"

"She did talk to him," Apple interrupted.

"How do you know?" demanded Cassandra, astonished.

"It was Ben James who recommended the detective to Jonathan," Apple explained. "This was before Ben became involved with the band of course. But Jonathan knew Ben through Verity, and called him up and asked his advice. Ben gave him the name of his detective—his name is Norman, I think, Something Norman—and Jonathan hired him. Then Jonathan died, and Verity got hold of him. She told him to start looking into Jonathan's death too. And he did, but then when he didn't hear from Verity again, he got worried, and called up Ben. Ben's been trying to get in touch with you. . . ."

"I've been moving," said Cassandra. "I haven't sat down in two days."

". . . so he called us this morning," Apple went on, "to see if we knew where you were. Ben's very upset about Verity's death. Very upset. But he didn't know Louise, really, and it never occurred to him that—"

"That she might have murdered Verity?" said Cassandra.

"Anyway," Apple went on, "he gave me the detective's name, and I'll give it to you now. He's in Manhattan, and he's listed."

"Thank you," said Cassandra simply. "I'm worried too, now. Put Rocco on again, will you?"

"What are you going to do?" Rocco asked, when the receiver had been passed to him.

"I don't know yet," said Cassandra. "I'll have to think about all this."

"I want you to stay out of Louise's way."

"I intend to," said Cassandra. "I'm certainly not going to give her the satisfaction of dying. I'm not convinced that Louise *did* have anything to do with all this—that's too crazy. But if she *did* . . ."

"Just be careful," said Rocco. "Be real careful. 'Cause I love you."

"I love you, too," said Cassandra absently. "Now tell me that detective's name."

Three days later, at her desk at the Menelaus Press, Cassandra received a telephone call from Louise.

Her stepmother was incensed. "You might have left word with me," she snapped. "You know how I found out? When I went down to the kitchen and asked Ida if she had seen you. Ida said, 'She moved out on Monday.' She wouldn't even tell me where you had gone." Louise paused. Cassandra did not tell her where she was now living.

"I thought," said Louise, "that you might have gone flitting after that Italian."

Cassandra said nothing.

"So you've left me with the responsibility of running that house. And with all the work I have to do running the agency."

"Louise," said Cassandra, "please don't do me any favors. Move out today if you like."

"I don't have any place to go!"

Cassandra sat back in her chair, rolling her eyes. "For God's sake, Louise. You run a real-estate agency. You've got more listings than anybody in town."

"Well," said Louise after a pause, "I'm not going anywhere for the time being. I'm much too upset about Verity."

Cassandra made no reply to this, but asked, "Where is Eric, Louise? Verity died one month ago. Why hasn't he come back here?"

"He's in New York," returned Louise vaguely. "He has a job, and it's keeping him busy. Very busy. But Cassandra, what I need from you is—"

"Louise," Cassandra interrupted, "I have to go. And please do me a favor and don't call me here anymore. Personal phone calls are very disruptive, and I'm just as busy as you are. Good-bye."

She hung up the telephone, grimly smiling at the discomfiture that had been apparent in Louise's voice.

"Feel better?" asked Sarah, pausing at the door of the room.

"Louise always makes me want to scream." Cassandra motioned for her assistant to seat herself in the chair opposite the desk.

"What's up?" asked Sarah.

"I got three letters today," said Cassandra, holding them up, "praising the job I did on the last issue."

"Hey, great!"

"Well, not so great," said Cassandra. "Since I didn't do any of the work. You did all the work."

"Well," said Sarah, "you were busy."

"Yes I was. With the band. And this month I haven't been any good either."

"Well, your sister—"

"There's no need to make excuses for me," smiled Cassandra. "I'm just lucky to have you here to take over."

"I'm hardly taking over," shrugged Sarah.

"The point is," said Cassandra, "you could. I wanted to let you know . . ."

"Let me know what?"

". . . that you ought to take as much responsibility as you can."

"I'm an overachiever," laughed Sarah. "You don't have to encourage me. Watch out, or when your back is turned I'll push you out the window and take over your job entirely."

"I trust you," said Cassandra. "I just wanted to give you a word of advice."

"What?"

"This job is good for about three years. Learn everything you can, then quit, and go out in the real world. The thing about working with *Iphigenia* is that you get to do a little of just about everything."

Sarah looked around the room. "How long have you been here?" she asked.

Cassandra only smiled. "I'm taking the afternoon off," she said, "to attend to personal business. Take over, will you?"

26

Louise stepped out of the library and peered first down the long hallway. Then she went to the bottom of the stairs. "Serena?" she called upward. "Cara! Where are you?"

There was no response to her summons. The stereo system in the living room had been set to an easy-listening station. Connecting speakers in various rooms produced an uneasy echo.

Once more Louise called the names of the servants, and then, perplexed and irritated, went back to the kitchen.

Ida stood at the counter, trimming the fat from a pork roast with a long, sharp-bladed knife. She looked up at Louise without perceptible reaction, and then went back to her work.

"Ida," said Louise, "where are those girls?"

"Ma'am?"

"Serena and Cara," said Louise, growing more irritated. "I was upstairs half an hour ago and my bed hadn't even been made up. It's four o'clock."

"They're not here," said Ida.

"This is Monday. Thursday is their day off."

"That's right."

"Ida," said Louise with growing impatience, "where are they?"

Ida put the knife aside and wiped her hands on her apron. "They're not working here any longer. They packed this morning. They left before lunchtime."

"What?"

"They quit, ma'am."

"They couldn't have! Quit? Just like that, they decide to walk out on me? No notice, no nothing?!"

"They gave notice last week," said Ida quietly.

"They did not," snapped Louise. "Neither of them said one word to me about quitting."

"They spoke to Miss Cassandra," said Ida.

The bracelets on Louise's hands jangled nervously. "*Miss* Cassandra doesn't even live here. Why on earth did they go to her and not to me?"

"Miss Cassandra is the one who always signed their checks, ma'am."

Louise began moving about the room, her heels clicking sharply on the quarry-tile floor. "This is great, just great!" she breathed. "*Why* did they leave?"

"I don't know, ma'am."

"Oh, yes you do. You just won't tell me."

Ida picked up the scraps of pork fat and threw them down the disposal. She did not reply to Louise's accusation.

"They should at least have the decency to tell me about this. Now what am I supposed to do?"

Ida still said nothing.

"It's just as well they're gone," said Louise in a calmer voice. "They were getting slack. I was thinking about replacing them anyway. Ida, you'll have to serve in Serena's place tonight. Mr. Strable and I will be eating at eight."

"No, ma'am," returned Ida calmly.

"What did you say?!"

"I was hired to cook. I don't serve."

Louise digested this, and then said in a hard voice, "I don't suppose you'd be willing to help with the cleaning either, then?"

"No, ma'am, I wouldn't. It doesn't make any difference anyway, because as soon as this roast goes in the oven, I'll be taking my leave as well. Keep it at three hundred twenty-five degrees, and it'll be done at seven-thirty."

Louise's jaw dropped in shock. In a voice of sharp anger, she said, "If *any* of you people think you're getting recommendations from me, you are dead wrong."

"Miss Cassandra has already found us places, ma'am." Ida began smearing the pork roast with a mustard sauce.

"Leave that alone," snarled Louise. "I'm eating out tonight. Just get out!"

Ida wiped her hands on her apron, untied the apron, folded it neatly, and laid it on the counter. "Good-bye, ma'am," she said, and walked out of the kitchen.

"What the hell do you think you're pulling?" Louise screamed into the telephone. "How am I supposed to live in this house without anyone to do the cleaning and the cooking, or make up the beds, and do the laundry? This house has twenty rooms, for Christ's sake, and I'm trying to run your father's real-estate agency. I—"

"Did you wish to speak to someone in particular?" interrupted a calm voice on the other end of the line.

"Who is this?" demanded Louise.

"Sarah Hardesty. This is the Menelaus Press."

"Give me Cassandra," growled Louise.

Sarah cupped her hand over the mouthpiece. She was sitting at the worktable by the windows while Cassandra sat at her desk busily blue-penciling a sheaf of manuscript on a clipboard. "There is an irate woman on the line," said Sarah. "I think she wants to yell at you."

Cassandra laughed and picked up the extension. "Hello, Louise," she said cheerily.

"Don't hand me that," said Louise in a low voice. "This is not going to work!"

"What isn't going to work?"

"What you're trying to do to me."

"I take it you're talking about the servants quitting. It was their decision. I had nothing to do with it."

"Oh, really? And what reason did they give?"

"It's really none of your business, but I'll tell you anyway. They left because of you. They had been running that house efficiently for a number of years, and then you come in and ride herd over them."

"You've got to keep a watchout for servants," said Louise. "They'll steal you blind."

"You're probably right, Louise. So you're better off without them. Good-bye."

"Wait a minute!"

"What?"

"I can't run this house by myself. Cook and clean and all that —this is a twenty-room house."

Cassandra said nothing.

"So I'm going to call the employment agency tomorrow, and hire new servants. I can get along with just two I think, since I'm the only one living here."

"No," said Cassandra.

"You don't have to worry," said Louise sarcastically. "I'll pay their precious little salaries."

"No," said Cassandra again.

"What do you mean?"

"I won't have strangers in the house."

"They're not strangers, they're servants!"

"I don't care," said Cassandra. "They're strangers, and I won't be there to supervise them. I won't allow them in the house. You drove away three very fine servants—I had no trouble at all finding other places for them, by the way—and now you're going to have to get along by yourself."

Louise gasped in rage. "I can't!"

"Then I guess you'll just have to leave," said Cassandra.

"I'll never leave this house!"

Cassandra didn't reply.

"You cannot stop me from hiring servants with my own money!"

"I can," said Cassandra, "and I will. I will lock them out. And I'll lock you out with them. The house is mine. What I say goes. No servants, Louise. And if you're not comfortable there, why don't you just pack up and leave?"

Louise began to sputter a reply, but Cassandra interrupted her: "One more thing, Louise. I asked you not to call me here any more, and you just did. That was my assistant who answered the phone. She's not going to put through any more calls from you, so you might as well not even bother dialing the number. Good-bye."

Cassandra hung up and smiled at Sarah, who had made no pretense of not listening to the conversation.

"My," said Sarah, "aren't you the hard woman!"

Cassandra shook her head. "I hate being like that. It's not me. I don't even sound like myself. But it's the only kind of talk Louise understands. You can't be nice to her—she'll take advantage. There's an old Russian proverb: 'Give her a table and she'll put her feet up on it.' That's Louise. She moved into the house last Thanksgiving because she had a little smoke on the ceiling of her apartment kitchen. I made a big mistake in not stopping her at the beginning. That's when I should have said no. Then I wouldn't be having all this trouble now." Cassandra shrugged. "It's my own fault."

"Are you going to move back into the house? It must be huge —she said it was twenty rooms. Is that true?"

Cassandra nodded. "Depending on whether you count bathrooms or not. I don't know what I'm going to do. The band is coming back next week, and the Prudential apartment is too small for three—Apple, and Rocco, and me. But the house is too big—especially without servants. We'll see." She looked down at her work again, but then raised her head almost immediately. "That reminds me."

"What?" asked Sarah.

"I'm going to be *very* busy next week, with the band and so forth."

"It's all right," said Sarah. "I'll cover."

After work, Cassandra drove to Brookline. She parked in the drive behind Eugene Strable's car, and walked around the house to the studio. A light snow had begun to fall earlier in the evening. She turned on a couple of space heaters near the desk, and prepared a pot of tea for herself. She glanced out the studio window over the sink, and glimpsed Louise standing at one of the French doors of the living room, holding back a curtain, and peering out at her. Cassandra did not acknowledge her. While the tea was steeping, Cassandra listened to the band's message tape, making notes. She began returning calls immediately. The first was to Ben James, whom she caught just on his way out of the office.

"Everything's going great," he said.

"I know. I talked to Rocco this morning."

"Listen, something's up. I got somebody from Columbia Records coming up for the Valentine's concert at the Orpheum."

"Columbia!"

"Yes. I hope you don't mind—you and I are splitting the bill on air fare, hotel, and . . . other things."

"Fine," said Cassandra. "How'd you get him? Pull another favor?"

"Didn't have to. Sent him the tear sheets and a tape. He said to me, 'Any band that has a dollar sign for a logo is all right by me.'"

"You think he'll take them on?"

"If he judges on the basis of talent, originality, and marketability, of course. But who knows why these people *really* make decisions?"

"It's great news," said Cassandra.

"But I need your opinion."

"On what?"

"Should we tell them—the band—that he's going to be there? They're already going to be keyed up, I wouldn't want to throw them."

"Nothing would throw them," said Cassandra. "I know that for a fact. They're real professionals."

"That's what I thought. So call them tonight, and tell them."

"It's your doing," Cassandra pointed out.

"Oh, well," said Ben, "I'll let you pay for the phone call."

Cassandra laughed. "Thank you. I never mind being the messenger of good news."

"Thank me when the album is pressed and in the racks and selling."

"Then too."

"Now to personal business," said Ben, in a lowered, more serious tone of voice. "You talked to that private investigator?"

"Yes, I did," said Cassandra. "In fact, I brought him up here."

"And? Are you going to go to the police?"

"Not yet. I'm still not convinced. I just find it difficult to believe anybody would be as stupid and as evil as to murder three members of the same family in the same year. I have the detective working on Jonathan and Verity now. If he comes up with anything else, then I'll go to the police."

"Well, I won't interfere or give my advice. Or I guess the only advice I'll give is for you to be very, very careful around that woman."

"Don't worry," said Cassandra. "I think I know what I'm doing."

"Louise," said Eugene Strable, "come away from the windows." He sat on the edge of the sofa, checking his watch against the clock on the mantel.

"I wonder what she's doing over there," said Louise, taking a swallow of vodka. The ice clinked loudly in her glass. "She pretended she didn't even see me."

"You just had a fight today," Strable pointed out.

"How can you be so calm about this?"

"Well, you called me up and said it was an emergency. It's not an emergency. Cassandra is not going to call the police if you go out and hire a responsible day woman."

"She's said she'd change the locks. And I wouldn't put it past her, either."

"Louise," said Strable, glancing at his watch again, "I'm due at the Harvard Club in half an hour. Traffic is still heavy."

"You don't care what happens to me. You think this is funny, don't you? Me running this house without any help."

"I think you're overreacting," said the lawyer quietly.

Louise swung around and stalked to the hearth. A fire was laid but not lighted. She raised one arm, grasped the corner of the mantel, and then laid her head down on her outstretched arm.

"I'll see what I can do," said Eugene quietly. "I'll speak to Cassandra."

Louise looked up. "You *make* her hire new servants. You know how to manage her."

Eugene stood up, straightening and adjusting the sleeves of his jacket. "All right, Louise."

"You're the one handling her trust. You remind her of that."

"No," said Strable quickly and earnestly. "Don't *ever* mention that trust to Cassandra, whatever you do. She might start asking questions. We're lucky that none of those children ever came into that inheritance. It was always a sort of fairy tale to them. I don't think any of them really believed that the money was there. They got their allowances, and that's all they cared about. They never really understood what their mother did for them. If two of them had to die, it's just as well for us that it was Jonathan and Verity."

"Why do you say that?" said Louise harshly.

"Because they were the oldest. It'll be another four years before we have to worry about Cassandra coming into all that money."

Louise said nothing.

"And of course," the lawyer went on blandly, "four years is a long time. Anything could happen. Anything at all." He smiled at Louise. "Feel a little better now?"

With a brightening smile, Louise went up to Eugene and put her arms around his shoulders. "Much better. I just got upset thinking Cassandra had gotten the better of me. But she hasn't, has she? Oh, Eugene, I'm sorry I snapped at you. You and I will figure out something."

"Louise . . ."

"Skip that meeting. Stay here with me." She pressed herself against him.

"Please, Louise," Eugene said uncomfortably. He eased himself out of her embrace. "I'll see if I can't speak to Cassandra tomorrow. I'll call you as soon as I know anything."

27

People Buying Things returned from New York on the thirteenth of February, the day before their concert at the Orpheum Theatre. Cassandra was waiting for Rocco and Apple at the Prudential Towers apartment. They walked in exhausted.

"We did a late show last night at Danceteria," said Apple, "and we were up again at five this morning to do an interview on cable."

Rocco laughed wearily. "It sounds like we're complaining. Six months ago, we would have killed for this kind of exposure."

Apple wandered blearily around the apartment. "At this point, I would kill for a down pillow."

"Go to bed," said Cassandra.

"What about tomorrow?" said Apple. "Don't things have to be arranged?"

"I've taken care of everything. You just have to make sure you're rested."

"Thank you. See you in the morning. Good night," said Apple, and swung through the door of her bedroom, slamming it softly behind her.

Rocco and Cassandra sat together on the sofa.

"I'm tired too," he said.

"I know," smiled Cassandra. "You need rest."

"You haven't seen me in six weeks," he reminded her, as if in wounded self-esteem, "and you're going to let me go to sleep?"

Cassandra laughed. "No, no. I guess not. I've missed you."

"I missed you too. I wish you had come with us."

"You needed someone to take care of things here."

"I needed someone to take care of *me*."

"I still have a job, remember?"

"Why don't you quit it?" said Rocco.

"I'll tell you a secret. I did quit it."

"When?"

"Yesterday. It came as a shock to Menelaus Press."

"It'll fall apart without you."

"No. I trained Sarah to take my place. She'll do fine."

"You know what that means?" asked Rocco.

"What?"

"We don't have anything scheduled after tomorrow night, at least not for a couple of weeks. So you and I are going to take off somewhere. By ourselves. No music, no friends, no telephones, no nothing. Just you and me."

Cassandra was silent for a few moments. Rocco lay at full length on the couch, with his head in her lap. He looked up at her and smiled.

"Don't think you could stand to be with me for a whole two weeks?" he asked. "Better get used to having me underfoot."

"I was just thinking where I'd like to go."

"It's February. That means we have to go to the Caribbean."

"All right."

"You're easy to please," said Rocco.

Cassandra smiled. "When it comes to you, I'm easy to please. It'll be good getting out of the city and especially good getting away from Louise." Cassandra shook her head. "That woman is impossible. I've been avoiding her as much as I can."

"Have you seen Eric? I couldn't believe he didn't show up at the funeral."

"Eric's in New York," said Cassandra with a peculiar smile. "That's all I know. Or, at any rate, that's all I'm going to say."

"You've got something up your sleeve, haven't you?" said Rocco. "Something about Eric?"

"Maybe," said Cassandra. "Maybe we'll have a little news tomorrow, or maybe even tonight."

"About Eric? About Eric *and* the Wicked Stepmother?"

"Maybe," said Cassandra.

"Well," said Rocco, rubbing his face against her stomach, "you're not going to have to think about Louise for the next two weeks, at least."

"I have to go see her tomorrow."

"About what?"

"I just want to clear up some business about the house."

"Like what?"

Cassandra smiled. "I'm tired of talking about Louise. I'm tired of talking. I think I'll pick you up and carry you over the threshold of our bedroom."

"Don't you want to hear the song I wrote about you?"

"What?" laughed Cassandra. "You didn't write a song about me . . ."

"I did too." He sang softly:

> Love reached out of the gutter,
> Love stuck a knife in my ribs . . .

"Is that what you think of me?" protested Cassandra.

Rocco laughed. "Don't you like it? We're playing it tomorrow night at the Orpheum. It's called 'Love Jumped Up and Bit Me on the Ass.'"

Cassandra shook her head unbelievingly. "Good God."

"But do you like it?" he asked.

"Yes," she laughed. "I do."

"Do you like it enough to marry me?"

Cassandra blinked. "Well," she laughed, "I guess I'm not going to have to be the one to ask, after all."

Rocco and Cassandra slept late that next morning. When they finally rose at eleven, they threw on robes and went out into the living room. They found Apple, with a serious expression, sitting at the kitchen counter. The morning edition of the *Herald* was spread out before her.

"You look glum enough," said Cassandra, taking mugs from the cupboard.

"I am," Apple replied.

"What's wrong?" asked Rocco.

Apple glanced at Cassandra. "There's something in the paper that concerns you." There was an ominous tone in Apple's voice that caused Cassandra and Rocco to exchange glances.

Cassandra put the mugs down and walked slowly, reluctantly over to the counter. Apple flipped the paper around, folding it back to the front page. Cassandra pulled it closer. As she read, she drew in her breath sharply and folded her hands into fists against the counter. She felt a sensation of coldness pricking down her spine. She lifted her eyes from the newspaper and stared across to the plate window, through which she could glimpse the bleak gray skyline of Boston. She let her breath out slowly and closed her fingers tighter against her palms. But she could find no words.

Later that Saturday afternoon, Cassandra drove grimly the familiar route to the mansion in Brookline. Louise's lime-green Toronado was the only car in the drive. A light snow had begun to fall, and the car was dusted completely white. Broad tire tracks were faintly visible farther up the drive. Those belonged to Bert and Ian's van, she supposed. They must have already left for the Orpheum, to start setting things up for the evening performance.

Cassandra folded the *Herald* and took it with her when she got out of her car. Inside the front door, she instinctively tossed her car keys into the basket on the marble table in the hallway. Then she stopped, and thoughtfully retrieved them. She thrust them into the pocket of her coat.

In the living room, the stereo was softly playing a Frank Sinatra album from the sixties. Cassandra peered into that room, and also opened the door of the study. Finding no one, she went through the dining room and straight into the kitchen.

Louise stood in the corner of the room, almost hidden behind the stacked electric ovens. Her black hair was bound tightly in a net. She wore no makeup but bright red lipstick. Her black corduroy shirt with red buttons had belonged to Verity. Louise's flushed face was gleaming with sweat. A streak of grime daubed one cheek.

"What are you doing?" Cassandra asked automatically, placing the still folded newspaper on the counter.

Louise wiped a trailing bead of sweat from her temple with the back of a yellow rubber-gloved hand. "What does it look like I'm doing? I'm cleaning house. Since you fired the servants, and won't let me hire any more, I have to do all this drudgery myself."

"You're scrubbing the floor," said Cassandra.

"Brilliant. Just brilliant. Is that what you majored in at Radcliffe—logic?" Louise leaned wearily against the ovens. "Ida was a layabout—you ought to see the grime down in the corners over here. And what's under the refrigerator!" She glanced at the expanse of tiled floor. "I don't think she'd waxed this floor since it was put down. By the time I finish with it, it will *shine.*"

"Louise, this is quarry tile. You don't put wax on quarry tile —ever. It ruins the finish. Just a damp mop."

"What?"

Cassandra stepped around the corner and sighed as she looked at the space Louise had already sponged with wax. It had begun to discolor.

Louise stood up. She wore a pair of black corduroy slacks and wooden clogs that had also been Verity's. She slapped the wet sponge down on the counter by the newspaper there.

"This wouldn't have happened if you hadn't bribed the servants to desert me. How was I supposed to know?"

"I didn't bribe anyone. Besides, Louise, you sell luxury accommodations—I just figured you'd know what quarry tile was." Cassandra opened one of the cupboards, evidently looking for something. "Is there any coffee?"

"There would be," replied Louise acidly, "if you hadn't closed the account at the market. I was in there yesterday and I was never so humiliated in my life."

"You can hardly have expected me to pay your food bills," said Cassandra. There was a tone of argumentativeness in her voice.

Louise picked up the bottle of wax from the floor, recapped it, and crossed over to the sink. She peeled off the gloves and tossed them aside. "Don't worry about it," she said, "I'll get down there again on my hands and knees and scrape all that wax up. Your precious floor won't be harmed."

Cassandra looked at her stepmother, and said, in a quiet voice, "Don't bother."

Louise had taken a small tube of hand cream from a drawer and squeezed a dollop into her palm. She paused now, glancing curiously at Cassandra. The lotion began to drip. Louise rubbed her hands together vigorously.

"Why not?" Louise asked suspiciously. "You mean that I can hire somebody to take care of this place now? I hope so. Do you have any idea how much of a *favor* I am doing you by just living here? Thieves watch houses like this. I've seen them parked out just on the other side of the stone fence out front, waiting for this house to be empty. If there weren't anybody living here, they'd walk right in and cart everything away."

Cassandra didn't answer. She went to the refrigerator and took out a bottle of mineral water. She unscrewed the cap, and poured it into a glass she took from the drain board.

"It's bad enough," Louise went on, glancing apprehensively at Cassandra all the while she spoke, "to have that band out here all day. It was so nice and quiet before they came back from wherever it was they had gone. That's not music they play, that's—"

Louise had grown more and more nervous as Cassandra maintained her silence. Finally she trailed off altogether.

Cassandra still said nothing.

"Eugene spoke to you, didn't he?" asked Louise. "You *are* going to let me hire somebody, aren't you?"

"Louise," said Cassandra slowly, "you're going to have to be out of this house in five days. By Thursday."

Louise's mouth dropped open. "What?"

"Five days," Cassandra repeated. "By Thursday. Everything out."

"I have *told* you: I have nowhere to go."

"Then you'll have to find somewhere," said Cassandra calmly. "Won't you?"

Louise's mouth tightened and became ugly.

"Why? So you can move in with your Italian? As if everybody in Boston didn't already know why you're walking around with that satisfied grin on your face."

Cassandra put her glass down and said, "Louise, you have to get out of here. I'm selling the house."

"You can't sell it," Louise whispered.

"I am."

"No, you can't," Louise cried. "Half this house belongs to Eric. He inherited it from Verity. Verity and Eric were still married when she died, and he gets everything that belonged to her."

Cassandra looked at Louise strangely. "Yes," said Cassandra, "everything that belonged to her. He gets the Lotus, and her jewelry, and all her clothes. The Lotus is in the garage—he can pick it up any time." Cassandra glanced at Louise's outfit. "It looks as if you've already cleaned out the closets."

"The house—"

"The house was left to Jonathan, Verity, and me. When one of us died, it went to the other two. Spouses were *not* part of the business. Of course if I died, the house would become part of the estate. It *would* be yours then, and so would the rest of the fortune that Mother left us. But the fact is, I'm not dead. I'm very much alive. I have every right to sell the house, and that money is mine to do with as I please. It doesn't go back into the estate. That's the way the will was set up, Louise. I thought you knew all that."

"You're a liar! The house is Eric's!" cried Louise vehemently. "You can't sell it. It's not legal."

"I'm passing papers on Thursday. I'm selling it to Richard Lake; he's a friend of Ben James's. He's paying cash, and I told him he could take possession immediately. So you're going to have to be out."

"This is illegal," Louise protested weakly. "Who handled this deal?"

"Richard Lake himself. He's a lawyer."

"I'm going to call Eugene! You're just trying to pull a fast one on me. Well, you're not getting away with it!" Louise shouted hysterically. "I'm your father's widow, and this was his house, and I'm going to live here for as long as I like. I don't care if you *do* own it, or if you *say* you own it. Eugene will throw the whole business in court, and you'll be an old woman before anything's decided. I'm staying right here, right in this house where I belong, and you can go to hell!"

Louise grabbed for the telephone.

"There's no point in calling Eugene Strable," said Cassandra.

Louise dropped her hand. "You don't want me to bring in Eugene, do you? You aren't really selling the house, either. You're lying. You don't need the money. You get that huge allowance from the estate. I'm going to call Eugene. He'll put a stop to the whole thing."

"Eugene's telephone is disconnected," said Cassandra dispassionately. "But go ahead and try."

"What? I think you've gone crazy, Cassandra. I think you've gone right off the deep end." She took the receiver, and quickly punched out a number. The telephone rang many times without being answered. "I don't know why I'm calling," said Louise, hanging up the telephone. "It's Saturday, there wouldn't be anybody there anyway."

Cassandra reached over and in one gesture flipped open the newspaper on the counter. She pushed it around for Louise to see. Down the entire front page, the bold headline screamed, LAWYER SKIMS SCAMS & SCRAMS.

Cassandra struck her knuckles against the paper. "That's why Eugene Strable is not answering his telephone," she said. "He's skipped town, Louise, with something over five million dollars of *someone's* trust money. I guess you and I can figure out whose, even if the reporters haven't found out yet. And apparently the rest of the trust was sunk into some completely disreputable waterfront scheme."

Louise stared at the headline in a daze, then looked up at Cassandra.

"Wha—what?" she said weakly.

"The full story is on page two," Cassandra answered shortly. "I suppose all the names involved will be released in another day or two. Then you and I will have to deal with reporters, and the news cameras, and so on."

With trembling hands Louise turned the page. At the top was a portrait photograph of Eugene Strable, smiling confidently for his thirty-fifth Harvard reunion.

"He's skipped town," Cassandra repeated, "and he's robbed me of nearly everything."

"This is a lie," Louise said distractedly. "This is a joke. . . ."

"I only found out about it this morning," said Cassandra. "I'm selling the house on Thursday of next week. I got four hundred thousand for it, furnished—and that includes permission to continue to use the rehearsal studio for the band." She shrugged, and said bitterly, "I guess I'll *need* that money now."

"He took everything?" Louise whispered.

"I spent this afternoon with Richard Lake. He's representing me. He's already hired a detective agency to get on Eugene Strable's trail. And of course the police and the FBI are going to be after him as well." Cassandra looked closely at her stepmother. "That's why I came over here, Louise. The newspaper says that a well-known Back Bay realty firm was involved in this scheme. I hope that wasn't you, because it would be too bad for the family honor if it turned out to be my own stepmother and her lover who cheated me out of my fortune. Wouldn't it, Louise?"

"You're making all this up! All of it! You've come over here and read me a pack of lies!"

"I'll be back on Monday and Tuesday, to pack up all my personal things. It's strange to think . . . ," began Cassandra.

"What?" asked Louise blankly.

". . . that soon you'll be the only Hawke left." She turned, and walked out through the swinging door.

Louise, after a few moments, looked down at the article before her. Her hands trembled slightly against the paper, and her ruby nails cut into the paper as she violently crumpled it between her hands.

28

At Cassandra's request Rocco and Apple had said nothing of the loss of her fortune, either to Bert and Ian, or to Ben James when he appeared at the Orpheum that evening with his friend from Columbia Records. Her name had not yet been released to the press, and she felt that for now it was easier to deal with the loss than with the sympathy for the loss.

She was backstage with her future husband and Apple in the dressing room before the show.

"I can't believe you're taking it like this," said Apple. She was applying lipstick and watching Cassandra in the dressing-table mirror. "I think if I had just lost five to eight million dollars, I'd be in a coma."

Cassandra shook her head. "I nearly was, when I first read that article. But at least I'll be getting good money for the house.

Richard Lake's buying it as an investment. I imagine it will be sub-divided into 'luxury estate condominiums.' When I made the decision to sell, I didn't realize that I'd actually *need* that money. But don't waste your sympathy on me for that. I'll be fine."

"You're being very brave," said Rocco, kissing her cheek.

"What else can I do? The law is after Strable. And if they catch him, then I'll get some of the money back—I hope. But this band is going to make a fortune, and since the drummer has asked me to marry him, I think I'm going to make out. Louise is the loser, and she brought it all on herself. I wouldn't be surprised to find out she's in on this scheme and that Eugene Strable has left her holding the bag. If that's true, then she'll be indicted."

"The poor thing," said Apple tonelessly, twisting the lipstick back into its tube. Setting it aside, she picked up a comb. "Well, like you said, Louise brought it all on herself. I just hope she really does get what's coming to her. There are some people who always seem to escape punishment. They always scramble up onto dry land somehow. That's Louise."

Cassandra smiled. "This time, though . . ."

"This time?" echoed Rocco curiously. "You *do* know some-thing, don't you?"

"I just talked to that private investigator I hired. He found Eric in New York this afternoon. That is to say, he and half a dozen drug cops found Eric in New York this afternoon. Eric had expanded his operations—he wasn't just dealing cocaine to his ex-wife any more."

"Heroin?" said Rocco, frowning.

Cassandra nodded. "And angel dust. And just about everything else. And they told him they had the vial of cocaine and angel dust Verity had died from. And the note that he had written to her. And they asked him about it. And you know what he said?"

"'I didn't do it,'" suggested Apple.

"Right," said Cassandra. "Eric said, 'I didn't do it. Ma did it.'"

Rocco shook his head. "Those two are a pair, aren't they?"

Cassandra nodded. "And you know what else the detective discovered?"

Apple shook her head. "What?"

"A wrench. A very heavy wrench. In the toolbox in Jonathan's boat. It still had traces of blood, and hair, and skin on it—Jonathan's. Eric evidently didn't wipe it off well enough. Jonathan didn't hit his head on the bottom of the boat. Eric beat him over the head with that wrench, and knocked him unconscious. That's why he drowned."

Cassandra closed her eyes, and tears welled out from behind the lids. Rocco took her by the shoulders and sat her down in the chair next to Apple's. "You'll be all right," he whispered. "You'll be all right."

Cassandra wiped away her tears, opened her eyes, and stared into the mirror in front of her. The naked bulbs surrounding it were violently bright.

"Louise killed Father," she said.

"Why?" asked Rocco curiously. "Wasn't she better off with him alive?"

Cassandra shrugged. "She wanted the trust fund money. Probably she asked him to set up the waterfront scheme as a way to defraud us, and when he said no, she killed him. On impulse, probably. That's how Louise worked. She did something utterly stupid just on impulse, and then she spent all her energy covering her tracks. So when Jonathan found out about her killing Father, she had Eric kill *him*. And when Verity found out about it, and accused her of it, she killed Verity. And she and Eugene Strable got together and tried to rob us of every penny we had. And probably she would have tried to kill me too, just to get her hands on that house and that money."

"Louise will get hers," said Apple.

Cassandra shook her head. "You were right the first time: we can't be sure. Louise isn't the type to go under without a fight. I just want to get out of here. I just want to go somewhere where I don't have to think about that house, and Louise, and Eric, and Eugene Strable. I don't want to have to think about any of it ever again."

Rocco dropped his chin onto the crown of Cassandra's head, and smiled at her reflection in the mirror. "That's what honeymoons are for," he said.

Louise sat at the desk in the chill, damp study. At her back the snow fell softly against the black windowpanes. She punched out a number on the telephone, reading it from a scrap of paper. While the line was ringing, she turned out the light so that she sat in darkness. With one hand she held closed the collar of her sable coat.

"Hello?"

"Barbara?" asked Louise in surprise. "Is that you?"

"Yes, it is," replied Barbara harshly.

"I'm *surprised* to hear your voice again. And none too pleased either. Would you please put Eric on."

There was a pause.

"Well," said Louise impatiently.

"Don't you know?" said Barbara.

"Know what?"

"He was arrested this afternoon. He was taken down to the Eleventh Precinct."

"*Why?*" demanded Louise. "What were the charges? Drugs?"

"Drugs," said Barbara, "that was part of it."

"What else? What else?" Louise persisted frantically.

"Something about Verity, and Verity's brother—I forget his name."

"Jonathan. What about Verity? What about Jonathan?"

"I don't know. Mrs. Hawke, I have to go. I'm going down and see if I can't see Eric. He was real upset this afternoon. Real upset with all those police in here. And there was a private detective too. Good-bye, Mrs. Hawke," Barbara concluded. "I'll tell Eric you called."

Barbara hung up. Louise continued to hold the receiver against her ear. After a few moments, she broke the connection, and dialed Eric's number again. After fifteen rings, she gave up. As she replaced the receiver, she heard the noise of wheels on the gravel driveway. Louise tensed but did not rise to look out of the window. She heard car doors slam, and footsteps on the gravel. Then, more ominously, she heard tinny mechanical voices—such as those that are emitted from a radio dispatcher.

There was a knock at the front door. She dialed Eric's number again, and listened to the ringing signal for a long while.

The knock at the front door was repeated. Louise hung up the telephone and went to the front window and peered out. The front light was off and she could see no more than the figure of a policeman standing at the front door. She saw him raise his arm, and a moment later the loud echoing of his knocking filled the hallway and rattled the door of the study.

Louise dropped into the chair behind the desk, and drew the collar of her sable coat tightly against her throat. After a little, the knocking left off, and she heard footsteps retrace their path back to the police car. She heard voices. Then she became acutely aware of the silence in the darkened mansion. The snow was flung blindly against the windowpanes, and with a sudden gust of wind, the casements shook. Louise was very cold.

Then more car doors slammed, and more footsteps pounded on the gravel, and knocking commenced not only on the front door, but on the French windows in the living room, and at the kitchen door in the back. Louise sat very still, staring through the darkened panes of the French doors into the dense evergreen foliage that closely bordered the house. And quite without warning, there appeared, in that limited vista, the prowling curious face of a policeman, the badge of his cap gleaming faintly.

The doors were unlatched, and as the policeman slowly pushed them open, Louise felt the icy draft of the winter evening blow in upon her. Flakes of snow swirled inside and brushed coldly against her face and the sable coat she held wrapped so tightly about her.